I Murder for the Dough

Lock Down Publications and Ca$h
Presents

I Murder for the Dough

A Novel by *Ambitous*

I Murder For The Dough

Lock Down Publications
P.O. Box 1482
Pine Lake, Ga 30072-1482

Lock Down Publications
Like our page on Facebook: Lock Down Publications @
www.facebook.com/lockdownpublications.ldp
Cover design and layout by: **Dynasty Cover Me**
Book interior design by: **Shawn Walker**
Edited by: **Lauren Burton**

Stay Connected with Us!

Text **LOCKDOWN** to 22828 to stay up-to-date with new releases, sneak peaks, contests and more...

Thank you!

Submission Guideline.

Submit the first three chapters of your completed manuscript to ldpsubmissions@gmail.com, subject line: Your book's title. The manuscript must be in a .doc file and sent as an attachment. Document should be in Times New Roman, double spaced and in size 12 font. Also, provide your synopsis and full contact information. If sending multiple submissions, they must each be in a separate email.

Have a story but no way to send it electronically? You can still submit to LDP/Ca$h Presents. Send in the first three chapters, written or typed, of your completed manuscript to:

LDP: Submissions Dept
Po Box 1482
Pine Lake, Ga 30072

DO NOT send original manuscript. Must be a duplicate.

Provide your synopsis and a cover letter containing your full contact information.

Thanks for considering LDP and Ca$h Presents.

Ambitious

Prologue

Summer – Ten Years Ago

"Please, please," the young girl begged with tears streaming down her face. "Don't shoot him! Don't shoot my daddy, please! Please, don't kill him!"

Fed up with her persistent protesting and whining, Snake pointed his thirty-eight at her. "Shut the hell up, li'l girl," he snarled.

In a desperate attempt to draw Snake's attention away from his daughter and back to himself, Jason spoke up. "Snake, man. Please, man," his voice cracked and he swallowed painfully. "I swear, I'ma get the money. Just gimme a few days, bruh. Please, man," he pleaded from his knees, just a few feet in front of Snake. His right eye was swollen shut and a deep gash over his left eye continuously dripped blood. Both wounds had come from being hit with the butt of the thirty-eight that Snake still had trained on his teenage daughter.

Snake looked at him and then back to the young girl with lust gleaming in his eyes. "C'mere," he barked at her.

Jason shook his head emphatically. "Nah, man, what you doing? She just a li'l girl, Snake! I'ma get you that money, man. My baby ain't but fourteen, shawdy! Leave her the fuck alone, nigga!"

Snake shot him a withering look, and Jason began to cry and plead quietly for his baby girl to be spared. It hurt him to his core to not be able to come to her aid. His hands and feet were tied with telephone cord.

The young girl shook her head and backed away, clumsily knocking over a broom that had been propped against a folding chair.

As he pulled the hammer of his thirty-eight back, it made a deadly clicking sound that seemed a lot louder than it actually was. "Don't make me tell ya twice. I already told ya once," he growled through clenched teeth.

Frozen in fear, the young girl looked her father in the eye, and for a split second she was sure – no, she was positive – all of this was just a really fucked-up dream. She was beyond sure that any second now she'd wake up and begin to get ready for her third day at Douglass High School. She even pinched herself a few times.

Just as quickly as that fleeting instant of assuredness came, it vanished when her father dropped his head and began to sob. Her heart cracked and shattered into a million pieces. All hope was lost. Her precious daddy wouldn't be able to make everything alright. Not this time.

She started to inch forward, and when she was in arm's length, Snake reached and ripped her long nightshirt as he tried to pull her to him, exposing her still-filling breasts. She screamed out at his touch and tried to recoil, but his grip was firm.

"Bitch, shut up," he roared as he backhanded her.

She immediately crumpled to the floor from the force of the blow and cowered as he stood over her. Jason never lifted his head. He couldn't stand to see his princess violated and do nothing about it.

"I would say I hate to do this shit, my nigga, but that would be a lie. You begged me to give you that shit, and yo' ass turned right around and fucked up all that work and my fuckin' money, bruh." He sucked his teeth and shook his head slowly with a pained expression on his face. "Yo' ass gotta answer for that shit, shawdy," he said as he unbuttoned his pants while kneeling over the whimpering teenage girl. "This aint nobody fault but yours, my nigga."

The young girl screamed out in pain as Snake's large erection tore into her virgin vagina, but a fierce blow to the head with the butt of his revolver knocked her unconscious as he continued to defile her young body.

***

Smurf winced and dropped his head when he saw Snake's black '72 Monte Carlo pull up and park across the street from where he and some other niggas from his hood were shooting dice. "Here come this ol' wack-ass nigga. I know he 'bout to be on some sucka shit," he mumbled under his breath to himself.

Snake had been on some extra-low-key shit for the past couple of weeks, giving the whole Jason incident plenty of time to blow over, and it had made him antsy. He liked to roam around the city freely and alone, and while he didn't like having to look over his shoulder, period, he'd much rather be looking over it for niggas he'd crossed in the streets than the law, because them muthafuckas just simply didn't play fair.

"What up, Smurf? What y'all niggas shooting for?" he asked as he walked up.

"Shoot ten, bet ten," another young nigga said before Smurf had a chance to respond.

"A, get the fade, bruh. I gotta dip," Smurf said, hastily stuffing money in all of his pockets.

"Damn, young nigga. What, you scared or something? Let a nigga try to win some of that money, bruh."

Smurf could see the bullshit brewing in Snake's expression. He heard it in his voice, so he didn't know for the life of him why he responded the way he did. "I can't stay long, man. I gotta go do some shit for my mama or she go' trip on me," he said with a slight frown and, against his better judgement, he kneeled back down.

"My next shot," Snake said.

"Nah, I shoot next, you can go after me."

"Man, who the fuck this nigga is?" Snake frowned and pointed at the nigga who had just spoke as he looked at everybody else for an answer. Some of them shrugged while others just looked away, but each and every single one of them kept their mouths shut. "Exactly, mufucka! Yo' ass ain't even from around here, shawdy. You lucky ain't nobody robbed yo' ass. My next shot, nigga," he finished aggressively, practically daring the guy to say otherwise.

The young nigga looked around and incorrectly assumed that he'd be outnumbered if some shit was to pop off between him and Snake, not knowing most of the niggas around would've loved to help him kick his ass, so he pumped his brakes, accepting the chump-off quietly. He knew who Snake was, and he really didn't want any problems with him. If push came to shove, he wouldn't lay down, but he figured why even let it get to that point when he saw it coming and could simply avoid it? Wisely, he kept his mouth closed and fell back.

When the nigga who was shooting crapped, Snake grabbed the dice. "C'mo', fade me, Smurf," he said.

"I got ya, bruh. It's my fade."

"Man, watch the fuck out," Snake snapped at the nigga who'd just crapped. "I want Smurf to fade me. He the one with all the money, all the grinding and shit he been doing around here."

"That's ya fade right there, Snake, the man just got off the dice," Smurf said in a tone that said *here we go wit' the bullshit.*

"That nigga go' be a'ight."

"Man wanna win some of his money back, shawdy," he mumbled, thinking that any time would be the perfect time for the nigga to stick up for himself.

It wasn't going to happen, though. From the look on his face, he'd already accepted defeat without so much as an argument, leaving Smurf to feel like a jackass for trying to help him stand up for himself.

"And I wanna win yours, nigga! C'mo'," he ordered

aggressively.

More than just a little intimidated, Smurf looked at the nigga who'd just crapped, loathing him for feeling the exact same emotion he was feeling at the moment – fear – and sucked his teeth. "Man. Shoot twenty, bet twenty. I ain't got all day. My mama go' be waiting on me," he said reluctantly and dropped a twenty dollar bill.

About twenty minutes later and close to eight hundred dollars under, Snake was so mad it wouldn't have surprised anyone if steam had started to rise from his head. Smurf had damn near beat him out of all of his money, fair and square, and the last of what he had was riding on a six and eight split. Snake picked up the dice, clicked them a few times, shook them, and tossed them at the wall.

"Gimme them," Smurf said as he kicked at the dice, trying to stop them. His hands were busy twisting the blunt Snake had suggested he roll. He missed them, though, and the dice hit the wall, bouncing and rolling to a stop on eight.

"Decatur, nigga! Shake back on these niggas, then," Snake exclaimed and started to pick up his money.

"What you doing, bruh? I caught them dice. Point no good."

"You ain't caught shit, nigga. You ain't touch them dice," he said as he stuffed money in his pocket.

"'Cause I'm rolling the blunt," Smurf said with a disbelieving, pleading look on his face. "I said hold them, and I tried to kick them."

Snake thought for a second, then shook his head and frowned. "Nah, Jones. Point good. Quit trying to be slick, young nigga, and put down. You know damn well you gotta stop the dice. We ain't pahtnas, nigga. I'm trying to win ya money. Now put down, bruh," he said while clicking the dice.

Smurf stared into Snake's eyes for a second and knew it was time for him to go. "You know what? You right, my nigga," he said with absolutely no aggression and no insinuation at all that he felt any type of way. "Just go on ahead and keep that shit." He waved off the rest of the pile of money that Snake hadn't stuffed in his pocket. "I'm gone, man. I gotta go do some shit for my mama, anyway."

"You crazy as fuck, nigga! You ain't about to leave, bruh. All that money you done won from me, I still got some to shoot." He squinted his eyes and frowned while shaking his head. "That shit you talking about just go' have to wait, young nigga, straight up!"

Smurf sucked his teeth and pouted. "Snake, man, I told you from the beginning I had to do some shit for my mama. I ain't about to sit here and shoot you all day, shawdy, especially when you start doing sucka shit, man. I ain't trying to be around all that shit there, man," he whined as he shook his head slowly while keeping his eyes downcast.

"Sucka shit?" Snake frowned and said, taken aback when he heard it. "I tell you what, mufucka," he pulled out his thirty-eight. "Get naked, nigga. Strip. I'ma show yo' li'l bitch-ass some sucka shit, nigga," he sneered.

Everyone else who was standing around scrambled away at the sight of the gun, leaving Smurf and Snake alone.

"Man, I'm sorry, man. I ain't mean the shit like that. I'm just saying," Smurf tried to beg his way out of the situation but quickly saw that it wouldn't work. "This shit fucked up, bruh," he said, shaking his head as he undressed.

"Life fucked up, young nigga. Kick them shorts over here to me."

***

Later that night, Snake was on a mission. He was about to try to flex an out-of-town nigga with a dummy brick that he'd made up. He had set the lil juug up for a place that would be perfect for him to do what he had to do and get the hell away quickly, and at the same time easy for the country nigga from Douglasville to find. The parking lot of the West End Mall.

He saw the car that his duck told him he'd be in, and he whipped into the empty parking space beside it. He watched as the nigga named Tim got out of his Pontiac LeMans and into the passenger seat of his Monte Carlo.

"What up, dog?" Tim said, closing the door behind him and reaching over to pound Snake.

"What's up, man?"

Tim nodded. "Listen, I got some other shit I gotta get to, man, so let's go on and get this shit done so I can bounce. You brought two, right?" he asked.

Snake frowned. The way the nigga was talking immediately put him on guard, but greed got the the best of him. "Two what?" he asked, confused a little.

"Remember, I changed my mind and said I was gonna try two of them, right before we hung up the phone?"

Hell no, he didn't remember hearing shit about two bricks, but shit was all good, though. The more, the better. He just had to nip and tuck his plan a little and go about busting this move another way. "Oh, yeah. Yeah," he acted as if a lightbulb had come on in his brain. Good thing he was just as good at lying and acting as he was at quick thinking. He nodded enthusiastically. "I got you. I thought you was talking about some other shit. I'm tripping. You got the cheese, right?"

"Yeah, this forty Gs right here, my nigga." Tim held up a small paper bag.

Snake inched his hand to his waist. *It's now or never!* He thought to himself as he whipped out his .38. "Drop that bag and get the fuck out! Slow, nigga! And don't try shit or I'ma bus' ya ass, homes, straight up!"

"Damn, dog. This how it is? I thought we was cool," Tim said, his eyes wide with fear and his hands slightly raised.

"Shut the fuck up, stupid-ass nigga," Snake snapped, angered by the stupid-ass statement. "Ain't no way in the fuck you thought some dumbass shit like that. I don't even fuckin' know you. I don't give two fucks about ya. Now drop that sack, nigga. Last time before I start shooting," he warned.

Tim dropped the bag and started to ease out of the car, but at that exact moment red and blue lights blazed everywhere. Snake whirled around in his seat to get a good look at his surroundings, and when he turned back to look at Tim, he found himself nose-to-nose with a nine millimeter.

"A.P.D., stupid-ass nigga! Move and I'ma put ya brains on the windshield," Tim – or whatever the fuck his name was – yelled.

"Man, I don't believe this shit," Snake muttered as he looked around at the narcs and uniformed police swarming the parking lot. He dropped his .38 to the floor of the car.

"You better. This ain't no dream, nigga," undercover Tim said matter-of-factly.

Snake smirked. "Y'all ain't got shit. That dope ain't even real, nigga. I'ma be out on bond tomorrow."

Undercover Tim laughed. "Fuck that dope, nigga. You just tried to rob an undercover officer. Not to mention all the other shit we go' stick on yo' dumb ass. It's go' be a minute before you see the streets again, nigga, bet that."

Snake thought so long and hard about what Tim had said that by the time he realized what was happening, he was being shoved into the back of a police car. He was driven to Rice Street, The Fulton County Jail, where he was booked for armed robbery and, just like the officer had told him, a host of other fucked-up charges they stuck on him.

***

Five months later, he sat handcuffed and chained to an

annoying young nigga from Bankhead while they made the trip from the courthouse back to the county jail. He'd just accepted a fifteen-year plea deal, serving ten years in prison, for the armed robbery while all the other charges had been dismissed. And after all of that, the sun had the audacity to come out, making the day pretty as hell.

"Hell yeah, though, shawdy, I been in this muthafucka forty-five days, man. First thing I'ma do is get me some pussy! Then I'ma go over my mama house. Got to have Dukes fix me a plate, ya feel me?"

Snake was trying his damndest to ignore the annoying-ass nigga, but he kept going on and on about some shit that he definitely wasn't trying to hear at the moment. And on top of that, the stupid-ass nigga kept jerking the chain they were cuffed to, causing the cuff to painfully dig into his wrist. *Man, if this young nigga jerk this chain one more fuckin' time without saying 'my bad' or something,* he thought to himself as he sighed while shaking his head.

And sure enough, when the young nigga was demonstrating how he was going to slap his girl when he saw her, he yanked on the chain again. Snake reached way back with his free right hand and slapped his ass so hard that blood spurted out of his mouth.

"What you hit me for, nigga? What I do," the young nigga demanded as he held his stinging face with his free hand, fear ablaze in his eyes and evident in his voice.

"Shut the fuck up, lame-ass li'l nigga, and stop pulling on this got-damn chain!"

Rubbing his face, the young nigga asked again, as if he didn't understand. "Why you hit me, man?"

"'Cause I fuckin' felt like it. Now shut the fuck up and stop yanking on this got-damn chain or I'ma slap the shit out of ya ass again, nigga!"

A few niggas on the bus laughed, thinking it was funny,

but not Snake. He was just setting the tone early.

Chapter One

Ten Years Later: Present Day

The light-skinned nigga with gray eyes stepped off of the Greyhound bus at Atlanta's Garnett Station. The bright May sunlight that streamed between the breaks in the overpass reflected off of his full head of extremely thick, wavy hair. Reaching into the pocket of his state-issued khaki pants, he pulled out a box of Newport 100's and tried unsuccessfully to not look at the disturbing images intended as a deterrent they now printed on the packaging. His skin had the healthy glow that only a nigga that was fresh off of a bid seemed to be able to attain, and his crisp white t-shirt and black-and-white bo-bos screamed chain-gang to anybody who knew exactly what to look for.

He lit a cigarette and cracked a smile as he turned in a slow circle, looking around at downtown Atlanta. "Home, sweet mufuckin' home," Snake said to himself as smoke came from his nose and mouth and he began to walk. "'Bout damn time."

"Aye, homeboi," somebody called out.

Snake turned instantly when he heard the prison slang, in search of whomever had yelled it out. The last thing he needed was to run across a nigga he'd had a beef with while he was in prison on his first day out. Scanning his surroundings, he spotted an old Chevy Chevelle SS with a set of ridiculously large chrome rims on it sitting in the middle of Forsyth Street, holding up traffic.

"What's hap'ning," he called back aggressively. He didn't think he'd ever laid eyes on the nigga behind the wheel of the car that looked like an old rollerskate.

"You just touched down, didn't ya, homie?" the driver of the little rollerskate asked as car horns started to blare behind him. He tossed a quick, unconcerned look over his shoulder, obviously unfazed by his fellow commuters' impatience, and refocused his attention back on Snake.

"Why, what's up?" he responded apprehensively.

"Shit, I'm just trying to help a nigga out if I can, bruh. I done been in them exact same shoes you in now, my nigga. Where you headed? I might be able to run ya by there."

Cautious of whether he should say or not, he winced a little and made a split-second decision. "I'm headed to The Bluff."

The nigga driving nodded slowly. "I'm slick-headed that way, right. I can run ya by there if you want me to."

Unconsciously, one of Snake's eyes squinted slightly in suspicion as he analyzed the situation. *Why the fuck this nigga just volunteering to help a nigga? Me, of all people?* he thought to himself. He looked at the nigga again, weighing the situation, and once he was one hundred percent positive he didn't know him, he shrugged and jumped into the passenger seat of the car. Fuck how backwards it sounded. Accepting a ride, even if from a total stranger, beat the hell out of having to walk from Garnett to The Bluff any day of the week.

As soon as he closed the door behind him, the nigga hit the gas, causing the dual pipes to growl loudly as the car snatched forward. "How long you was down, homie?" he asked as he made the left onto M.L.K.

"Ten and a li'l change. I fell around the summer of Two Thousand," Snake said as he looked out of the window at the Georgia Dome, Phillips Arena, and the Richard B. Russell Building, awed to finally be seeing such familiar landmarks again after so long.

"Damn, bruh, a whole decade." He shook his head and said in a tone that clearly conveyed the message he couldn't even begin to fathom doing that much time. "I ain't do but three and a half, but that shit was more than enough for me, though." Noticing how Snake was looking around, amazed at his surroundings, he slowed down a little and chuckled lightly.

"The city done changed a whole lot since you been gone, shawdy, but shit, you go' see."

"Yeah, I bet," he said, still looking out of the window as they made the right onto Northside Drive. "Money still talking and hos still fuckin', though, ain't it?"

The nigga driving laughed and nodded his head. "More than ever, my nigga, more than ever. Where you got out from?"

"Shit, I just maxed from Hayes, right."

"I did my li'l bid at that ol' bullshit-ass Dodge," he said with a nod. "What they call ya, bruh?"

"Tonio, or T.O., it don't really matter which one." Snake lied convincingly with no conscious.

"Check that, my name Ant," he said, and they made small talk, mostly about prison life, for the remainder of the ride to The Bluff.

Just before Ant got to a small, three-bedroom house with burglar bars covering all entrances and exits, Snake said, "Right here, bruh," while pointing. Once they stopped, he opened the door and started to get out, but then paused and shut the door back. It may not have been an elephant in Ant's room, but it was definitely one in his, so he did the only thing he knew how to do in those types of situations: he addressed it. "Aye, check this out, my nigga. I ain't trying to be all in ya video or nothing, right, but shit, you seem like a pretty good nigga, so that's why I don't feel fucked up telling you this shit. I'm fucked up, my nigga. I ain't got a bean. I ain't got shit but the clothes on my back, man," he said and pulled at his t-shirt.

Ant immediately started to fumble with his pocket. "Shit, I got ya homie," he pulled out a small knot of bills and peeled off a hundred. "It ain't much, right, but shit, you know," he said with a slight shrug of his shoulders.

Snake did his best to come off as humble as he possibly could while accepting the money. "Aye, look, don't feel no type of way about what I'm about to say, 'cause I swear, I 'preciate it, man. But I really wasn't looking for no handout or nothing, right? I'ma hustla, my nigga. I like to go get my own shit, ya feel me? It's just, right now im kinda..." he crinkled his face to finish his sentence while holding his hand out flat and turning it from side to side quickly, hoping he had pegged the nigga right.

"What you saying, man?" he asked, not quite seeing what he was getting at.

"Shit, my nigga, I see how clean you riding and shit."

"And?" Ant cut him off, his tone and expression both quickly turning uneasy.

"Look, I'm just saying, man." Snake knew he had to just let it flow or he might miss out on an opportunity to juug. "Listen, man, I know we don't know each other from a can of paint, but on some real shit, my nigga, I'm a solid nigga. I know you or nobody else don't owe me shit, but straight up, bruh, I can stand a li'l fuckin' with, just to get on my feet, shawdy. I'm just asking ya to fuck with me one time, man. Or point a nigga in the right direction or something, bruh."

Ant stared into his passenger's eyes for a few tense seconds, trying to read him before he eventually nodded slowly as his expression softened back to normal. Tonio seemed to be an alright nigga to him, and he felt where he was coming from. He couldn't really identify, but he felt him. He knew he needed to be careful all the same, but he'd made up his mind. *Just to see what homes is about*, he thought to himself before he said, "You got a phone?"

"Hell nah," Snake laughed. "I got a pen, though," he said while reaching for his pocket.

"Take down this number and hit me in about two or three days, bruh. I'ma see what I can do for ya." He called out his number slowly.

Once Snake was sure he had the right digits, he said, "Aye, look, my nigga, I 'preciate it, man. For real, homes," he said earnestly as he stared Ant directly in his eyes and dapped him up.

"Yeah, ain't shit. Just make sure ya hit me, man," Ant said while nodding.

"Don't even worry about that, bruh. I'ma hit ya up," Snake said, opening the door and getting out of the car.

Bonk bonk. Ant hit the horn twice and sped off.

Pocketing the number, Snake turned and looked at his grandmother's house. It looked exactly the same as it had ten years ago. Raggedy and run-down on the outside, but it had always been kept spotless and squeaky clean on the inside. He made his way up the weed-strewn walkway, up the crumbling stone steps, and rang the doorbell. After waiting a few seconds and not hearing any movement inside, he knocked on the door.

"Wait a damn minute! I'm pretty sure whoever you is, you already know I'm old as hell. Gimme some damn time!"

Snake smiled and shook his head slowly. "Seventy-six and still kicking," he said to himself.

"Who the hell is it, any damn way? I ain't 'spectin' no damn comp'ny," she said as she swung the the door open.

"Hey, gramma," Snake said with a bright, genuine smile.

"Lawwwd," the old woman clapped both of her hands over her mouth and said quietly. Tears instantly came to her eyes as she looked at her only grandchild standing on her porch again after so many years. "Hey, Siree, baby! C'mo in here, boy, hurry up." She opened the screen door and pulled him inside by his arm.

He had only planned on staying for a little while, but after taking a bath and filling his stomach with a good homecooked meal, all of the things he used to dream about and even say he would do on his first day out were a million miles from his mind. The fact he really didn't have anywhere else to go played a role, but for the most part he was content with just sitting around the only person in the world that he knew gave a damn about him, the only person who loved him and actually cared whether he lived or died. The only person where, with him, those feelings were mutual.

"You know what, baby?" his granny said later that evening while they were watching an episode of C.S.I. "I blame yo' damn daddy. I always used to tell his ol' crazy-ass about having you out there ripping and running all in the streets with him. You was just a li'l boy, and he used to have you out there all times of the night while he was doing God knows what. Then he go off and get his self kilt like that." With a deep sigh, she shook her head slowly as tears filled her eyes at the thought of her only child and the way he was murdered.

Snake reached and grabbed his grandmother's hand. "It's a'ight, Gram. I'm good."

"No, it ain't, baby. I did the best I could with you and ya daddy. You know, I done heard about some of the things you supposedly done while you was out there in them streets."

"Ain't none of it true, Gramma. Don't believe none of..."

"I don't, baby. I don't," she cut him off while patting his hand tenderly. "But, I pray to God that ain't none of it true, 'cause I ain't raise you like that. That's why you gotta do right this time, Siree. Show everybody you ain't a bad person. Just like everybody else, you just done made a few mistakes." Her eyes pleaded with her grandson. She needed him to straighten himself up and fly right, because she didn't want to have to bury him, also. She couldn't stand to, didn't have the strength to deal with it.

Snake began to fidget a little. He was uncomfortable as hell because in all actuality, he was a bad person. The worst. His granny had all kinds of trust and faith in him, which was what was making him uncomfortable. Only if she knew half of the shit not many people besides himself knew he'd done, he wouldn't have been able to look at her right then. But it was way beyond too late to change now, because he had indeed grown into a true West Side nigga a long time ago. That slimy, cut-throat shit flowed proudly through his veins. It was embedded in him, had been since birth. The shit came naturally, like breathing.

And as a matter of fact, he was already kicking a scheme around in his head that involved resorting back to his old ways. He'd been gone for ten long years. Catching up at any and all costs was first and foremost on his brain, but his sweet, little old lady of a grandmother with her kind, rheumy eyes and sparkling personality didn't need to know all of that. She needed only to believe and be aware of what made her happy at this stage of her life.

He cleared his throat. "I need somewhere to stay for a minute, Gram, just until I can get my own spot," he said quietly.

She was delighted, but tried unsuccessfully not to show it. "Yo' old room ain't got nothing in it. Li'l ol' lady like me could use some comp'ny, anyway. All my good neighbors left a long time ago when this neighborhood first started going to shit. Bums and drug dealers everywhere you look nowadays."

"I'ma go on up to bed, then, Gram," Snake said and nodded while stifling a yawn.

"I'm right behind ya, baby. I'ma just check all the doors first," she said as they both stood up and headed in separate directions.

When he stepped into his old room, a flood of old memories slammed into him. But as soon as he lay down, a deep, comfortable sleep overcame him.

Ambitious

Chapter Two

Snake woke early the next morning to the hearty smell of breakfast being cooked. After washing up, he wolfed down a generous plateful and was on his way out of the front door when his grandmother called him. "Yes, ma'am?" he answered.

"Wait a second, baby," she said as she pattered into the front room. "Here you go. It ain't a lot, but I know you prob'ly need it a lot more than I do." She offered him three one hundred dollar bills.

"Nah, Gram, I'm straight. I got a li'l money," he protested, not even attempting to accept the money she was offering.

"Boy, quit being foolish and take it." He eyed the money warily. "If you don't, it's just gonna sit here," she said in an exasperated tone.

Smiling at the firm look she gave him, he took the money from her outstretched hand. "Thanks, Gram," he said. After pocketing the money, he began to to pat his other pockets in search of something and frowned slightly. "I think I left that form I need in the room. I'll be right back," he said before bounding up the stairs and heading straight to his grandmother's room. He put the three hundred dollars on her nightstand and took off, never having the slightest of intentions of keeping her money. He was dead set on going out and getting his own shit like he'd always done. Accepting money from his seventy-six year-old grandmother wasn't even an option for him.

Counting the hundred dollars Ant had given him the day before, he had one hundred and eighteen dollars to his name. No car, no place to live, nothing except a few of his old clothes his granny still had. And his hustle, which he knew he was going to have to turn up to catch up. He knew there was no way he could replace the past ten years he'd missed, but he could damn sure try to make up for lost time.

He kissed his grandmother's cheek when he went back downstairs and quickly left the house before she had a chance to discover he'd put the money back.

He planned on staying away from most of his old haunts and stomping grounds for a while because he wasn't ready for everybody to know he was out just yet, so he walked the short distance to Vine City Train Station. Even though things looked completely different from how he last remembered them, he wasn't completely lost, in terms of surroundings and direction, that is. He still had absolutely no idea about what he was going to do as far as getting money. One thing was for certain, though: he knew he wasn't about to start filling out job applications. That wasn't even a remote option.

He also knew that it took money to make money, and one hundred and eighteen dollars definitely wasn't enough to get something started to generate the kind of money he was after.

He got on the eastbound train, heading to no place in particular with the intentions of gathering his thoughts. The first conclusion he firmly arrived at was he needed a pistol. Fuck the whole convicted felon firearm law, he'd crossed and slimed so many people in the streets and in prison that he'd rather be caught with a strap than without one.

He threw his arm over the little partition by one set of the sliding doors on the train and stretched his legs out into the aisle as the wheels of his mind began to churn again. Before he knew it, the train was sliding to a smooth stop at King Memorial Station. A bell donged twice from a hidden speaker somewhere in the train car, and the doors in front of him and the ones a little to his left slid open with a mechanical whiz. He had a direct line of sight to all of the oncoming passengers, and in this case there weren't very many.

Two cute young chicks stepped onto the semi-deserted and quiet car, talking loud as hell, clearly in their own little world. Snake eyed them interestedly, surprised that he'd been out for a full day after serving a long-ass bid and right then was the first time he'd really noticed a female sexually. He wouldn't have minded smashing either – if not both – of them. Unconsciously staring with total disregard for manners, he took in everything about the duo, from their tiny tennis-shoed feet and skin-tight jeans to their two hundred dollar braids.

"Girl, guess what that fuck-nigga did. I swear, you ain't go' believe this shit," one of them said loudly to the other and then paused for dramatization.

"What the fuck he do, bitch? Damn, what, you waiting on me to die from suspense or some shit? What he do?"

They both laughed and sat in the two empty seats directly across from Snake. Once they got situated in their seats, the girl telling the story covered her mouth with her hand and leaned over to whisper in her friend's ear.

"You fuckin' lying, girl," she exclaimed in disbelief.

"Swear to God, girl," the storyteller said, the corners of her mouth just barely turning up in a sad smile as she nodded solemnly.

"I know that ol' trifling, bitch-ass nigga didn't," she'd started saying when she noticed Snake staring directly in her face. "Excuse you, ol' nosey-ass nigga! You got a damn problem or something?" she snapped and rolled her eyes slightly.

Completely caught off guard by her aggression toward him, Snake was at a loss for words. The handful of other passengers in the car tuned in discreetly in hopes of seeing some kind of altercation while one middle-aged black woman boldly reached in her purse and dug out her iPhone, ready to start recording.

"You gotta excuse my friend, man," the other girl said with a small laugh when she saw the shocked expression on Snake's face. "She kinda off a li'l bit."

"No, the fuck I ain't, and no, you don't, nigga. You just

need to mind yo' damn business! All in a bitch's mouth and shit. That's why muthafuckas be getting shot: being damn nosey."

"Jazmine, chill!" the other girl hissed quietly to her friend through clenched teeth. "That nigga big as hell, and I ain't got my fuckin' taser, girl. Be the fuck quiet, please, before he do something to us." She finished and turned to Snake with a bright, desperate smile on her face, her eyes begging him to forgive her friend and not attack them. "Please, don't worry about her," she said in a forced upbeat tone.

"Aye, look here, crazy-ass lady, my bad for staring, right?" Snake's deep voice boomed throughout the train car, although he wasn't yelling. "But I was really wanting to say something, and I was just about to, right before you went all postal on a nigga."

Obvious relief showed on one of their faces as the two girls sat quietly for a few seconds, appraising his handsome features. A look of approval came over one of their faces while a blank, uninterested expression made it's way onto the face of the one who'd been called Jazmine, once they both were sure and satisfied the handsome stranger posed no immediate threat to either of them. The lady who'd shamelessly been looking forward to some kind of altercation slipped her phone back into her purse and, with a loud and obvious sigh of disappointment, she turned back around in her seat.

"Well, what you waiting on? Say something," the one that seemed to have a bit more sense than the other said sweetly with a sexy little smile. By that time her friend's expression had turned from one of uninterested blankness to uninterested boredom as she prepared herself to listen to the inevitable flirting she knew was sure to come.

"Aye, you pretty, too, right, but I was really talking about ya li'l buddy right there beside ya," he said and pointed to the chick who had snapped on him.

"Who, me?" she said with a confused frown while pointing at her own chest, embarrassed as hell all of a sudden for how she'd acted, but not exactly knowing why.

"Yeah, you," he flashed a handsome smile and nodded. "You pretty as hell, and I think I was just about to tell ya so, right when you started blasting a nigga. Is attacking random niggas on the train, like, something you do in ya spare time? I mean, like, is that a hobby of yours or something?"

Even though he had a serious expression on his face, the aggressive chick noticed the glint of humor in Snake's gray eyes, and she smiled as her friend laughed and nudged her.

"I'm sorry, but you was—" she started, but Snake cut her off.

"Nah, my bad. I shouldn't have been staring, no matter how pretty you is. That's my fault, shawdy. But, look, though…"

He got up and moved closer to the pair of girls, and by the time they got off the train at Decatur Station, he'd learned their names were Jaz and Tasha. Both of them were twenty-six, and while Tasha was from Hollywood Court, a set of projects on Atlanta's West Side, Jaz was from Pink City, a very small set of projects in Atlanta's 4th Ward. It took a little prodding and convincing, especially after finding out he didn't even have a phone, but in the end he convinced Jaz to give him her number, and he told her she could count on hearing from him real soon.

The next time he checked his watch, it was 9:53 a.m. He had to go and check in with his probation officer sometime before noon. "Might as well go on and get this shit out the way," he said to himself when the train started to move again, heading westbound back toward Five Points Station.

When he got to the probation office downtown, he signed in and told the lady at the desk his name.

"Have a seat, Mr. Ellis, and I'll let your probation officer know you're here," she said while pointing to a row of empty chairs.

A few minutes later a prematurely-balding black man wearing a pair of black-framed prescription Polo glasses appeared from behind a door that led deeper into the building. "Ellis! Si – Si," he paused and squinted at the paper he held in his hand. "Si-ree? Siree Ellis!" he called out.

Snake stood up. "Yeah, that's me," he said.

"Come with me," he said and led the way down a cluttered hallway to a small, cramped office with paperwork scattered all around it. "You can sit down. How you say ya first name, man? I know I prob'ly fucked it up."

"Siree."

"Siree?" he asked in a questioning tone.

Snake nodded. "Yeah, that's right."

The P.O. nodded. "A'ight," he said. "My name is Mike. No Mr. This-or-That, just plain ol' M-I-K-E. Got it?"

Snake nodded again, not really knowing what to make of the guy. He knew he hadn't been expecting him to come off as okay, either, but he would wait until the meeting was over before he made an assumption.

"Good. Now," Mike fumbled around on his unorganized desk until he found what he was looking for. "Says here you just did a decade for armed robbery. You planing on doing it again?"

"No, sir."

"Good, 'cause you'll end up right back in the slamma, and for life if you do it again and get caught. And, uh, no, sir's. Just Mike." He flipped a page in Snake's file and continued. "You drink, man?"

"Just a li'l, yeah."

"Smoke weed?"

Snake hesitated a second before going with his instinct over his gut. "Nah, I don't smoke," he lied, preferring not to tell on himself.

All movement stopped for a few seconds as Mike stared pointedly into Snake's eyes. He took off his glasses, closed his eyes, and rubbed his temples. "So, basically, what you saying is the first time you piss dirty, you want me to violate ya and send ya back to the can?"

"Nah, man," Snake shook his head slightly. "I be smokin' a li'l."

"A'ight, listen. We go' get this shit straight, right here, right now." Mike put his glasses back on and used one of his hands to wipe his mouth. "When I ask you something, you tell me the truth. Example: you killed anybody lately? If you have, then this is how you respond: yeah, I had to shoot a muthafucka two days ago 'cause.... You get me?" he said through a little laugh, but he was dead serious. "I ain't go' ask you no shit like that, but you get my drift. Be one hundred percent honest with me, and I'll go to bat for you whenever you need me to. I know it's hard as hell out there, man, especially for a convicted felon, so I ain't applying no pressure, but I do want you to at least try to find a job. It'll keep you occupied and give you less time to get into some bullshit."

He puckered his lips like he was about to start whistling and made a ticking sound with his tongue as his eyes devoured the words on the page of Snake's file that he was looking at. "All I need you to do is report twice a month. When you find a job, you can come in once a month and report by phone once a month. I know you smoke, so I won't piss you often. Can you pass a test now," he looked over the top of his glasses and asked.

Snake shook his head no. "I smoked the night before I released."

"Okay. Anyway, listen, I hate to lock people up, but I will. You can pretty much do what you want as long as you stay out of trouble, but if you don't report, I'ma book ya. Lie to me one time, and I'ma book ya," he said in a no-nonsense tone. "That's about it. As long as you don't catch any serious felonies, I'll try my best to have you out of Rice Street in thirty days, if I can. Here's my number." He handed him a card. "You report every other Thursday. Cool?"

"Got it," Snake said, looking at the card.

"You can go now, man. I know you prob'ly anxious as hell to get out there in the world. Just be careful, big man. A lot's changed in ten years."

Snake nodded and stood up, turning to leave as Mike answered his ringing phone. "Hold on a second, honey. Hey, Siree?"

"Yeah?" Snake looked over his shoulder just as he reached the door and saw Mike with the phone to his ear, his hand covering up the end.

"Welcome home, black man."

"'Preciate it, man," Snake responded with a small smile and nod of his head as he opened the door and stepped out into the hallway.

"Umph!" The wind was briefly knocked out of him when he bumped into someone walking past the door. "Oh, shit, my fault, I ain't even see ya. Smurf?" he exclaimed as he closed his P.O.'s door behind him, surprise registering in his squinted eyes.

"Yeah, what's up?" Smurf said, and then recognition dawned on his face when he got a good look at the brick wall that just bumped into him. Recognition quickly turned to hate, fear, and worry all wrapped up in one.

"What's up, young nigga?" Snake said with a gleam in his eyes that Smurf didn't like.

"Shit, man. I ain't got shit going on. When you got out?" he asked, his voice sounding exactly how he was feeling: shook.

"Damn, my nigga. You act like you seeing a ghost or something. Relax, fool. You ain't glad to see a nigga back out?" he asked with an evil little smirk.

"Yeah, man. A nigga really just shocked," he lied unconvincingly. If truth be told, Snake was the last nigga on the planet he wanted to see. He had hoped and prayed for a long time that somebody would kill his ass while he was in prison, but unfortunately nobody had wanted to do the entire world that favor. And now, because of that selfishness, he was back. And if his expression was any indication, nothing had changed. He was still on the bullshit.

"I been hearing good things about ya, boi. Ol' Fif' Ward Smurf." He quietly clapped his hands together and started to rub them. "Yo' name ringing even behind them prison walls, young nigga," he said as his evil grin widened. "You know I'm looking for a blessing, right? I'm fucked up, bruh. Cut a nigga a check or something, pahtna. Tear it off."

Completely taken aback, Smurf just stared at him, unblinking. *This nigga done went crazy,* he thought to himself. *Don't you know I would rather die and go to hell before I even pissed on yo' ass if you was on fire, nigga?*

He shook his head and blinked rapidly a few times, trying to clear his head. "Uh, yeah. I got ya, bruh. Take my number and holla at me tonight, and I'ma fuck with ya," he said and called out his number while Snake wrote it down. "But yeah, though, man, I gotta get back to my P.O. office before that ho start tripping. I'ma holla at ya," he said and rushed off before Snake could even respond, but it didn't really matter.

"I got yo' ass, nigga," he mumbled and thumped the piece of paper with Smurf's number on it as he started to leave the building. He walked back to Garnett Station, paid his fair, and got on the northbound train. He stepped off the train at Five Points, the station that sat in the heart of downtown Atlanta, and moved with the flow of other people toward the escalators. It was still pretty early, only 12:15 p.m., when he walked out of the train station, and his stomach rumbled loudly as he emerged into the bright spring sunshine. "What's up with chow, man?" he complained to himself while rubbing his stomach. Then he realized what he'd said and a smile came to his face. "I can eat whenever the fuck I want to, man. I'm fuckin' tripping," he mumbled quietly while shaking his head as he walked to the Chinese restaurant on the side of the train station.

After paying for his food, he crossed Peachtree Street and walked over to Underground Atlanta, where he sat on the concrete steps to eat and watch the fascinating, bustling flow of foot traffic around him. When he finished eating, he got out his cigarettes and saw there were only seven left. "Damn, man," he mumbled and sighed before lighting up. He needed a plan, and a damn good one, fast!

He smoked the Newport until the filter started to fizzle before thumping it away and standing up. He did a quick stretch and wiped his mouth free of crumbs with his hands before walking back to Five Points. He had just passed through the turnstile when a young nigga walked by him and mumbled, "I got sacks of the gas, shawdy."

Snake looked at the kid and saw he couldn't have been more than fifteen, sixteen at the most, and that was pushing it. V-neck, True Religion jeans, and a pair of Prada shots on his feet, he pegged him as a young hustla. "What's hap'ning?"

"Come to the bathroom," the young nigga said and kept walking.

Snake followed him to the bathroom, which reeked of urine so strongly it could be smelled a good ten feet from the entrance. Under the pretense of taking a piss, he stood at one of the urinals and waited for a white man in a cheap suit, carrying a briefcase to leave. "A'ight, li'l homie, what you got?" he said calmly.

The young nigga looked up at Snake. "You just got out from down the road?" he asked.

"Hell yeah. How you know?"

The young hustla shrugged. "Shit, I just can tell," he said disinterestedly before digging in his pocket and pulling out a big bomb of exotic-looking weed. "Since you just got out, I'ma fuck with ya. Gimme thirty dollars and get you five of these dimes."

Snake struck as fast as lightening. Before the young nigga even had a chance to think about what had hit him, he was crumpling to the filthy, pissy floor of the restroom, unconscious from a precisely-aimed, left-handed jab to the chin. He quickly fluffed the kid's pockets and found a big bomb of gas and a fat wad of cash rubber-banded together and cuffed in the youngster's crotch. For some reason when he felt the steel barrel of the pistol, it angered him. "Ya li'l bastard. Prob'ly would've tried to shoot me, wouldn't ya?" he said as he was tucking the forty-cal in his pocket. He looked down at the unconscious kid and kicked him in the face before he hurried out of the restroom and to the westbound platform.

As soon as he stepped off the escalator, the train destined for Bankhead Station was getting ready to pull out. "Right on muthafuckin' time," he said to himself as he stepped through the sliding doors of the train. The doors closed smoothly behind him right after he boarded, and Snake watched as the platform turned to a blur.

Ambitious

Chapter Three

"It's $23.17, sir," the cab driver said in a heavy Indian accent as Snake closed the back door of the taxi after he got out.

"'Preciate it, Abu, but I ain't paying," he said sarcastically to the cabbie and started to walk away, ignoring the irate shouts and protests to come back and pay. He could've easily paid the fare for the ride – he'd taken close to thirteen hundred dollars from the kid at Five Points earlier that day – but why not jam on the cabbie if he could? He was a foreigner. "Prob'ly ain't s'posed to be over here, any-damn-way," he shrugged and said to himself, chuckling at the cab driver's angry rant as he walked through Grady Homes.

He was headed to Jaz's spot, the crazy broad he'd met on the train earlier that day. He had called her just like he'd told her he would after trying unsuccessfully at least three times to contact Smurf. In the end, he'd resolved that the nigga had given him the wrong number on purpose, so he'd filed it in the the back of his mind with the intention of straightening it up the very next time he saw the little sissy. But right now, some potential pussy was waiting. "Fuck Smurf," he mumbled aloud while looking at the piece of paper he'd written her address on to make sure he was about to knock on the right door. After checking, he stepped up to the door and knocked.

Jaz answered in a pair of electric blue tights and a cut-off v-neck t-shirt. "Hey, what's u? You can c'mo' in," she said softly with a smile before moving aside so he could enter.

"What's hap'nin', shawdy?" Snake said as he stepped into the newly-rebuilt Grady Homes apartment. Before he went to prison ten years ago, Grady Homes had looked like an ordinary set of inner city projects. Now they looked a bit better than they had.

"Shit. You smoke, right?"

"Don't ya smell it on me?" he said, pulling out a few grams

of the weed he'd taken earlier.

Jaz smiled, glad she could keep her little weed. "Well, roll up. Wraps is on the coffee table. I'll be right back."

She hurried to the back room and was back in under a minute after putting on a bra and a pair of tight-fitting True Religion jeans. "So, you from The Bluff, right? I know a few people over that way. Who yo' folks is? I might know them." She sat on the opposite end of the same couch Snake was sitting on and turned the TV on.

"Shit, most of my folks dead or locked up. Ain't nothing but some new and young niggas running around over there, now. I don't know too many of them, so I don't fuck with them," he said in a distracted tone as he focused on rolling the weed.

"Oh," she said and nodded when she saw there was nothing else forthcoming from him about that.

"Where ya li'l buddy at?" he cut his eyes up at her and asked, but immediately returned them to his busy hands that were rolling the blunt.

Jaz didn't seem to mind the change of conversation at all. "Who, Tasha?" she asked eagerly with a smirk. "Stupid-ass bitch back over that lame-ass nigga she in love with house. She go' be back ova here again crying in the next few days about some shit that bitch-ass nigga done did, watch. Shit don't never fuckin' fail," she shook her head knowingly.

Snake paused and looked at her with a small frown on his face. He was a bit confused. Shaking his head, he shrugged it off with a little laugh. "I thought that was ya pahtna. How you just go' take her ass out like that? Here, fire this up," he said while passing her the rolled blunt.

Laughing lightly, which was pleasant and sexy sounding to him because it was so feminine, she took the blunt from him and had to stand up to work the lighter from the tight front pocket of her True's. "'Cause that shit true. She stupid as fuck, man. I been knowing Tash since, like, the sixth grade, and I love that bitch like a sister, but she a–" She caught herself about to cross the line and lit up the gas instead of finishing up what she'd been about to say. "Bitch ain't no saint," she said with a shake of her head. "And she do be causing a lot of problems for herself, but she be letting Ant ol' slick, gay ass get away with too much shit just 'cause he got a li'l money." She inhaled the weed smoke and looked at Snake as if she was waiting for him to agree whole-heartedly with what she'd just said. The fact he didn't know Tasha too well, or her nigga at all, obviously didn't matter not one bit to her, judging by the expectant expression on her face.

"What the fuck? Why you say her nigga gay?" Snake laughed and asked with a shocked and puzzled look on his face.

Jaz looked at him pointedly before saying, "This fuck-nigga be wanting her to stick 'er tongue in his ass and shit, and that's just what she told me about. Faggot-ass nigga prob'ly be wanting her to strap up on him and put him in the buck, too," she said with a giggle. "But for real, though, what kinda real nigga be wanting they ass played with like that? That shit suspect as hell to me, I'm sorry."

Seeing that she had a valid point and agreeing with her one hundred percent, Snake nodded slightly. "That shit do sound suspect as fuck. Her nigga getting a li'l paperwork, though?"

Jaz sucked her teeth. "Man, hell yeah, that lame ass nigga loaded. Him and his pahtna Smurf. Wait, you know Smurf? He from over your way. We went to alternative school together." She hit the weed again and passed it.

Snake thought for a second on the best way for him to respond, the world all of a sudden seeming two times too damn small. "Yeah, I know bruh. He a young nigga, though. We ain't neva fucked around."

Jaz threw both of her legs over the arm of the couch and

exhaled a stream of smoke. "Smurf older than me by a few years. How old you is, nigga?" she sat right back up quickly and asked, realizing that if Smurf was a young nigga to him, then he was a hell of a lot older than she had assumed. The whole time she'd been thinking that she was older than him.

Snake took a deep pull on the blunt. "How old I look?" he asked, his voice strained a little because he was holding the smoke in his lungs.

She stared into his extremely handsome face, taking in his full, nice-colored lips and his strong jawline, the perfect bone structure of his face and prominent cheekbones, his handsome nose and his icy-gray eyes and had no choice but to blush. He was even more attractive than she remembered. He was an outright masterful work of art, if it was okay to use that term in reference to a man. "You look like you about twenty," she said truthfully.

It was Snake's turn to blush then, his light-skinned cheeks and forehead turning a little rosy. "I'm twenty-three," he said with a serious expression and exhaled the smoke.

"You lying, nigga," she said with a playful laugh.

Snake laughed, too. "Yeah, I'm bullshitting. I wish I was fuckin' twenty-three. I'm thirty-five, though, shawdy."

The smile abruptly vanished from Jaz's face, and she hit him with a deadpan stare. It wasn't until it became apparent he wasn't joking that she spoke again. "You serious?" she asked, beyond shocked.

"Yeah, you don't believe me?" He smiled, showing off his straight and even teeth, assuring her he was the poster boy of physical perfection.

With a skeptical frown, she inhaled through her clenched teeth. "I do," she said, and then she started to shake her head slowly. "But at the same time I don't," she laughed lightly. "You don't look no damn thirty-five. You look like a kid, honey."

"'Preciate it," he shrugged and smiled again, and then hit the blunt. "Good genes, I guess."

Jaz nodded, then began to frown slightly as her mind started racing. "Where yo' ol' lady at? And I know you got one, so don't even lie," she demanded accusingly.

Caught off guard by her tone and expression, he cleared his throat. "What make ya say that?" he asked with smoke slowly coming from his nose and mouth.

"I'm just saying," she said with a shake of her head. "You don't think she would have a problem with you being over here like this? 'Cause I think she would if she knew. Plus, I don't get down like that. Fuckin' with other bitches' niggas ain't my thing," she finished matter-of-factly.

Snake frowned and stared into her eyes for a few tense seconds as a thin stream of smoke billowed up slowly from the lit end of the blunt. He concluded right then that she was a bit mentally unstable, which was too damn bad because he'd really been feeling her before she went berserk for no apparent reason, accusing him of shit he had absolutely no idea how she concluded in the first place. And that was exactly the type of shit he could do without, but damn, she was sexy as hell. "Man, what the fuck was that?" he asked quietly with a confused frown.

"'Cause I know how niggas play all kinda–"

"Nah," he cut her off while shaking his head. "You don't know me, though," he pointed at his chest with both of his thumbs. "You doing way too much, shawdy. You should've just asked me if you wanted to know if I had a girl or not. Don't just start accusing a nigga and shit. I ain't got no ol' lady. I don't know how the hell you even came up with that shit, and what's up with all this ol' extra aggressive-ass, bi-polar-ass shit you on? We was just sitting here, kicking shit, and then you just spazzed on a nigga for no fuckin' reason. What's up with you, man?" he asked disgustedly as he shook his head again.

Taking a split second to consider the fact that she might've jumped the gun a bit, Jaz started to apologize. "Look, I'm sorry," she managed to say before he cut her off again.

"You good, fuck that shit. Just be cool. Here," he passed her the burning blunt. "Let's just smoke this shit and chill, man. Kick it. You got some more wraps? It wasn't but one on the table," he said, trying his best to put her at ease so the psycho-aggressive bitch would go away and the cool, sexy one would come back.

They watched TV as they talked about this and that, oblivious to the hours passing by, and it was close to 2:30 a.m. before either of them noticed the time. "Damn, it done got late as fuck," she mumbled after glancing at the clock.

Snake was high as hell, but her little statement brought on a brief stint of sobriety. After smoking his weed up, he hoped like hell she didn't think he was just about to leave. That would defeat the purpose of him not taking off earlier when she went all crazy on him. No, leaving empty-handed just simply wasn't an option for him. She had to come up off the pussy, or at least some money or something. "Yeah, it is, ain't it?" he mumbled slowly, being sure to put the ball in her court before exposing his hand, maybe without it even being necessary.

"Aye, look, you ain't go' be no dirty-ass nigga and go and steal up all my shit, is you?" she asked with squinted, suspicious eyes.

And just like that, the crazy bitch was back! Right then and there Snake decided it might be best if he just left after all, but before leaving, he just had to know. "What the fuck?" he said, pointing at her with a frown on his face as he pulled his slumping figure upright on the couch. "Where the fuck all this other shit coming from, shawdy?"

"'Cause I done had a few bad experiences with some lame-ass niggas that will steal all a bitch shit if she slip," she said defensively.

"Oh yeah?" Snake raised both of his thick eyebrows and said in a tone that conveyed how little he cared.

Angered by his patronizing tone and expression, Jaz continued her defensive stand. "Hell yeah, nigga! Lame-ass, childish-ass niggas get mad 'cause they can't have they way, and then they start stealing and trying to take shit!"

"And once again, how the fuck do any of that shit relate to me?"

Her cute, almond-shaped eyes flashed anger. "It relate to you 'cause I don't wanna have to go through that shit again. I was about to tell you that you could stay here tonight 'cause it's so late," she snapped.

With only one brow raised, Snake frowned slightly. "C'mo, man, I done came all the way over here, done smoked my weed with you. We was just major kicking it, shawdy. How the fuck you go' turn right the fuck around and ask me if I'ma try to steal from ya? I ain't gave yo' ass not one reason to think I would do some sucka shit like that. You just tried the fuck out of me.

"Well, my bad. I ain't mean to piss you off, but it is what it is 'cause niggas do bullshit like that, and I'm just trying to protect myself."

"Yeah, only a sucka," he said and stared into her pretty face for a couple of seconds before he relaxed with a sigh and shook his head.

"Anyway, it's some food and stuff in the fridge. It ain't much 'cause I just got my stamps today. I'ma go grocery shopping tomorrow, but you can get you something if you want to, though," she said while standing up to stretch.

Snake eyed her flat stomach lustfully. He noticed the piercing in her belly button and was imagining himself playing with it with his tongue when he realized she was watching him stare at her.

"What?" she asked hoarsely when he looked into her eyes. The bickering back and forth between them from only a few seconds ago seemed to be long forgotten by both of them, and now the atmosphere felt like it was charged with extreme sexual tension.

"You already know *what*. C'mere, shawdy," he said quietly as he stood up and gently pulled her toward him.

Horny as hell just from the thought of screwing him, she allowed him to pull her to him. "Uh-uh, boy, stop," she protested weakly as he caressed her plump ass and bare stomach. Her breath caught in her throat and she bit the corner of her bottom lip while closing her eyes when he began to place soft little kisses and nibble on her neck. What he was doing to her felt amazing. Her heart was pounding, her pussy was getting hotter and wetter by the second, and she wanted him.

She desperately wanted to succumb to her desires and indulge in a few rounds of hot, sweaty, frenzy-paced sex with the modern-day black Adonis that was currently feeling her up, but she couldn't. For one, she didn't know him, and she definitely wasn't in the business of fucking random niggas she met. And two, she'd learned from past experiences she couldn't let niggas smash too quick, especially if she wanted him to look at her as anything more than just another piece of ass, and she definitely wanted Tonio to stick around so she could get to know him. Something about him was drawing her to him.

So, as much as it pained her to do so, she put her foot down and stopped him when he started to ease his hands to the button of her Trues. "Uh-uh, stop," she said just above a whisper as she grabbed his hand and took a step away from him, her eyes pleading for him to understand that she just couldn't do it. "I. I want to, but I can't." She steeled herself with a deep breath. "I ain't like that. Plus, I'm on my period," she said with an embarrassed look on her face.

"No, man." Snake mumbled as he dropped his head, devastated. He stood there, looking down at his feet for a few seconds before he started to shake his head slowly.

When he began to pat his pockets and look around for his things, Jaz spoke up. "Don't go. You ain't gotta leave, Tonio. It's late as fuck. I told you that you could stay here until tomorrow," she said in a soft voice.

Stay for what? he wanted to say, but he didn't. Then he thought about having to make the trip back to his grandmother's spot and sighed with a slight frown. "Where I'm s'posed to sleep at?" he asked with another sigh.

Jaz couldn't hide her smile. She'd been one hundred percent positive he was about to leave when he found out he wasn't about to smash, so his reaction was a pleasant surprise. She pointed at one of the two sofas in her living room. "I'ma get you a pillow and some covers," she said while turning to leave the living room. "Now, I just hope he don't try to rob me blind," she mumbled to herself.

Ambitious

Chapter Four

It was early afternoon when Snake opened his eyes and saw Jaz sitting on the other couch, fully dressed and staring at him. "What's up, man? Why the fuck you watching me sleep like that?" he snapped as he bolted upright, his eyes sweeping from left to right in search of a possible threat.

"I'm sorry, I ain't mean to scare you," she said, and then her eyes squinted as she pointed at him. "Something ain't right about you, though. I don't know what it is yet, but it's something," she accused as she wagged her finger at him.

"What the fuck is you talking about now, man?" he frowned and asked.

"You s'posed to be from The Bluff, right?"

With a smirk, he said, "I am! What the fuck you mean, 's'posed to be'?" he challenged quietly.

"So you know Ms. Betty then, right," she asked.

Snake gave a loud, sharp laugh. He'd forgotten all about Ms. Betty over the years since he'd last seen her. "Who don't know her nosey, old ass? What about her?"

"Well, I saw her this morning while I was at the store."

"So?" he shrugged and frowned.

"I asked her about you, and she said ain't no Tonio over there that look like you," she said matter-of-factly.

"So what?" he shrugged again. "Fuck her, she don't know what the fuck she talking about. It ain't like her old ass know every damn body that's from the hood, anyway," he said, swinging his legs to the floor.

Jaz stood up. "I said the same damn thing 'cause I wanna believe you. But then I thought about how every time we started talking about you last night, you changed the subject."

"You tripping, shawdy," he said, glaring at her with angry gray eyes. "You the same muthafucka that blasted me on the train about being nosey the other day. You ain't my bitch, you ain't even gave a nigga no pussy. How the fuck can you possibly think it's cool fa yo' ass to be going around asking folks about me?"

"'Cause, nigga, so many of these niggas out here be so watered down or on some undacover fag shit nowadays. I like yo' ass, and I wanted to know what was up with you," she snapped. It was just that simple. She'd be a damn fool to not do a background check on a nigga she wanted to fuck with now because she was absolutely determined to not wind up fucking with another busta or nigga that had a history of pushing fudge.

"How the fuck you like me? You don't even know shit about me, shawdy. I could be a damn serial killer or some shit for all you know," he said with a mocking smirk on his face.

"That's why I asked her about you. Didn't I just say that?" She frowned and shook her head. "And anyway, nigga, if you was go' do something to me, you would've been did it. And I'm just a bartender you met on the train, honey, so I know it ain't my vast fortune you trying to play up under me for, so don't try that shit, either, Mr. Serial Killer. So what's up, what's the deal with you?"

When Snake made no attempt to speak, she began to get frustrated. "Look, nigga, yo' ass about to tell me something or you about to get the hell out my house, simple and plain," she snapped.

"Damn, man! A'ight! Since yo' ass just gotta know every fuckin' thing," he exploded. "I just got out of prison, shawdy. I just did ten got-damn years, and I been out for three fuckin' days! I ain't got shit! No money, nowhere to stay, nothing! There! You fuckin' happy? Still like a nigga now?"

Jaz frowned. "Nigga why the fuck you ain't just tell me all that shit from the get-go? I don't give a damn about you not having shit or going to jail, nigga! Hell I'ma care about some punk-ass shit like that for? I wanna know why you made up all that other shit."

"What other shit, man? What the fuck is you talking about?"

"All that shit about being from–"

"Listen to me," Snake cut her off and sighed before speaking again in a much calmer tone than either of them had used in a while. "I been born and raised right there in The Bluff. Twelve forty-six, James P. Ms. Betty know me. Her old ass go' turn a flip when she see me again."

"Why she say she ain't know you, then?" she asked with an unbelieving expression on her face.

Snake dropped his head and cut his eyes up at her. "'Cause my name ain't Tonio, shawdy," he mumbled.

"Wait, what." She shook her head quickly like she was trying to shake off a daze. "What you just said, nigga? I know good and got-damn well I just heard yo' ass wrong."

Snake cleared his throat and looked at her. "I said my name ain't Tonio," he said loud and clear enough for her to hear.

"What!" She blew a gasket. A big vein appeared in her neck, and it was pulsing rapidly. "What the fuck you mean? That's what the fuck I'm talking about right there, lying and shit!"

"Just relax, man."

"Relax! Nigga, is you fuckin' slow? All this fuckin' time I been thinking yo' fuckin' name was Tonio! I been calling yo' ass that shit, and that ain't even yo' fuckin'–" She paused, took a deep breath, and exhaled loudly, trying to get ahold of her anger. "What's yo' muthafuckin' name, nigga?" she snapped while scowling at him.

"Snake."

"Snake ain't on ya birth certificate, nigga. What's ya government? Lemme see some I.D. or something," she snapped again because she just knew he was trying to push her buttons by telling her his name was fucking Snake.

Snake frowned and shook his head. "You doing way too

much, jones. I'm about to just get my shit and get the hell on."
He started to put his shoes on.

"Wait, nigga, is you really fuckin' slow or something? You telling me you would really rather walk out on a bitch that wanna get to know you and fuck with you, that's taking care of her shit, with her own place while you ain't got nothing or nowhere to go, than tell her yo' real fuckin' name and the truth about you?" she asked with a disbelieving look on her pretty face. She knew once she laid out the facts, he wouldn't leave when he really thought about it.

Snake smirked. "Yeah, 'cause that shit you kicking sound good but it really ain't. On the outside looking in, it might seem like you the perfect bitch for a nigga but you fronting," he shook his head and pointed at her. "You got issues, shawdy, and for a minute I was thinking maybe it was 'cause you on ya period. But after this shit, I'm realizing that ain't it. It's way deeper than that with you. So to answer yo' question, you fuckin' right! I swear, I would rather walk out this bitch and go sleep under a fuckin' bridge tonight than have to put up with yo' ol' crazy, bipolar-ass for a second longer when I ain't got to," he said and made his move toward the door.

"Nigga, you a dumbass," she said while glaring at him. "Get the fuck out." She pointed toward the door. "Don't ever worry about calling me again," she followed behind him saying.

"Whatever, psycho bitch, I wouldn't even dream of calling yo' ass no more. Ain't nobody got time for that crazy-ass shit you on, anyway," he said, patting his pockets to make sure he had all of his stuff and then hit the door without so much as a glance back at the beautiful psycho known as Jaz. *Good riddance!* he thought to himself while crossing the threshold.

"Stupid-ass nigga." She slammed the door shut behind him and raced to get her phone.

***

"Stupid-ass, nosey-ass bitch. And got the fuckin' nerve to blow on me on the train for being nosey, and her ass turn right the fuck around and go to trying to interrogate a nigga and shit. Nosey-ass ho prob'ly went looking for Ms. Betty old ass," Snake vented to himself as he walked to King Memorial Train Station just across the street from Grady Homes.

As soon as he reached the street level bus terminal, gunshots rang out. *Boc boc boc boc boc!* A bullet whizzed by just inches from his arm, prompting him to duck a little lower and run a little faster.

"Pussy-ass nigga! I'ma kill yo' bitch-ass!" *Boc boc boc boc boc!*

Snake heard somebody yell from his right, so he shot a quick glance that way and saw the young nigga he'd robbed the day before at Five Points Station standing about 25 yards off, gunning at him with no regard for the other people around. "Where the fuck this nigga come from?" he exclaimed as he kicked into high gear and began to take the long flight of stairs up to the platform by threes and fours. He could hear a train approaching.

Boc boc boc boc!

He just hoped like hell it was the westbound, because the platforms were separated and that was the one he was running to. By now the young nigga had made it to the bottom of the flight of stairs he was practically flying up.

Boc boc boc boc!

"What the fuck this nigga shooting?" Snake yelled to himself because it didn't seem like the nigga was ever going to run out of bullets.

Police sirens wailed in the distance, and pure pandemonium had erupted as soon as the first shots were fired, but through it all Snake had kept running. Up, up and up the extremely long flight of stairs, over the turnstile, and across the platform just in time to stick his hand between the doors of the train as they slid closed. They slid back open and he rushed onboard, panting and out of breath. A few people eyed him curiously as the doors closed again and he shrugged. "Them niggas shooting down there."

***

"What up?" Ant answered his phone after the third ring.

"Can I speak to Ant?"

"This me. Hold up," he said and moved the phone away from his mouth before yelling. "Aye, Tasha! Bring yo' ass here, girl!" When he came back on the line, he spoke in a much calmer, normal tone of voice. "Yeah, man, this me. Who this?" he asked.

"This Tonio. You had gave me a ride the other day when I first got out."

"Oh yeah, yeah. I remember ya, bruh. What's hap'ning?"

"Shit, I can't call it, man. I was–"

"Hold up, man," he cut Snake off and moved the phone away from his mouth again. "Didn't I tell yo' ass to go on ahead and do that shit? Now look, stupid-ass girl! Clean that shit up, shawdy!"

Snake heard a female mumbling something in the background and then Ant's angry voice again.

"Man, shut the fuck up and get that shit up," And then he was back on the line again. "Hello," he said.

"Aye, I can hit ya back if you want me to, bruh," Snake volunteered.

"Nah, you good, man. My ho just did some stupid-ass shit I told her ass not to do. Shit straight. What's up, though?"

"Shit, man, you had told me to halla at ya in a couple days."

"Yeah, yeah, yeah," he said quickly. "I remember. You caught me at the perfect time, too. Check the move, right. I'ma be on yo' side a li'l later on. You think you can meet me at The Flame at about eleven, homie?"

Snake nodded. "Hell yeah, I can do that."

"Well, check that. I'ma holla at ya then, jones," Ant said and hung up before Snake could even respond.

He hung up the phone and lay back across his bed at his grandmother's house. A Newport burned slowly in his fingers as he thought about what had happened earlier after leaving the nosey broad's crib. He didn't know if she had anything to do with the young nigga shooting at him, but it sure as hell was funny how that little bastard just popped up out of nowhere. What were the chances of them being in the same place at the same time that soon after he'd knocked his ass out and robbed him? It was one hell of a coincidence, if it was one, but in the end he took a long drag on his cigarette and shrugged, deciding to say fuck it. If he saw the young nigga again, he would just kill his ass. And as for the crazy bitch Jaz, if he ever saw her ass coming, he would be sure to run the other way.

Ambitious

Chapter Five

The Blue Flame had once been considered Atlanta's cream of the crop of strip clubs. It had risen to prominence during the mid- to late eighty's and remained there all throughout the nineties. At the turn of the millennium, it began it's extremely slow-paced, but steady downslide, mainly because many of the up-and-coming new clubs and a few of the older ones had stepped it up a notch or two and had a little more to offer. Located in the heart of one of the city's most dangerous and gutter hoods, Bankhead, it could still draw a more than decent crowd of good, paying pussy-watchers and tricks on any given night. Local and nationwide rap, movie, and sports stars still slid through occasionally to throw their money around, so it was nothing to see exotic whips parked in the V.I.P. out in front of the club.

That night, though, it was just the local dope boys and average Joes patronizing the establishment. Snake got out of the taxi and looked around for Ant's car before paying the cabbie. He pulled his new True Religion snap-back hat low to cover his eyes and walked to the entrance of the club where he paid one of two bouncers before the other one started to pat him down.

"You can't bring that pistol in here, homie," the bigger of the two said in a booming voice when he felt the strap.

Snake had honestly forgotten he had the pistol on him. "Shit, my ride just left, man. I'm just supposed to be meeting somebody up here. I ain't go' start no shit, man."

"You gotta leave it outside, dude. It can't go in there with you," the same bouncer said. He was all business, and he wasn't going to budge.

Snake shook his head. He thought about trying to slide them a bill to let him in with it, but said fuck it. He'd just find somewhere to hide it outside of the club. "I'ma be right back, man," he said and headed around to the back of the club where he found a good enough hiding spot for the pistol between some crumbling bricks and quickly returned to the entrance of the club.

The second pat search was a little more thorough than the first one, and the bouncer gave Snake a long, hard stare before stepping aside to let him pass through the curtain made of shiny blue beads.

Rick Ross and Nicki Minaj's *The Boss* was blasting from the club's hidden audio system, and the smells of pussy and perfume were heavy and intoxicating. It instantly hit him that after ten hard-ass years of being in prison, he'd been out three days and still hadn't had any pussy. He looked up at the stage as a dark-skinned dancer slid slowly down a pole. The couple of hundred bucks in his pocket felt like it had ignited when she noticed him staring at her and beckoned for him to come closer. He did so immediately, and she crawled toward him on her hands and knees. Once he was as close to the stage as he could get, she got to her knees and began to roll her body and move in rythm with the music as she stared boldly and seductively into his grey eyes, hoping all the while that he wasn't a cheap skate.

He pulled a fifty dollar bill from his pocket and dropped it on the stage in front of her after a few minutes of watching her sexy ass dance. "Come find me when you leave the stage, shawdy," he said, and she winked to acknowledge she'd heard him before he turned and walked away.

The crowd in the club wasn't large, so he was able to find an unoccupied seat and table easily. He chose one off in a corner that gave him a good view of the stage and an unobstructed view of the entrance of the club and began to wait on Ant to show up. It was only a quarter until eleven, anyway. Turning down offer after offer of lap dances from one pretty dancer after another while he waited, he was determined to save his little money in hopes the chocolate stripper chick would let him pay for a shot of the pussy a little later on.

He was in the process of turning down yet another dance when he saw Ant stroll through the entrance of the club. It was just before eleven, and it looked like he was rocking by himself. "Shouts out to Zone Three! The South in this bitch," the DJ announced into his mic, cutting into Young Money's *Bedrock*, immediately upon spotting Ant, who gave a lazy salute and pulled a half-naked waitress close to him. Jonesboro South was a set of projects in Atlanta's zone 3.

The strippers seemed to come to life when he walked in, and from the way they were buzzing around the place now, it actually seemed to be a bit crowded in the club, Snake noticed. They must've known he had a li'l paper.

By that time he had pretty much figured out the Ant who was helping him out was the same Ant the crazy bitch Jaz was telling him about the night before, and once again he thought about how small the world seemed to be.

He waited for him to to sit down before he stood to go over and talk to him. Holding his hat in his hands, he walked past a nigga getting a lap dance from a big-bootied, pretty-ass redbone, and when she turned around to grind her ass on the nigga's lap, she and Snake made eye contact briefly. Her expression changed to one he couldn't quite read before she looked away from him.

"What's hap'ning, homie? You good?" Ant said when he saw Snake approaching.

Pulling his attention away from the badass redbone, he answered as they dapped and he sat down, placing his hat on the table. "Yeah, bruh," he drawled. "What up."

"Nothing major. Same ol' shit. You drinking?"

"Yeah," he said with a nod of his head.

Ant threw his hand up, and a waitress came over to their table. "Hey, boo, what's up? Hey, cutie," she said to Ant, and then to Snake with a pretty-ass smile once she got a good look at him. Gently touching her perfectly cut and styled bob, she became more and more self-conscious with each passing second as she stood in Snake's presence, not quite able to bring herself to tear her eyes away from his handsome-ass face.

"What up, Bri-Bri? This my pahtna, right here. But before I introduce y'all so you can try to sink ya fangs in him, bring me a double shot of Remy."

"Shut up, boy!" she said playfully and and smacked him on the arm with her little notepad. "Don't pay him no mind, he crazy," she said and made a big deal of rolling her eyes at him. "Anyway, what you drinking, handsome?"

"Gimme a double shot of Hen and Alize," Snake said, staring directly into the waitress' eyes.

"Uhhnn," she said and started to fan herself with her notepad. "I know that's right, honey. I wouldn't mind a li'l of yours," she mumbled under her breath. "I'll be back in a second," she said as she turned to head to the bar, still fanning herself.

Ant laughed when he saw how Snake was locked in on the waitress' ass as she walked away, and an idea came to him. "That bitch there ain't shit, my nigga. I got a li'l ho fa ya," he said with a smile and nod of his head.

The sound of Ant's voice made him snap out of the trance the waitress' booty had him in. "What ya say, bruh?" he asked, looking over at him.

"I said I got a li'l ho for ya, hold up. Aye, Princess! Jay-Z here?" he called out to an amazon redbone chick who had been walking a bee-line toward them.

"I seen her earlier, why?" she stopped dead in her tracks and said with an obvious attitude.

"Man, just go tell the girl to come here. And quit frowning yo' damn face up like that. It's ugly."

"Whatever, nigga. I'll tell her if I see her!" she snapped,

but changed directions. Ant knew she was going to look for Jay-Z.

"Man, that bitch pussy smell so bad, bruh."

Snake looked at him like he was crazy. "Who," he asked.

"That big, pretty-ass, red ho I was just talking to."

"Naw, man," Snake said slowly while shaking his head in disappointed disbelief. "That big bitch fine as a mufucka, shawdy."

"I know, right? But that pussy was on fi' that night I was about to smash. I couldn't even fuck her, bruh," Ant said with a disgusted frown on his face. "I had to tell the bitch to put her clothes and shit back on 'cause my mama was texting me some emergency shit.

"No, bruh," he said with a laugh.

"Hell yeah, shawdy," Ant nodded. "But yeah, though, this li'l ho Jay-Z so bad. Li'l brown-skinned, pretty-ass, babydoll-looking li'l bitch. Fat li'l ass on her and everything, and I ain't never smashed her."

Snake nodded his approval. He couldn't wait to see if this Jay-Z broad Ant was hyping up was as bad as the chocolate stripper chick he was waiting on, or even the waitress who had took their drink orders.

He didn't have to wait long. He looked away from the dancer on the stage when he heard a glass slam down on the table. "You know damn well I can't stand that ol' stinking-ass bitch. Why the fuck you sending her to talk to me? And what the fuck you want anyway, nigga? You know I can't stand yo' ol' busta-ass either"

Ant frowned and a look of utter dislike came over his face before he snapped on her. "That's why yo' ass miserable and lonely as fuck now, without a nigga, 'cause of yo' smart-ass mouth and fucked-up attitude. I was trying to introduce you to–"

"Tonio," Snake blurted out as he stood up. "My name

Tonio, shawdy. Wus hap'ning." He couldn't fucking believe it! He wanted to scream out a million curse words right then, right there! Of all the bad bitches in Atlanta, a city where women outnumbered men ten to one at the least, this Jay-Z bitch just had to be the same psycho bitch Jaz from the train. He had the luck of a fucking buzzard.

"What the fuck?" Jaz frowned and said when she looked at Snake for the first time.

Ant frowned at her. "What the fuck wrong with you? You need to lose that ol' nasty-ass attitude, man. That shit ain't cute."

"Nigga, fuck you," she snapped back at him, but Snake cut her off.

"Aye, let me holla at ya over here for a second," he said, pulling her away from the table. When they were far enough away to not be overheard, he stopped. "What's wrong with you, man? Why you blowing on homes like that?"

"'Cause I fuckin' hate that nigga. The only reason I be being nice to his bitch-ass at all is 'cause of Tasha."

Snake frowned and shook his head. "You wasn't just being nice."

Jaz raised her eyebrows and nodded. "Uh, yes, the fuck I was," she said, and then looked directly into Snake's eyes, and somehow he knew from her expression what was about to take place. "Why the fuck you worried about it, anyway? And why the fuck you told him yo' name was Tonio?"

"He know my name Snake," he started saying in his best unconcerned voice, but Jaz knew better.

"You telling a damn lie, nigga. You just told me yo' name was Tonio, right in front of him. I know what, how about I just go ask him," she said and raised an inquisitive, elegantly-arched brow.

When Snake didn't protest, she made a move toward Ant before he grabbed her. "Hold up, shawdy."

A bouncer immediately shined a flashlight on them, but Jaz threw her hand up to let him know everything was cool, and the small spotlight vanished. "What the hell is you up to, Tonio? Snake? Whatever the fuck yo' name is, you?" she said and poked him in the chest.

He looked over her head at Ant, who was watching them, fully entertained although he couldn't hear a word of what was being said. "Look, I met homes the first day I got out and told him my name was Tonio 'cause I ain't know him. Now, why the fuck you had that nigga shooting at me?"

"Boy, what the hell you talking about," she frowned and said. "Quit trying to change the subject, nigga." She knew exactly what he was attempting to do, and she was determined to not let him get away with it again.

"Nah, fuck all that," he waved his hand back and forth. "Ain't nobody trying to change shit! I wanna know why you had that nigga shooting at me as soon as I stepped a foot out of yo' 'partment this morning."

"I don't know what the fuck you talking about, nigga," she said and scowled warningly at him.

"So, you ain't hear them gunshots when I left yo' spot this morning?"

Jaz thought for a second, and then remembered she did hear some gunshots after he left, but she didn't think much of them. Gunshots, sirens, and ghetto birds all played a melody she heard on a daily basis. "Yeah, I did, but—"

"Well, that was a nigga I thought you sent at me." He conveniently neglected to mention the fact it also happened to be the same nigga he'd knocked out and robbed.

"Now, why the fuck would I want somebody to shoot you?" she asked with an attitude and confused frown on her face.

"I thought you was mad 'cause I had left or some shit. I don't know," he said with a shrug.

Jaz burst out laughing. "Look, I know you prob'ly used to having yo' way with girls, and I know I said I like yo' ass and all that, but don't flatter yaself, boo-boo," she rubbed the back of her hand against his cheek. "I mean, you all cute and fine as hell and shit, but if you don't wanna fuck with me, then it's whatever. I ain't about to have nobody try to shoot you, though. You fuckin' tripping," she said and laughed again, causing her pretty eyes to twinkle like stars.

"Yeah, I might've been," he rubbed at his little chin stubble and said thoughtfully to himself.

"Ain't no might to it, nigga, you was. Now, what the fuck you doing in here with this ol' lame-ass nigga?" She jabbed her thumb over her shoulder in the general direction of where Ant was sitting.

A lie was on the tip of Snake's tongue when he felt an arm circle around his waist. "Hey, cutie, I had to wash up and dry off, that's why it took so long for me to come back out. You ready for me?" It was the stripper he'd been waiting on since seeing her on the stage when he first walked in the club.

He took a step back and looked at the two beautiful chicks in front of him. Jaz, although she had a murderous facial disposition at that moment, was looking good as hell in a pair of skin tight black jeans and black halter top. Her braids were pulled back into a high pony tail that made her almond-shaped eyes and high cheek bones look almost exotic. On the other hand, the smooth, dark chocolate-skinned dancer was flashing a beautiful, pearly-white smile that gave her an angelic look. She wore a pair of blue-and-white, horizontally-striped boy shorts that molded perfectly to her big stripper booty, and a matching blue-and-white-striped sports bra her titties were threatening to burst out of at any second. Her hair was a pixie cut and styled with spikes at the top.

The few seconds it took for Snake to take in all of that seemed like an eternity, and he honestly didn't know what to do. He wanted to smash the stripper broad bad as hell, but at the same time, seeing Jaz again and learning she didn't have anything to do with him getting shot at made him feel a certain kind of way about her. And to be completely honest, she really was the baddest of the two. She just had on more clothes at the moment.

He made a split-second decision, one he hoped and prayed wouldn't come back to bite him in the ass in the end. "I'll catch up with ya a li'l lata on. Lemme holla at shawdy real quick," he said to the dancer and gave her a $20 bill.

Smiling even harder, she said, "Okay, then. My name Coco, whenever you get ready to find me." And then she winked before walking away.

"Rude-ass bitch. I swear, I hate these stinking-ass hos in this muthafucka," Jaz said incredulously. "I'm saying, though, what if you was my nigga, or if you was trying to holla at me or something?" She scoffed and shook her head.

"She a'ight. She just trying to make a li'l money, fuck it. But look, though." He paused a second to make sure what he was about to do was something he was really prepared for and wanted to do. He swallowed and then continued. "How about me and you just, like, start over or some shit? What time you get off?"

"I'm about to leave in a few minutes, why?"

"I got a li'l business to take care of with bruh, but I want you to let me slide through and check ya when me and homes finish up," he said in an asking tone.

Jaz took a moment to think it over. She really wouldn't like anything more than to start over with him, but on second thought, "Only if you go' tell me the truth and stop with all the bullshit," she stipulated.

"I'ma tell ya everything you need to know, shawdy."

"Fair enough," she said with a nod of her head. "You still got my number?"

"After what happened this morning, hell naw. I tore that shit up as soon as I left yo' spot," he lied.

She smirked at him before pulling a pen and napkin from her pocket and scribbling her number on it. "Don't tear this one up, and call me when you on the way."

He looked at the number and pocketed it. "Already. I'ma run back over here with bruh real quick. I'll holla at ya a li'l later on tonight."

"Yeah, you do that," she said quietly to herself as she looked at his retreating back.

As he made his way back over to where Ant was, he caught the thick, light-skinned stripper from earlier staring at him. She looked away quickly when he smiled at her.

"What she talking about?" Ant asked when Snake sat back down with him.

"I got her number and shit. I'ma holla at her tonight and see what's up."

"I'ma tell ya, bruh, that ho crazy. Her and my girl best friends. Bitch get on my damn nerves, man, always getting in a nigga business and shit. Bitch be telling Tasha I be fuckin' these hos up here and everything. Shawdy really just need a nigga to make her mind her own damn business though, ya feel me."

"So you just go' push the ho off on me," Snake said with a grin. "Why you ain't tell me she was fucked up before you turnt me on to her?"

Ant chuckled. "Nah, man, it ain't nothing like that. You ain't gotta fuck with her if you don't want to. Bitch can't keep a nigga, anyway, that ho mean as fuck. Tasha be telling me how she be handling her niggas wheneva her ass luck up and find one crazy enough to try to put up with her shit. Bitch look good as a muthafucka, though, don't she? I told ya. You might be the one that can tame her ass," he shrugged and sipped his drink.

"Yeah, I got her," he said, and Ant chuckled skeptically. Snake sipped his drink while casually looking around the club, and when he caught the light-skinned stripper staring at him again, they locked eyes. That time, though, she didn't turn away. She stared right back into his eyes until he turned away.

"Man, who the hell that li'l chick right there is?" he asked as he patted Ant on the arm.

"Who?" He put his drink down and looked in the direction Snake was pointing.

"Right there in the red-and-white polka-dots, that's her running to the back."

"Oh, that's Jayla," Ant said and waved his hand dismissively. "That's my pahtna Smurf ho. That bitch 'bout two-thirds crazy, too. She won't talk to nobody but Smurf. Bitch won't say shit to none of the other dancers or nothing," he said and shrugged.

"I know I don't know her, but she kind of look familiar," Snake said with a pensive look on his face.

"You might know her. I think Smurf said she from the West Side somewhere. She young, though. Anyway, I got some other shit to get into tonight, so this what I'ma do. You say you a hustla, right?" he asked, turning his chair a little so he could face Snake.

"One of the best of them."

Ant nodded. "Well, you don't know me, and I don't know you, right? But I wanna see any nigga win, though, shawdy. Especially after doing a long-ass bid like you just did, ya feel me? So, I'ma give ya a li'l work, and you don't owe me shit for it. All I want you to do is fuck with me when you get ya money right, and I got ya. Sound good?" He sipped his drink again.

"Nigga, hell yeah," Snake said enthusiastically.

"C'mo, let's go on out here to the car right quick," Ant nodded and said as he stood up and led the way out of the club.

"I gotta go get my pistol, man," Snake said once they'd

taken a few steps outside into the warm night.

"Where it's at?"

"I hid it behind the club 'cause they wouldn't let me bring it in with me."

"Why you ain't just leave it in ya car?"

"Shit, if I had one, I would've. I caught a cab up here. Hold up, I'ma be right back." He sprinted 'round to the back of the club, got his pistol, and ran back to the front.

Ant hit the alarm and led him to a clean, black-on-black Dodge Challenger. A set of black, 22-inch Asantis with chrome lips capped off the hemi-powered beast, making it appear even more aggressive than it already looked. He opened one of the rear passenger doors, and there on the floor sat a plastic shopping bag he picked up. "Here ya go, my nigga. What you do with it is on you. If you fuck it up," he paused and winced, "it's on you. It is what it is. I tried to look out."

"Trust me, bruh, I know exactly what to do," Snake said as he grabbed the plastic sack from him.

There wasn't a word in the English language to adequately express the amount of shock he felt when he felt the full weight of the bag that Ant, a total stranger, had given him.

"Oh, yeah, here go a li'l something, too." He dug in his pocket and pulled out five neatly-folded $100 bills and handed them to Snake. "That's to help make sure you don't fuck ya money up, 'cause I'm really investing in ya, my nigga, but I'm trying to see ya with something at the same time, too, though."

Dumbfounded, Snake slid the money in his pocket. "Man, I 'preciate ya, homie. Real nigga shit, bruh," he said as he dapped Ant and pulled him into a quick embrace.

"It's all good, my nigga. Where ya headed at, though? I can prob'ly drop ya by there," he said as he walked around to the driver's door of the Challenger.

"Shit, my nigga, if I can use ya phone for a quick second, I can let ya know." Snake got in the passenger seat and buckled his seatbelt. The work was in his lap, along with his pistol.

Ant handed him his phone and turned the volume down on Young Jeezy's classic album *The Recession* so he could hear. He fired up a blunt of gas and cracked the sunroof before pulling out of The Blue Flame's parking lot onto Bankhead Highway.

Ambitious

Chapter Six

The smell of fried chicken hung thick in the air. Jaz had decided maybe Snake would keep it real with her this time, being he was the one who had suggested the truce in the first place. The food she'd cooked for him was only to be sure he was nice and comfortable, hopefully, so he'd open up completely. She didn't want any surprises later on down the road she had a funny feeling she was about to set out on. "A'ight, cutie, let's hear it. And don't try to be slick and leave li'l shit out. Just hit me with everything ya got," she said as she sat back down on the couch across from him after washing up their plates.

"Where you want me to start at, shawdy?" he asked while nodding.

"Let's see." She closed one eye and cocked her head. "How about you just tell me enough to make me feel like it's everything?"

Snake nodded again. "A'ight, uh, let's see," he said and thought about where he should begin.

Jaz stared at him with rapt attention. She'd burrowed down into her seat, placed her elbows on her knees, and rested her chin in her palms, ready to listen and, from the looks of it, maybe even afraid to breathe or blink because she didn't want to miss anything.

"My mama was from Dixie Hill. She dead. O.D.'d on heroin when I was a baby. My daddy dead, too. A dread nigga named Milt had him killed and his head chopped off for running off on him with a couple bricks of cocaine when I was about fourteen. He used to move a li'l heroin through The Bluff. It wasn't nothing major, but I don't know why he was even trying to fuck with no cocaine, anyway. Anyway, my gramma pretty much raised me. She been staying on James P. Brawley since the sixties. That's about it," he said and hit her with a look that said, *what more could you possibly wanna know?*

Jaz sighed and scooted to the edge of her seat, clearing her throat in a dainty, girly way that wasn't a turn-off. "I see you go' make this shit hard, so how about we start with this: what's ya real name?"

Snake pondered whether he should tell her or not for a second. "Siree," he said slowly.

"Siree?" she raised her eyebrows and asked.

Snake nodded. "Yeah."

"That's cute. Original as hell without being all extra ghetto and shit. I ain't never knew or heard of a Siree," she said, liking the way his name sounded.

"That's 'cause it's only one," he said with a grin.

Jaz smiled again before moving along. "Where Snake come from? I don't like that."

"It was Li'l Snake. My daddy was Snake, too. When I got older, I made folks stop that *li'l* shit. I'm six-foot four, two hundred and thirty pounds, shawdy," he closed his eyes and shook his head. "I ain't about to be answering to no *li'l* nothing."

Jaz nodded her approval as her mind lustfully munched on his measurements. "So, you just did ten years. You ain't, like, gay or bisexual or no shit like that, is you? And getting ya dick sucked by a dude still mean you gay to me, for the record," she looked him straight in the eye and said.

Normally he would've blown on anybody who asked him some bullshit like that, but given the situation and the times, he reasoned she did have a right to ask, no matter how much it angered him. But her ass was most definitely going to have to come up off some pussy the instant she got off her period for questioning him about that type of shit, no doubt about it. So, he checked his temper and said calmly, "Hell nah. Don't stereotype me 'cause I been to prison, shawdy, I hate that shit."

Feeling the vibe, she quickly moved on. "What you was locked up for?" she asked while nodding.

"Some bullshit, man," he said and winced at the memory as he rubbed his little stubble goatee. "A li'l move I was trying to bust went sour on me. Fucked around and caught a li'l armed robbery in the West End."

She nodded again. "So, like, what you do?"

"'Bout the armed robbery?" he asked with a curious expression.

"Nah, like, how you get money? You rob folks, sell dope, work, run scams, bust checks, taxes, what? What do you do?"

"D. All of the above," he smiled. "But I ain't limited to just that, though. I'll do whatever it take. I'll even murder for the dough," he said pointedly.

His smile is what caused her to brush his comment about murdering for money off. She assumed he was just talking to try to impress her. She picked up her cup of apple juice and sipped from it. "So, how you know that ol' wack-ass nigga Ant, again?" she asked between sips.

Snake told her how he and Ant had met and how the nigga had looked out for him a couple of times since he'd been out. He realized that moment was the perfect opportunity to lay a foundation for his future plans, so he grabbed her hand, looked into her eyes, and with as much sincerity as he could muster, he laid on a coat of hot bullshit, as thick as he possibly could. "Listen, shawdy, it's some niggas out here that want me dead, man. That's part of the reason why I been telling folks my name Tonio, too. I done told you all this shit about me 'cause I'm trusting you to not say nothing to nobody about none of it. Not even ya friend, Tasha. Especially not her. She might tell Ant, and homes be in the streets. He know them niggas already. Next thing you know, somebody that don't need to know what's up with me go' be somewhere in a cut, lying to blow my ass off. All 'cause he might slip up and say some shit around them niggas, not knowing what's really going on. You might not understand how serious this shit is, but really, it's some life-or-death-type shit. You know my name, but we just stick wit the whole 'Tonio' thing, a'ight?"

Enraptured by his bullshit, Jaz looked into Snake's grey eyes, and the seriousness she saw in them penetrated to her soul. She'd never betray his trust. Never. Not in a million years.

She cleared her throat again before she answered. "A'ight," she nodded. "What you do? Why they wanna kill you?" Her voice was barely more than a hoarse whisper, and her own heart was beating fast out of fear for him, as if she was the one people were trying to kill instead of him.

He was expecting a question of the sort so he had more lies ready and on hand for her. "I had to kill a nigga before I went to prison, right? It was some me-or-him type shit, and his ass got it first before he could do it to me. His folks wasn't trying to hear that shit, though. Still ain't. So shit, it's still guns-up wheneva we see each other," he finished somberly.

Jaz's heart melted. How could it not? Looking into Snake's freakishly handsome face and hearing about all of the bad luck and misfortune he'd endured in his life, she wanted to scream and cry for him. She sat her cup down, climbed over into his lap, and looked into his eyes. "I swear, I got you. I ain't go' say shit to nobody," she said softly and kissed his lips. Breaking the connection, she pulled her t-shirt over her head and undid her black lace bra, exposing her pretty, caramel-colored C-cups.

"I thought you was on ya period, shawdy," Snake said with a hesitant look in his eyes.

"I lied. You want some pussy or not?" she asked huskily as she ground against him.

In response to her question, he greedily popped one of her titties in his mouth and teased her stiff nipple with his tongue.

She moaned with pleasure from being sucked and groped on as he leaned forward so she could pull his shirt off. Now, she already knew he had tattoos because both of his arms were covered with them. And she also knew he had muscles, too, but nothing could've prepared her for the sight before her eyes. Fine wasn't even the word for him. Snake's body looked like a replica of a chiselled Greek statue. Fully-clothed, his 230-pound physique came off as slim and strong, but boy, was that an understatement for what it actually was! Unclothed, it was obvious the boy was a workhorse! He had muscles stacked on top of muscles. Everywhere. And he was as hard as a brick. Everywhere. And he had tattoos. Everywhere! There wasn't a square inch of his torso that wasn't inked except for his face, and she was loving every inch of what she was seeing.

Mentally licking her chops and devouring the perfect specimen of a man, she rubbed on his chest and rock-hard stomach until he could stand it no longer.

"Jaz!" he barked.

"Huh," she flinched and said. He had startled her out of the zone she'd unknowingly fallen into.

"What the hell you doing, shawdy?" he asked with an impatient and confused frown.

"Oh, sorry," she giggled goofily and stood up. Down went her Ralph Lauren sweatpants and thong until she finally stood before him naked except for a pair of blue Sponge Bob footies with individual slots for each toe. Bronze kissed caramel with a beautiful body, and just as beautiful of a face to go along with it.

"Damn, you bad as fuck, shawdy," Snake said with a wince as he shook his head and stared at her.

"Thank you," she said quietly, then sent a silent thanks to God for something telling her to pull out the weed wacker and trim her garden after he had stormed out of her place earlier that day. When a girl wasn't getting any or planning on it, who cared how wild the bushes grew? She sure as hell didn't.

She grabbed his hand and pulled him up, leading him to her bedroom with her naked ass bouncing and shaking the whole way.

'Bout damn time, Snake thought to himself as he kicked the door closed behind them.

***

Jayla thrashed around wildly in her sleep. She was having the nightmare again, the only one she ever had, now. His face, panting and distorted with pleasure, an evil grin playing at his lips. She would never forget that face. Or those eyes. She screamed out loudly. *"Ahh!"*

"Jayla! Jayla! Jay!" Smurf grabbed his girl and yelled urgently, trying to wake her so she would calm down and realize she was only having a bad dream, but the look on her face when she regained consciousness was one of wild terror, and he knew from the look in her eyes that who he was wasn't quite registering in her brain yet. "Jay, baby, it's me. Just relax. It's okay now. You just was having a bad–" he started in a calming, pacifying tone and reached out to touch her again, but she recoiled so violently she fell out of the bed and landed with a muffled thud on the floor.

She was up and on her feet in under a second, though, and quickly backing away from the strange man who was speaking to her as if they knew each other. "No, no, no," she said repeatedly, as if she was having trouble believing something. Tears flowed freely down her face, and she shook he head no at a dizzying, frantic pace.

"Jayla, baby, calm down," Smurf said, getting out of bed. Bad move. Jayla picked up a heavy glass candleholder and hurled it at him with every ounce of strength she possessed. He was barely able to weave it in time, and it shattered into a thousand shards when it slammed against the wall right where his head had been just moments before. A few seconds later a door slammed shut, and when he turned back around toward her, she was gone.

"Baby, please, everything is a'ight. It was just a dream. C'mo' out and let's talk about it," he said while hearing her fumbling to turn the lock on the bathroom door. He sighed and looked at the clock on his nightstand with tired, bleary eyes. 9:23 a.m. "It's too fuckin' early for this shit," he shook his head and mumbled to himself while walking over to Jayla's nightstand. He pulled the top drawer open and picked up her weekly pill dispenser. It was Thursday. The Sunday through Wednesday compartments still had her medication in them. "Shit, man!" he hissed under his breath and rubbed his closed eyes with the tips of his fingers. Jayla hadn't been taking her medication, and it was nobody's fault but his own. He was responsible for her. He was supposed to check daily to make sure she took her meds, but he'd been so busy for the past week or so he'd forgotten to actually check. The most he'd done was ask her if she'd taken her pills, and her ass had told him yes every time. He chuckled sadly at the thought of it, because he should've known better than to take her word for what it was about that. He of all people knew how much she really hated to take her medication sometimes. Now she'd locked herself in the bathroom again, and no doubt about it, it would take hours of sweet-talking and coercion from him to get her to calm down and come out.

"Okay, baby, I'm ready to talk about it. You wanna tell me about the nightmare?" he said as he got his pillow off the bed and dropped it on the floor beside the bathroom door.

***

Jayla sat curled into a tight ball on the floor. Her knees

were drawn into her chest, and she had squeezed into the corner beside the toilet. Even now that she was awake, she could still see his face, his eyes just as clearly as if he were standing right in front of her again. It had been ten years since Snake had raped her and forced her to watch him murder her father. Ten long years, and now he was back, looking exactly the same as he had the night he'd destroyed her young life. She wondered what she was supposed to do. What did he want? Did he recognize her? Those were just a few of the questions that were running through her highly-disturbed mind as she sat there, crying.

Then, out of nowhere, she slapped the shit out of herself. *Calm the fuck down, bitch, and think!* she heard a voice say. Her tears stopped instantly and her body snapped to rigid attention. *This is our chance to fix this shit, once and for all!* the voice said again.

Jayla frowned a little. "What? How?" she mumbled quietly, scared as hell.

Easy, you ol' simple-minded-ass bitch! That nigga raped us and killed daddy while we was too young and scared to do something about it. We grown now, though, Jay. We can handle our own now. All we gotta do is find a way to get close to that nigga so we can kill his ass.

"Uh-uh, Tab! Is you crazy? We ain't about to kill nobody, girl! I'm about to call the police so they–" Jayla hissed quietly as she started to get up.

Sit the fuck down, scaredy-ass bitch! the voice ordered Jayla. Her hand slipped off of the rim of the toilet, which she'd been gripping to help push herself up, and splashed loudly into the toilet water as she fell back to the floor with a thud. *Now, yo' ass is about to fuckin' listen to me, you punk-ass ho! You been fuckin' listening to them damn doctors and Smurf ol' sissy-ass about taking that fuckin' medicine to stop you from hearing me when I'm talking to you. Well, now it's time for yo' ass to start back listening to me.*

"No, Tab, please. You always get us in trouble," Jayla whined as she dried her hand on her shirt.

Stupid bitch, that's 'cause you always find a way to fuck up somewhere! Now, shut the hell up and listen. All you gotta do is sit the fuck back and ride, 'cause I'm about to drive this muthafucka. And as an afterthought, the voice added, *And if yo' ass was so serious about the police catching that nigga, yo' dumb ass would've listened to me when I was trying to tell you we shouldn't take no bath before the police came the night he fuckin' raped us! Genius!*

"I was scared, and I felt dirty," Jayla hissed back.

Yeah, whatever. Just let me handle this shit, a'ight? the voice said, and not too nicely, either.

Jayla just sat there, quietly brooding.

A'ight? it demanded.

Jayla sighed angrily and pouted. "Okay, Tab, but—"

Ain't no fuckin' buts, Jay-Jay. Not this time! That muthafucka raped us and killed daddy right in front of us, just in case yo' ass done forgot! We gotta get his ass! You know I'm good at this type of shit, and you always saying how you wish it was something we could've did about it. Well, this the chance to do something about it! Now's the time to boss the fuck up, bitch. Is you with it or what?

Jayla nodded slightly. Tab had a point. She often thought about how she wished they could've done something to stop Snake, but she was still unsure and wary of what Tab was suggesting.

Good. Now, the first thing we gotta do is find out everything we can about this ol' perverted-ass nigga. We seen him talking to Jay-Z last night. Maybe she know him? You gotta talk to her and pick her for information about the nigga. He was wit' Ant, too, but we can't say nothing to him about it 'cause he might tell Smurf you asking about another nigga, Tab said thoughtfully and then reassured Jayla. *Just chill, Jay, everything go' be cool, we go' bake this nigga a real nice cake. Just do exactly what the fuck I tell ya, when I tell ya.*

"A'ight, Tab," Jayla said and nodded again.

A'ight. Now, get up and straighten us up, girl. You got us looking a damn mess. And Smurf pussy-ass, been at the door for forever, talking to you. I don't see how you put up with his ol' soft ass.

"What I told you about talking shit about him, Tab? I love Smurf," she said in a firm, but quiet tone as she worked on their appearance in the mirror.

I know you do, girl, so I guess I do, too. Kinda. But he a bitch, though, honey.

Jayla frowned. "Tab," she hissed.

I ain't go' say nothing else, boo, I promise.

Jayla smoothed her hair with her hands and gave her reflection a once-over. With a satisfied nod and a deep breath, she unlocked the door and swung it open.

"Baby, you a'ight?" Smurf scrambled to his feet and said in a relieved tone when the door opened.

Jayla stood in the threshold with a sheepish grin on her face before she nodded and rushed forward to hug her Smurfy-Poo.

Remember, Jayla, Tab's voice said in her head. *Don't take that fuckin' medicine or you won't be able to hear me when I'm talking to you.*

"I know," Jayla mumbled.

"What ya say, baby?" Smurf asked as he stroked her hair.

"Nothing," she shook her head and buried her face in his neck.

Chapter Seven

Later that afternoon, after a few hours of some good fucking and lounging, Snake sat in the kitchen and watched as Jaz cooked up a few ounces of the quarter-brick of cocaine Ant had given him the night before. It didn't surprise him in the least that she knew what she was doing. In fact, with her being born and raised in 4th Ward, he would've been a bit shocked if she didn't know how to handle the work. And that was a major plus for her in his eyes, because he liked the fact she wasn't green to the struggle and everyday life in the streets. The more they had talked and gotten to know about each other, the more he realized she'd actually experienced more than her fair share of hard times and bad luck. And from the looks of things, they hadn't even come remotely close to breaking her.

"So, look, I ain't about to keep calling you Tonio. I don't like it," she said, pulling the pot off the stove while thinking about another nigga she knew and had a very strong dislike for named Tonio.

"We been through this already, ain't we?"

"Yeah, I know," she said slowly. "But I know a nigga named Tonio, and that nigga so fuckin' whack," she rolled her eyes quickly and shook her head. "I don't even want to associate you and him in no kind of way if I ain't got to. I'ma call you Smoke," she said thoughtfully and pointed at him with the fork in her hand as she smiled a little.

"Smoke?" he asked, a confused little frown settling over his features.

"Yeah," she said in a preoccupied tone as she tapped the cookie of coke with the fork. "You got the prettiest set of smoke-gray eyes."

"My eyes ain't pretty, shawdy, but if that get you off," he shrugged in a dismissive manner. "You gotta work today?"

"At five," she said.

"I'ma get me a room, see if I can get off this shit. I need to holla at my gramma, too. Aye, how you got home so fast last night?"

She looked at him with one eyebrow raised and said in a high-pitched voice, "I drove, how you thought?"

Snake scratched his head, confused. "You got a car?"

"Hell yeah, nigga, a bitch ain't got time to be walking and depending on MARTA," she said with a scandalized smirk on her face.

"How come you was on the train the other day when we met?" The lines of his confused frown deepened.

She was tempted to say *fate*, but instead she went with something she knew would be a bit more believable for him. "I was headed to pick my shit up out the shop in Decatur. The A/C had been fuckin' up on me."

He nodded. "What kind of car you got?" he asked.

Sitting the pot with the work in it to the side, she stood at the sink to wash her hands. "A '96 Impala SS," she said, looking back over her shoulder at him.

"Oh yeah?" Snake smiled and said, surprised and impressed. He'd been expecting her to say she drove some ridiculously feminine car like a Honda Civic or maybe even Pontiac Sunfire or something, but definitely nothing packing as much muscle as her Super Sport.

"Yep," she nodded. "I done had that car about five years now. A nigga I used to fuck with sold it to me for the low 'cause he was fucked up and needed some money to bond out of Rice Street," she said, turning around to face him. She began to dry her hands on the bottom of her T-shirt, exposing her thick, creamy, caramel-colored thighs. "It was just a few things wrong with it, so I got it fixed and been riding good ever since."

"So you can drop me off somewhere before you go to work then, right?"

She smiled and looked into his smoky eyes. "I might," she said and pulled off her long t-shirt, baring her sinfully beautiful body. "It depends on what you go' do for me."

Snake watched her seductively walk over to him with lust smoldering in his eyes as he stood to his feet. When she reached him, she threw her arms around his neck and pressed her body close to his rock-hard frame.

"You want me to give you a ride?" she said huskily, looking up at his lips and mouth, wishing he would kiss her.

"I do," he said and quickly spun her around so her back was to his chest. He pinned her to him and began to grind against her bare ass as he placed hot kisses on her neck.

"Ooh," she chirped and giggled from the unexpected exhilarating sensation of being spun. "Where to?" she asked as he nibbled on her neck.

In response to her question, he cupped one of her plump titties with his large hand and slowly moved his other hand down her body and between her legs. "Right here," he said as he slipped three of his fingers inside of her, causing her already quick, shallow breaths to catch in her throat. A moan escaped her slightly-parted lips when he started to work his fingers inside of her, and pretty soon she was grinding on his fingers and against the bulge in his pants. She started to scream out when she came, but his sexy mouth was on hers a second before the sound could escape, and she found herself sensually kissing him back as the last little quivers of her orgasm shivered up her spine.

Breaking the connection, he took his fingers out of her and wiped her wetness on her round ass as he gently pushed at her back. "Bend over, shawdy," he said with a patience he didn't feel, his throbbing dick feeling as if it was about to burst as he hurriedly undid his pants. His erection sprang free, and he stepped up behind Jaz, who was bending over, holding onto the edge of her wooden dinner table. Rubbing the head of his dick up and down against her opening, he used her own fluids as lube before he squeezed into her tight pussy from behind.

She gasped through clenched teeth from the sensation of his dick penetrating her, and then with a smile she looked back over her shoulder at him. With a swoop of her hand, she gathered all of her braids to one side of her head and bracing for the pounding she knew she was about to get, she leaned most of her weight against the table and stood wide-legged to receive him.

He started out with slow, little pumps, but quickly moved to long, hard, and fast strokes that had Jaz beside herself with pleasure and begging him to never stop. He came before she did but to his credit, she followed right behind him with an ear-splitting high note to accompany it. After both of their heart rates slowed back to their normal paces, Snake pulled out of her and said through a lazy yawn as he squeezed her ass. "Yo' li'l horny ass trying to wear a nigga out, ain't ya."

Jaz stood up and laughed a tired, shy laugh. "It been a while since I had some, especially any that was any good. So no, I definitely ain't trying to wear you out," she said with a small giggle as she gave his semi-hard dick a caressing tug on her way to the bathroom with him following close on her heels.

*****

"A'ight, I'ma call ya later, and please don't lose my phone, cutie. I just got that shit," Jaz said, standing in front of Snake who was sitting on the bed in the room she'd rented for him for the night.

"You can take that shit with ya. I told ya I don't really need it," he said, tossing the phone down on the bed.

"Well, what if you out of the room? How I'ma call ya then?" she looked at him pointedly. "Just keep it," she said, not even attempting to pick it up.

"Whatever," he shrugged.

"Well, I'm about to go. I'ma call ya right before I get off, and you can tell me then if you want me to swing back by here."

The look on her face told him what she wanted to hear. "Yeah, just come on back when you get off. You ain't gotta call."

After she left, he looked around the forty dollar-a-night motel room. One bed, one bathroom, a TV, two lamps, a table, and two chairs. Simple. It was surprisingly clean and in good shape for the area, though. The whole Fulton Industrial Boulevard was a strip of motels, gas stations, and truck stops where the only things going on were pimping, hoing, and hustling. It was classified as one of the top five drug trafficking areas in Atlanta's Zone 1, but the violence in that particular area wasn't as bad as some of the others so the police didn't patrol it as often as they should. As a result of the sporadic police presence, the whole strip was a goldmine for whoever was dedicated and determined enough to stay down with whatever their craft was.

He pulled the paper-thin curtain back to look out the window and saw a fiend walking through the parking lot with two brown paper sacks in his hand. "Time to get it," he grunted to himself as he got to his feet. Grabbing a handful of sacks and stuffing them in his pocket along with his pistol and Jaz's phone, he hit the door.

He walked a full circle around the motel twice, just scoping out the scene, before walking to the the store right up the street and buying a pack of Newport's, a soda, and stealing a couple of things. He made his way back to the motel and discreetly observed all of the foot traffic and transactions taking place around him, from the wino with a black can of 211 malt in each of his back pockets getting served to the old lady pushing a stroller with a missing front wheel full of tissue and baby clothes she was trying to sell, flagging down a nigga with some work. He watched it all, taking note of how the hustlers served, out in the open, unconcerned with whether the police or anybody else saw them and knew what they were doing or not.

When he got back to the motel, he was walking by one of the breezeways on his way back to his room when he heard two voices, raised in anger, coming from within it. The mention of dope is what really grabbed his attention, so he stopped and eased a little closer, careful to not be seen or heard as he eavesdropped on the strangers' argument.

"Y'all nigga tripping, homes. Look at these li'l-bitty-ass sacks! And y'all niggas talking about twenty fuckin' dollahs? These li'l shits ain't barely even worth five! Y'all niggas need to straighten these sacks up, man. We ti'ed of spending our money on this bullshit, Trell."

"Man, look, Rambo," Snake heard a different voice say calmly, but he could tell the owner was trying to stop his anger from manifesting itself through his speech and tone. "You want this shit or not, nigga? Damn! Yo' ol' grumpy, shell-shocked ass always fuckin' complaining. If you and the rest of these mthaufuckas don't like the sacks me and my niggas is pumping, then I got a newsflash fa ya, dummy: y'all muthafuckas quit fuckin' buying them! Take y'all ass ova there to the HoJo or Best Inn or some shit and buy them niggas' watered-down-ass, whipped-up-ass dope. All this fuckin' whining and causing problems and shit, man. Yo' ass the reason everybody else done started that shit!"

"Naw, muthafucka. Muthafuckas is complaining 'cause y'all niggas is shitting on us! I tell ya what, though, nigga, don't straighten them sacks up. I bet ya by this time tomorrow, this bitch go' be a ghost town."

"Fuck you, junkie-ass nigga. You ain't talking about shit! Get the fuck outta here."

"Just watch," Snake heard the voice that belonged to

Rambo say and some feet shuffling. "If y'all don't fix them sacks, Popeye a fuckin' sissy if y'all niggas get off anotha gram at this muthafucka! Watch!"

Snake heard the unmistakable sound of a pistol being cocked, and the next thing he knew an old man with a nappy-ass salt-and-pepper afro and scraggly beard ran past the spot where he stood listening, seeming to not even notice he was there before quickly ducking into another breezeway and out of sight.

Snake peeked around the corner of the building into the breezeway and saw who was obviously the other person who had been arguing walking away, shaking his head. He still had his pistol in his hand.

Snake waited a few seconds before he set off in search of the old man who had just run by him, nodding occasionally as he mapped out a blueprint with every step he took.

***

A'ight, there the bitch go, right there, Jayla. Now take yo' scaredy-ass on over there and see what's up. Tab's voice echoed in Jayla's head.

She had just come from the dressing room where she'd cleaned and freshened up after finishing up on the stage. She wore a gold thong, a gold-tinted, see-through sash, a gold bra, and a pair of gold tie-up stiletto sandals by Roger Vivier. "I'm scared, Tab. What am I s'posed to say to that girl? What if I mess up?" Jayla asked quietly, barely moving her lips as she looked over at the bar.

All you gotta do is go over there and start a fuckin' conversation with her, Tab started in an exasperated tone. *It can be about anything, bitch. Money, gas prices, niggas, something! It ain't fuckin' rocket science, Jay! Just get the ho to start talking, and then ease the shit in about the cute, light-*

skinned nigga with cat eyes you seen her talking to. This shit is real fuckin' simple!

Warily, Jayla looked over at the bar again. Jaz was pouring a shot of Patron for a nigga she recognized as one of the club's regulars. She swallowed and nodded slightly before nervously licking her lips and starting toward the bar.

"Aye, let me get a dance, shawdy," a nigga grabbed her wrist and said while waving a bill at her.

She snatched her hand away and frowned at him like he was the most disgusting thing in the world. She had business to handle, and she needed to get it done while she had the courage to. All that idiot was doing was trying to hold her up. She shook her head no and kept it moving.

"Hey, girl, what's up?" she said, sitting down on one of the bar stools.

Jaz looked up from the place she was wiping dry on the bar and saw Jayla staring at her. Glancing over both of her shoulders to see if anyone was behind her, she turned back to Jayla and pointed at herself. "You talking to me?" she asked with a confused expression on her face.

Jayla nodded and smiled.

Jaz was stupefied. She'd heard all of the "she crazy" rumors about Jayla, and the entire year and few months she'd been bartending at The Blue Flame she had never, not once, heard her say one single word. Now, she spoke to her like they were, at the least, polite strangers, and once she thought about it, she realized that they were so she shrugged, mentally, and said, "What's up," in a conversational tone. There was no harm in being polite in return to the girl, no matter how crazy she was rumored to be.

"Girl, on God, I'm so sick of this shit. These ol' trifling-ass niggas and hos that be in here is a fuckin' trip. Let me tell ya about one of them," Jayla started saying.

***

Snake peeked out of the window when he heard the knock at his door. Rambo, the disgruntled smoker he'd heard arguing earlier in the breezeway, along with two other rough-looking niggas he took to be junkies, were standing around talking while waiting on him to answer the door. It had gotten dark outside, and he noticed a bunch of bugs were flying around the light by his room that illuminated the three men. After grabbing the forty-cal, he opened the door. "Y'all c'mo' in," he beckoned for them to come inside with the same hand that held the pistol.

The two strangers looked at each other warily for a split second and then, as if one brain sent one impulse to each of them simultaneously, they turned those same wary expressions to Rambo in synchronized timing with each other.

"It's a'ight y'all, he straight," Rambo assured them, shaking his head quickly while stepping into the room. Hesitantly, the two strangers followed his lead, and as soon as the three of them had crossed the threshold, Rambo started rambling. "A'ight, Tonio, this right here is, C.J.," he said, pointing at the shorter of the two men. "And that's Nate, right there," he pointed at the other man. "These is two of my pahtnas that be around here all the time."

Snake gave C.J. and Nate a quick once-over and then tossed the strap on the bed behind where he was standing. "What up?" he said.

C.J. and Nate both literally sighed in relief and visibly started to loosen up when he threw the gun on the bed.

"What's going on?" they said, speaking at the same time.

"Ain't shit," Snake said expectantly and waited for them to state their business.

"Shit, man," Nate spoke up. "We wanna see these sacks everybody bragging about. All nicks, right?" he asked.

"Yeah, that's all I got," he said, reaching into his pocket.

"A'ight, let us get four of them," Nate said. He lifted one pant leg of his ashy-black jeans and pulled a crumpled $20 bill out of his dirty-ass, blue-striped tube sock.

Taking the money, Snake dropped four sacks into his waiting hand.

"Yeah, them muthafuckas right there is straight," C.J. said excitedly, peeking over into Nate's hand and prodding the sacks around with an abnormally-long, ET-looking index finger.

"Hell yeah, man. If yo' shit any good and they stay like this, I'ma keep fuckin' with ya," Nate said with a pleased expression on his face as he looked at the sacks.

Rambo winked at Snake and said to Nate, "Hell yeah, all of them go' be like that."

"A'ight, young blood," Nate said with a satisfied nod as he and C.J. turned to leave the room with Rambo in tow. "I'ma be back to fuck with ya."

Once they were gone, Snake sat on the bed and couldn't resist the urge to sniff the $20 bill Nate had just given him to see if it had a funny odor to it. It didn't, and he put it with the rest of the money he'd made. Investing in Rambo had turned out to be a pretty good idea so far. He'd promised to give him a sack for every few sales he brought to him or sent his way if they were spending twenty dollars or better, and with his help he'd made a little over $2,100 in just a few hours. The only problem now was he was getting low on work, and the rest of it was back at Jaz's apartment. At the rate Rambo was bringing him plays, he would sell out within the next hour or so, but had he known that the hotel was jumping the way it was, he would've come prepared. *No worry, though,* he shrugged. The next day when he went back, he'd be sure to be strapped.

Another knock sounded at the door. He looked and saw it was Rambo, and he was alone that time, but he still grabbed the forty-cal again and let him in.

The nigga's mouth seemed to be powered by some kind of motor or something, because he took flight the second he stepped foot in the room. "What I told ya? I told ya, didn't I? Keep showing love like you doing and everybody over here go' fuck with ya! I got a whole lot of more pahtnas to bring ya, too, I just ain't seen them yet. I told ya, man, everybody over here fuck with me, man. I know everybody. You-you. You still got me, right," he sputtered.

"Calm down, man," Snake said with a grin and tossed him a sack. He guessed he had went and smoked with C.J. and Nate, because he was high as hell. That was probably why he was babbling on and on. All business again, his little grin a part of recent history, Snake said, "Look, right, I ain't know I was go' get off like this. I'm almost out of work, so don't worry about bringing nobody else through tonight. When I come back tomorrow, I'ma be straight again."

Rambo nodded. "I told ya it was some money over here. Just keep fuckin' with me and I'ma get you rich. Them other niggas down there at the other end some bullshit. That li'l-ass shit they been selling niggas," he said with a frown while shaking his head.

"Yeah, you know, I had heard you and one of them niggas arguing earlier, right? Who them fools is?"

Rambo sucked his teeth and frowned even harder. "Them niggas from Bowen Homes. They came over here about eight or nine months ago when some of them ol'-school Perry Homes niggas ran them away from the other motel down the street. They say one of them niggas' uncle or some shit got it, but I can't tell, not from what they crabass been selling. It's just more convenient to fuck with them niggas 'cause they closer than going somewhere else. But when everybody find out about you, though, them niggas' li'l run go' be over."

Snake nodded. He knew then he was probably about to

step on a few toes and piss some niggas off, but it wasn't intentional. And even if it had been, he wouldn't have cared. All he wanted to do was get a li'l money. If he could do so without any problems, cool. But if not, then so be it. "I'ma be back tomorrow around one or two, man. Come back through around then and I'ma fuck with ya again."

"A'ight," Rambo nodded and turned to leave.

Jaz's phone rang as soon as he closed the door behind him, and he searched high and low for it before realizing it was in his pocket the whole time. Whoever was calling had hung up by the time he got it out, and he really wasn't interested enough in finding out who it was to look and see. Ignoring the flashing *missed call* indicator, he tossed it on the bed and went to the bathroom. It rang again just as he was coming out.

"Yeah?" he drawled and heard muffled music in the background.

"How you go' answer the phone like that?" Jaz asked.

Snake shrugged slowly as if she could see him. "Shit, I don't know."

Jaz chuckled. "What's up, though? You about ready to leave?"

"Yeah. What time you get off?" he asked.

"I'm about to now, that's why I called. I can be there in about ten minutes. You want me to bring you something?"

"Nah, I'm good. I'ma be outside waiting on ya, shawdy."

"A'ight, be there in a minute," she said and hung up.

Chapter Eight

Bitch, can't you do anything right? Tab scolded Jayla as they watched Jaz leave the club. *All you had to do was coax the ho into talking about the nigga, finesse the bitch, bitch! Yo' dumbass done asked the girl everything about the nigga except how big his dick is! You make me ashamed of yo' ass sometimes, you know that?* Jayla dropped her head. She wanted to cry, but Tab was merciless. She kept right on blasting her ass. *Ain't no way in the fuck we grew up together, as green and square as yo' ass be acting sometimes. West Side of Atlanta raised me. I don't know where the fuck you was at, but it damn sure wasn't with me. I tell ya what, though, you lucky she didn't go in on yo' dumb-ass fa asking all them stupid-ass fuckin' questions! This the main reason why I always be mad I ain't got full control of our brain and body. You fuckin' stupid, Jay!"*

"I said I'm fuckin' sorry, Tab! Damn!" Jayla hissed with tears in her eyes. Her feelings were beyond hurt.

Don't be sorry, dizzy bitch. You gotta be fuckin' smarter! How many times I gotta tell yo' ass that shit? Damn! Now quit all that pussy-ass crying and just be cool while I try to think of a way to patch this shit up. In the meantime, stay the hell away from that fuckin' medicine. You hear me?

Jayla nodded slightly as she dabbed at her eyes with a napkin.

Good. Now, don't worry, boo, Tab said in a softer, consoling tone. *Everything go' be cool, I'ma fix this shit right on up. We go' get this nigga.*

Jayla just nodded again.

***

Snake was standing in the parking lot of the motel when

Jaz's deep burgundy Impala pulled up beside him. "What's hap'ning," he said when he climbed into the passenger seat.

"Shit, ti'ed as fuck. You hungry?" she asked with a smile as she turned the wheel and tapped the accelerator. Just seeing him again made her a bit giddy.

He thought quietly for a second before answering. "Nah, not really. But I can eat, though."

She nodded and hit her blinker. They got take-out from Waffle House and then headed straight to her spot where, after showering, they ate, smoked, and then fucked until sleep overcame them.

True to his word, Snake was back at the motel the next day at around one in the afternoon. Jaz didn't have to work until later, so she decided to stick around and keep him company for a while.

Soon after they got there, a knock sounded at the door. "See who that is, shawdy," Snake said. He was busy cutting and sacking up some of the work.

Jaz pulled the curtains back and looked out the window. "What the fuck?" she said to herself, but loud enough for Snake to hear as she quickly moved toward the door.

Snake immediately clutched the strap. "Who that is?" he whispered, praying it wasn't the police.

"My damn uncle," she said to him and opened the door.

Rambo stepped into the room with a big-ass smile on his face. "Girl, what the hell yo' ass doing over here?" he asked in a booming voice, happy and surprised as hell to see his niece.

"Shit, just cooling, unk. Me and my friend just kicking shit. What's up with you, though? You been a'ight?" she asked with a genuine smile.

"Hell yeah, hell yeah. You know me, one day at a time," Rambo said as he rubbed his chest. He looked over at Snake. "What up, young blood? You ain't tell me you knew my niece," he said, scratching his scraggly beard.

"Shit, man, I ain't even know I knew ya niece," he replied with a small chuckle.

Rambo nodded and shrugged. "Word is, them Bowen Homes niggas been asking around about ya, man," he said in a serious tone.

"Sho'nuff?" Snake asked with a quizzical look.

"Hell yeah. Say they been trying to see who you is and where you from and shit." He was still nodding as he eagle-eyed the work on the table.

"Fuck them niggas, they can keep asking," Snake shrugged. "Long as they stay out of my video, all of us can get a li'l money and won't be no problems."

Rambo agreed while Jaz looked between the two of them with a lost expression on her face. Snake tossed him a few sacks and asked him if he was ready to crank up. He quickly affirmed he would be as soon as he finished smoking one of the sacks he'd just got, and after a hug and a promise to come back later so he and his niece could catch up, he left.

As soon as Jaz closed the door behind him, she turned to face Snake and leaned back against it. "So, what's up with them niggas he was talking about? What they asking about you for? Who they is?" She fired question after question at him, and had it not been for the worried look on her face, he probably would've thought she'd transformed into the psycho bitch again.

"Them niggas ain't nobody, and they ain't talking about shit. Everything straight. Just relax," he said coolly and calmly to assure her nothing major was going on. Hell, he wasn't even aware anything at all was going on.

She stood up straight and sighed. "I don't want to see nothing happen to you or see you get in trouble again, that's all," she said with a little less worry in her voice.

"Ain't nobody about to do nothing to me. Ain't nobody even go' fuck with a nigga that even look like me, shawdy.

Trust me when I tell you I got this shit," he scoffed arrogantly, his words oozing so much confidence and assuredness they actually made her feel a bit better. "Just chill, shawdy." He flashed a cocky grin at her. "Rambo yo' real uncle, or y'all just know each otha?" He changed the subject so she would relax.

"Yeah, that's my mama's baby brother. I love the hell out that nigga, too, with his ol' crazy ass," she chuckled as she walked over to the bed. Kicking off her Jordans, she plopped down on the bed to watch TV.

As time passed by, the room started to bump harder and harder, and by the time Jaz had to leave to go get ready for work, Snake was in desperate need of some triple zeros. He knew the store down the street sold them because he'd seen them when he bought his cigarettes the day before. He had Jaz take him and he told her he would just walk back, but she insisted against it. After being gone for only a few minutes, they pulled back into the motel parking lot and saw somebody looking, or better yet, trying to look into his room through the window. Luckily he'd left the curtain closed, but he still wasn't having anything of the sort.

Before Jaz could even get the car stopped good, he was out, forty-cal in hand, and yelling. "Aye, say, bruh! What the fuck you doing, nigga? Why the fuck you looking all in my shit like it's yours?"

The kid, Snake saw as he got closer, looked like he was about thirteen or so. "Nah, man, m-my big cousin Trell had told me. He had told me to come and see-see if you had some weed or something they could buy," he sputtered and had a hard time swallowing. He was scared as hell, for one, because Snake was big as hell and obviously a grown man. And two, because he was clutching a pistol, although it was lowered to his side. "I was just looking for ya so I could ask you. I ain't mean nothing by it. I'm sorry."

The kid was trembling visibly as he cowered before

Snake. "Tell yo' cousin I ain't got shit," he said, slipping the strap in his pocket just as he felt Jaz slightly brush up against him to let him know she was there beside him. "And you don't bring yo' li'l ass back down here looking all in my shit. Next time I'ma start shooting, li'l nigga."

The kid quickly nodded his understanding and walked away at a brisk pace.

"You go' be a'ight?" Jaz asked as she and Snake walked into his room.

"Hell yeah, everythang cool. Come get me when you get off," he said calmly as if what had just transpired only a few seconds ago hadn't even happened.

Jaz nodded. "You know I am," she said and squeezed his arm lightly before going back to her car.

He stood in the doorway watching her pull off, and then went back to sacking up the rest of his work. He had only been sitting down for a few minutes when he heard a forceful knock at his door. A slight frown creased his face as he wondered who the hell was banging on his door like they'd lost their damn mind. Moving the curtain aside to take a look, he recognized one of the three people as Trell, the same nigga he'd seen arguing with Rambo the day before, but also the older cousin of the young nigga he had just run off. "And the bullshit begins," he said to himself as he picked up the forty-cal and opened the door. "What up?" he asked in an even tone and with a deadpan expression on his face.

"My li'l cousin say you drawed down on him, bruh. What's up?" Trell said with a hint of bravado in his tone.

Easy, Snake thought to himself. He could deal with this situation without it getting out of hand because he could understand where Trell was coming from. If somebody was to pull a pistol on any of his folks, he would've checked it, too. Plus, no type of disrespect had taken place, so he decided to diffuse the situation before it got ugly. He kind of figured all three of the niggas were strapped, and it was obvious he was, too. His pistol was in his hand.

"Yeah, I had done caught that li'l bastard peeking in my window, bruh. I ain't know what the fuck was going on. When I seen he was just a li'l boy, I put the strap up, though. He said some shit about selling some weed or something." He paused and looked at each of them before he continued. "I ain't got nothing but what I'm smoking, shawdy, and I don't sell it."

Trell shot one of his pahtnas a quick, nervous little glance. This little encounter was obviously going nothing close to how the three stooges had planned and assumed it would. They had come with the intention of telling Snake he had to stop selling his dope at their motel, and by it being three of them to his one, they'd been sure he would tuck his tail and leave quietly. Now, though, with the way he'd answered the door, pistol in hand and all, and just his overall demeanor that said fuck you, the three of them were thinking otherwise.

But Trell had a bit of pride and an image to uphold in front of his pahtnas, so he tried to save face and ease on around to what they had really come for. "Yeah, but I had thought since you was over here slowin' a nigga money up and shit–"

Snake yawned and with a lazy, unconcerned expression on his face, he politely took a step back and slammed the door in their faces. Nobody short of the law was about to tell him he couldn't trap out of a motel, and somehow, some way, he had known those three clowns were headed in that direction. Taking a deep breath, he shook his head with a little laugh. He didn't know which one they thought they were working, but they were really begging for some serious trouble by fucking with him.

As soon as he got back to sacking up the work, another knock sounded at the door. Irritated because he just knew it was Trell and his pahtnas again, without a second thought he grabbed the strap and went and yanked the door open.

"Whoa, man! Hold up! What the fuck I done did?" Rambo exclaimed. He'd instinctively raised his hands chest high and leaned back, away from the barrel that was still just inches from the tip of his nose.

"My bad, man. I thought you was them other niggas." Snake lowered the gun as Rambo entered the room.

"What other niggas?" he asked, his heart still pounding from being scared shitless as he closed the door behind him.

***

Okay, now remember, Jay, don't say shit about him. Just go over and talk to her about anything, whatever, just as long as it ain't dealing with him.

"A'ight," Jayla nodded as she weaved between the patrons in the club that night. "Hey," she said and smiled when she reached the bar.

Jaz looked Jayla's extremely sexy, half-naked body up and down suspiciously before responding. "What's up?"

"Nothing much, girl. Gimmee a Hen and coke," she said, handing Jaz a $20 bill.

"Keep ya money, girl. You know y'all drinks is free until y'all get too drunk to make money," she said, fixing the drink for her.

"Well, you keep it, then, since you doing all the work," she insisted.

Jaz paused and stared at the bill Jayla held out for her. *Why not?* She grabbed and pocketed the money, and then fixed herself a drink also before sitting down across from her to chat, gossip, and talk shit about the girls and niggas in the club.

Ambitious

Chapter Nine

The next few weeks or so passed by in a blur for Snake. He had pretty much moved in with Jaz at her unofficial invitation, of course, and so far it was working out beautifully for him. He liked her, and she was the type of bitch a nigga could really kick it with, so he liked being around her, too. He'd also copped some work from Ant, who had looked out for him again with four ounces on top of the quarter brick he paid for, just on the strength of him being able to tolerate dealing with Jaz.

"This just for putting up with that crazy ho and keeping her ass out of me and Tasha business, bruh. I know that bitch prob'ly about to drive yo' ass crazy," he said in a serious tone of voice.

Snake just laughed a little and nodded as he accepted the gift. Ant didn't need to know he and Jaz were working perfectly together if he was going to give him a few thousand dollars' worth of cocaine just for assuming he was having a hard time dealing with her. He needed to keep assuming and believing whatever kept the free work coming. He even considered telling him he was thinking about cutting her ass off just to see what that would get him, but he decided not to, electing to keep that little strategy in the tuck for a later date. But what he did do is make a mental note to ask Jaz exactly what the hell she had done to become such a pain in the ass to Ant.

The only minor problems on his radar were the whack-ass niggas out at the motel. Their little run at the place was pretty much over, thanks largely in part to his and Rambo's collaboration, but they were still holding on for dear life. They had thought themselves smart when they made their sacks bigger to try to compete with him, but the dope was whipped, and that was when even their most loyal of customers had started fucking with him.

For a day or two immediately after their bad business decision, they began to shoot him all kinds of sideways and envious glances, like he was in some way responsible for what they'd done. Every time they saw him, it was the same thing until one day he got tired of it and flat-out checked Trell and his two flunky pahtnas about the off-color looks. But of course the pussies had feigned ignorance and screamed peace, so he let it go, even though he was reluctant to. He could feel the tension building, and he knew that sooner rather than later, something was going to have to happen one way or another for him to continue being comfortable trapping at the motel. And being that he wasn't in the business of going out bad, it didn't look too promising for that particular crew from Bowen Homes.

One night he and Jaz pulled into the parking lot and saw Trell and one of his flunky pahtnas posted up on the railing in front of their own room, apparently just chilling.

Jaz knew she didn't know even an eighth of the things she would have liked to know about Snake and his personality and what not, but she figured by that time she had gained a good enough bead on him to know when something was amiss with him. "Listen," she said softly to him as she eased through the parking lot of the motel. "I don't want you to start no shit with them niggas over there. Just mind ya business and let them niggas mind theirs."

A frowning smirk came over Snake's face. "What you talking about, shawdy?" he asked. He'd done nothing he knew of to make her say some shit like that.

Right then, Trell spotted Jaz's Impala and flicked his cigarette away before taking off his shirt and going into their room with his pahtna following right behind him. No sooner than when the door closed behind them, an unmarked A.P.D. Crown Victoria whipped up behind Jaz's Impala.

"Shit! Gimme all that crack and stuff that pistol in my seat. Hurry up, nigga!" Jaz ordered in a panicked tone while leaning forward for him to stick the pistol in her seat, her heart thundering madly.

Snake moved quickly and watched her stick her hand in her panties and bring it back out empty of all the work it had held before going in. By the time the police officer came and asked them to step out of the car, everything was in place. All paperwork and documents were in order, but in the end, after a lazy search of the car was conducted, Jaz was booked for misdemeanor possession. She'd forgotten all about the seven grams of gas in the cupholder because she'd been more concerned with stashing the crack and pistol for Snake. It wasn't a big deal, though. She'd be out of pre-trial more than likely just as soon as she got there, she and Snake both knew.

As the officer put her in the backseat of his car, it didn't go unnoticed by Snake how the Bowen Homes niggas kept peeking out of the window in their room down at the scene in the parking lot. He fired up a Newport as the officer rode off with Jaz. "Bitch-ass niggas better not be playing police games," he said to himself, smoke escaping from his nose and mouth as he got behind the wheel of the Impala. He needed to get down to pre-trial to wait for her to be released. They were lucky the officer didn't have the car towed. Had he found the pistol stuck between the seats, he would've had to.

***

It was close to two o'clock in the morning when Jaz was finally released. There had been some kind of mix-up with her name, which had prolonged the process. She was dog-tired, so instead of going back out to the motel, Snake took her straight home where they showered together and fell asleep naked as soon as they hit the bed.

The next afternoon when he woke up, she was already awake, watching some show on the Oxygen channel and balancing a plate of food on her thighs. "Hey, cutie, you hungry?" she asked when he stirred. She speared a forkful of eggs and a small piece of sausage and fed it to him.

"Hell yeah, I ain't eat shit last night," he said with a scratchy voice while chewing and swallowing as he stood up to stretch.

She couldn't resist the playful urge to give his naked backside a little squeeze and pinch.

"The fuck!" he jumped and yelled as he whirled around to face a giggling Jaz. "Hey!" he said, giving her a stern look while slashing his hand through the air as if to say *Enough*!

Still giggling, she brushed him off and he walked to the bathroom, mumbling something under his breath. When he came back, she was gone and her plate sat on the nightstand. He lay back down and turned his attention to the reality show on TV, and a few minutes later she walked back into the room, still ass-naked, and carrying a plate of food for him.

He eyed her clean-shaven pussy hungrily while his stomach growled from nutritional hunger. It didn't take long for one urge to overpower the other, and in the end he decided the food, which was most important, could wait. He ordered Jaz to, "Put that shit on the dresser and get yo' li'l ass over here!" as he scooted to the edge of the bed.

She saw his throbbing dick sticking straight up at attention and, with a slutty little smile and smirk on her face, she obeyed his command. Not able to take her eyes off his erection, she purposefully made her way over to him as slow as she possibly could, but once she was close enough, he grabbed her and threw her on the bed roughly. "Ooh!" she screamed out with a confused smile on her face. She didn't quite understand why he was being so rough with her all of a sudden when he knew she wanted the dick.

Not knowing whether to be scared or turned on by the over-aggressiveness he was showing, she looked directly into his smoky eyes for some sort of indication of how she should be feeling. Along with lust, she saw a ton of rage in them, and that was when she became positive she should be feeling only fear, fuck being horny or turned on.

Her pulse quickened, and she was just about to start whimpering and begging for him not to touch her when he spread her legs with his hands roughly and dropped to his knees. "I'm about to eat this pussy!" he growled to himself.

Wait, what? Jaz's face unconsciously screwed up in utter bewilderment, and she raised her head a little to look down at him. His smoky eyes met hers again, and she no longer saw even the slightest touch of rage in them, only pure, unadulterated lust, tinged with a bit of humor.

In complete contrast to the aggressive way he was handling her just a few seconds ago, he lightly caressed her pussy with his hand. He brushed his thick lips against her lower lips, and from her point of view, all she saw was the top of his head, full of thick, wavy, jet-black hair next to her cat.

Oh! It took her seeing that, and just that long for her to realize what his intentions were, and she gushed. Not having time to feel like an idiot, she lay her head back with a little smile and spread her legs wider to make sure he had enough room to do what he wanted to do, and boy was she glad she hadn't panicked and done something stupid, like tell him to stop or scream for help like she'd been about to do. She felt his silky-smooth tongue search for and find her swollen little spur, and when it did she convulsed immediately. She arched her back and screamed out as he teased her clit with his tongue, and when she was about to come, she grabbed the back of his head with strength he wasn't aware she possessed to hold him steady. "Right there! Eat that pussy, boy! Eat that shit! Don't fuckin' stop! I'm about to come!" She screamed and raked her fingers through his waves. She started to soak his face with her juices, and she arched her back even more, trying to push all of her pussy into his mouth.

Snake took it in stride. Horny as fuck, he rubbed his entire face around in her wetness. Once he was positive she had finished coming, he stood to his feet.

"Breakfast of a champion," he smacked his lips and joked with a devilishly handsome smile, but for some reason his little comment, coupled with the sight of her fluids glistening all over his face and even in his hair at the front, turned her on even more.

She sat up and pulled him to her. She kissed his lips and then moved to licking her juices from his face before focusing on his tattooed and muscled stomach and chest. Before long she was cupping his balls in the palm of her hand and opening up to take as much of his large dick in her mouth as she could work with. Snake groaned and grabbed the back of her head as he watched her gobble his dick while she played with his balls and spread her legs wide. All of the groaning and grunting he was doing turned her on even more because she knew she was the reason behind his pleasure, and she began to rub her clit.

Before she could rub herself to another orgasm, Snake pulled his dick out of her mouth and shot a thick stream of come all over her neck and titties. "Ooh!" She gave another little scream as she closed her eyes and jerked back, trying to avoid a facial or getting it in her freshly-done $200 braids.

Satisfied his semen didn't go where she didn't want it, she grabbed one of her titties and pushing it up as far as the stubborn thing would allow her to, which wasn't very far. She stuck her tongue out and played with a small pool of his nut there. Cutting her eyes up at him and wearing a slutty expression, she saw she was turning him on. His flaccid dick began to harden and throb with every beat of his heart until it was standing strong and proud again.

Snake smiled. "Yo' ass is a real freak, girl," he said, watching her like a hawk.

"I can be, sometimes," she purred and slid back on the bed. She started to rub his semen into her skin as she spread her legs as wide as she could, giving him an excellent view of her lady business.

Snake just stood there, staring, admiring her naked body for the beautiful piece of work it was. The girl was virtually perfect.

She cleared her throat. "Me and this pussy waiting," she said with mock attitude.

He snapped out of his zone and climbed on top of her little frame. Jaz purred and squeezed both of his naked ass cheeks when he slipped into her wet pussy. Wasting no time, he started to pound her off the rip, and the fact she'd wrapped her legs around his waist and was using them to pull him into her harder and deeper with every thrust spurred him right along like he was a prize-winning thoroughbred. Before he knew it, he lay on top of her, spent and chest heaving as he sucked oxygen into his lungs at a desperate rate.

Jaz lay beneath him, panting herself as she kissed and nibbled at his face, beyond satisfied. "You ready to start round two?" It was her turn to joke.

***

Later that day, Snake had Jaz take him out to the motel where everything appeared to be normal until they reached his room. When he tried to unlock his door, it put up no resistance and swung inward on squeaking hinges with ease. He looked at Jaz and then down the walkway towards the room the niggas from Bowen Homes rented before going inside.

Everything he saw had been touched. The entire room had been thoroughly ransacked. The bed flipped. The lamps broken. The table overturned. Everything had been disturbed. Rage seeped through his body as he looked around at the shambles. Snatching the forty-cal out of his pocket, he chambered a round with authority and started for the door, but Jaz beat him to it and blocked his way. "Hold up, nigga. Wait a muthafuckin' minute! What the fuck is yo' ass about to do, nigga?" she demanded with a scared look on her face.

Fighting to control his breathing and his voice, he scowled. "Man, I'm about to kill them puss-ass niggas. Move, shawdy," he said and tried to move her away from the door with one hand.

"Hell naw, boy! I ain't about to move so you can go and do some dumb-ass shit," she said, struggling with him but refusing to budge. The only reason she was able to hold her ground was because Snake held the pistol in his other hand, and he didn't want to be rough with her. "It's broad daylight out there, and yo' ass talking about you about to go kill something."

"You fuckin' right! Now move, girl, before I move yo' li'l ass." His scowl deepened as he growled the warning at her, putting the pistol in his pocket. At that moment a big bolt of lightening flashed and a loud thunderclap followed close behind it. It seemed just that fast, the weather had adjusted to fit Snake's mood.

Knowing that physically she was no match for the big man, Jaz decided to attempt a different tactic to try to get him to think rationally. "You ain't lost nothing. Everything you got that's worth something is back at the apartment. Them niggas ain't get no money, no dope, nothing."

Shaking his head, Snake sucked his teeth and cut her off. "That ain't even the point," he said angrily.

Jaz grabbed his face by his chin and looked directly into his eyes. "Think about what you about to do. Just take a second and think about this dumb-ass shit you about to try, please. You ain't go' get away with it. You go down there and do something to them niggas, I'ma be right here waiting to drive yo' ass away from here, but it's the middle of the day. Somebody go' see yo' high-yella ass, and they go' fuckin' tell it. Yo' ass go' be on Crime Stoppers within a hour. Please, don't do this stupid-ass shit. Just think, Siree," she said softly with tears brimming in her eyes and moved out of his way.

Snake stood rooted to the spot, as still as a statue. She was right, and he knew she was right, but boy how he wanted to murder them niggas! "You right," he said calmly while shaking his head. "'Preciate it, shawdy," he pulled her close to him and kissed her on the lips, "'cause I was damn sure about to do some stupid-ass shit." He rummaged around the room and grabbed a few things he wanted to take with him, and then told Jaz, "C'mo' le's dip."

The two of them made their way out to her car, and as they were leaving, she nodded toward the room the Bowen Homes niggas rented. "Look," she said.

Snake looked and saw one of Trell's flunkies standing in the window, holding a choppa with a smirk on his face. "Humph," he grunted with a very slight nod and rested his hand on Jaz's thigh.

***

That night arrived and brought a hard, warm rain with it. Snake had his collar turned up against the weather with his back turned toward the door and was busy brushing little beads of water from his jacket when his knock was answered. "Got yo' ass!" he muttered while turning and swinging the butt of his pistol ferociously. Blood splattered, and he heard as well as felt bone crunch from the impact before he forced his way into the room, kicking the door closed behind him. The nigga he'd hit with the pistol lay on the floor, moaning and clutching his bleeding face while a sudden movement to his right caused him to swing his pistol that way and fire a single shot. "Next one of y'all niggas move, ya dead," he warned quietly, stopping the nigga who had been closest to the choppa from trying to get to it.

"Get the fuck on the floor, all of y'all!" he barked quietly as he stepped over to where the choppa was leaned up against the wall and kicked it out of the potential reach of any of the four people he held at gunpoint. "I ain't playing, nigga. Get the fuck down!" he barked again and rushed over to one of the niggas and slapped him across the head with the pistol for slow-poking. The nigga lost consciousness immediately and crumpled to the floor awkwardly. "Y'all bitch-ass niggas wanna play li'l games and break in my shit, right?" he said matter-of-factly while nodding his head. He'd worked himself into a calm, but deadly rage.

The first nigga he'd hit with the pistol dared to risk a quick peek up from his spot on the floor over by the door to see what was going on around him, and in the brief second he saw Snake, he knew instantly he was psychotic. Right then, at that very moment, he really, really started to regret he and his pahtnas had broken into the nigga's room the night before.

No matter, though, because what was done was done, and he had more pressing issues to worry about right now, anyway. Like why he was being snatched to his feet by the back of his shirt and hearded over toward the rest of his pahtnas. And why was a fucking pillow being shoved into his face?

Although the gunshot was muffled considerably by the pillow, the reaction of the other two conscious people Snake was holding at gunpoint was nothing short of dramatic.

"Y'all niggas shut the fuck up," he hissed furiously. The nigga he'd just shot in the face twisted as he fell to the floor, exposing the ugly-ass exit wound in the back of his head from the slug. Snake grabbed another pillow and walked over to the nigga he'd knocked unconscious a few moments ago. He was lying on his stomach, and the slight rise and fall of his back could be seen with every breath he took. His head was turned to his left, and Snake covered it with the pillow before he squeezed off another round from the forty-cal. "Pussy-ass nigga," he said while pulling the trigger.

By that time the horrid smell of human feces had started to grow stronger and stronger throughout the room. "Nah, bitch," he said with one hard, sinister-sounding laugh. "It's too late for all that ol' shit there. Y'all muthafuckas wasn't scared enough to be pooting and farting and shit while y'all was breaking in my shit." He grabbed another pillow off the bed. When he stood over the kid he'd caught peeping through his window a while back, he turned up his nose. The ungodly stench was undoubtedly wafting up from the kid's trousers.

"Don't shoot him, man. That nigga just a kid, man," Trell begged for his little cousin's life to be spared. "All the work and money is in the bathroom in the top of the toilet. Just let bruh go, man."

Snake looked at him with an exasperated frown. He honestly couldn't believe his ears. "Now, why the fuck," he said as he stopped what he'd been about to do to step over to Trell, "would I do some shit like that?" he asked. "Fuckin' dumbass," he growled and kicked Trell in the nuts just for being stupid.

While he lay there writhing and moaning in agony, Snake moved back over to the kid. Kneeling down and pushing the pillow over his teary face, he put him out of his misery. Then, suddenly, after the bullet tore through the kid's skull, the only sobs left to be heard were Trell's own.

Snake grabbed the last unused pillow in the room and stepped over to him. Knowing death was imminent, he tried to scream out for help, but almost no sound came out at all. In fact, the effort and force he'd put into his pitiful excuse of a cry for help caused him to shit his pants also, but it was preceded by a loud, long fart.

"Bitch-ass nigga," snake shook his head and said as he smothered Trell's face with the pillow. He thrashed around and threw a few wild blows before Snake put a bullet through his face, causing all of the reckless thrashing about and carrying on to cease abruptly as a deafening silence descended over the room.

Snake stood and listened for the telltale sound of sirens to alert him of police proximity but heard nothing other than the driving rain making impact with the roof of the building and the ground outside. He looked around for a second before stripping the sheet off of one of the two beds in the room and heading to the bathroom to raid the stash in the toilet.

***

When he walked into Jaz's apartment, he went directly to the bedroom the two of them were sharing, dropped the sheet with the pilfered goods wrapped up inside of it, and turned the TV on to Fox 5 to await the news.

Thinking it strange of him to come in and not say anything at all to her, not even one of his many playful jokes, Jaz frowned. Upon seeing how interested he was in watching the television, she scooted down to the foot of the bed beside him and began to watch also. When the news began to air, he pulled a pack of Sour Skittles from his pocket and quietly started to munch on them. He and Jaz still hadn't spoken one word to each other, but when she nudged him he automatically knew what she wanted. Without taking his eyes away from the TV screen, he poured some of the Skittles into her open palm as they both stared intently at the TV.

Just as he had figured it would whenever it made its debut, the murders at the motel over on Fulton Industrial Boulevard were the night's top story, and Jaz's mouth gaped open as she listened in horror to the details of what had happened. Snake blinked for the first time, it seemed, when the reporter spoke of a witness, but his heart rate slowed immensely when it was reported that the witness could only say she'd heard a single gunshot.

Once that story was completed and one of the anchors began to report about another murder over on Cooper Street, Jaz jumped up and stood directly in front of the flat screen TV on the wall. Her eyebrows were knit together as she stared at Snake with her very best *What the fuck!* expression, but she didn't say a word.

"What?" Snake asked with a frown as he chewed his Skittles. When she didn't move or say anything, he offered her some more of his candy by holding the bag out for her. "What, you want some more or something?" he asked with a shrug.

"Really?" she exploded and slapped his hand, causing Skittles to fly everywhere. "Get that got-damn candy out my face! You gotta be fuckin' kidding me, right? Are you fuckin' serious right now?"

"What? Wus wrong with you, shawdy?" he asked, his tone of voice and facial expression showing deep concern for her wellbeing.

Jaz stormed out of the room, mumbling something about the last time she would ever let him use her car.

Shrugging, Snake started to pick up the candy she'd made him waste. "I wonder what the fuck she mad for," he said to himself before popping one of the Skittles he'd picked up off of the floor into his mouth.

Ambitious

Chapter Ten

The next day, after fiercly denying he'd had anything to do with what had happened out at the motel and arguing back and forth with Jaz all morning about it, once she calmed down, he asked her to take him over to his grandmother's house. Although she'd agreed to stop fussing and chill out, she was still unbelievably pissed off at him. Fuck what he was saying about not knowing anything about them niggas getting killed, she knew he'd done it, but the kids in hell would get a snow day before she allowed her anger, however justified it might be, to cause her to miss out on such a grand opportunity. She liked Snake a hell of a lot, but he was always so damn secretive and sneaky, especially about his past and things of the sort. So, when he asked her to take him to see his grandmother, the woman who raised him and no doubt was probably bursting with the kind of information she wanted to know about him, despite all her frustration and fear and anger geared toward him at the moment, she'd smiled and quickly agreed to do so. She was sure if no one else could help her fill in some gaps about her Adonis, his grandmother would be able to. Plus, with the way he doted on her, he'd painted a pleasant picture of a wonderful little old lady with a ton of personality and spunk in the eye of Jaz's mind, and she honestly couldn't wait to meet her.

The two of them set out together and made it to his grandmother's house a little before noon. All of the rain and bad weather from the previous day had blown through, and now the sun shined brightly in the cloudless sky, warming the city and drying up the little puddles of water that still lingered here and there.

"Hey, Gram, how you been?" Snake smiled and said as he hugged his grandmother and kissed her cheek when she answered the door.

"Worried sick about you, baby. I ain't heard from ya in days. C'mo' in here." She fussed lightly over him as she held on to his hand. "Let me fix ya some lunch. Oh, hello," she said when she finally realized her grandson wasn't alone. She looked from Jaz to Snake, and then back to Jaz again with a questioning gaze.

"Hi, I'm Jazmine. I'm a friend of Siree's," she said with a pretty smile as she looked at the frail little old lady in front of her, liking her instantly. Everything about her from the wispy, unruly grey hair sticking up on her head to the powerful motherly aura with a strong pull she seemed to not be able to resist put Jaz in the mind of a loving grandparent.

"Oh, good!" she exclaimed and clapped her hands lightly. "I need some great babies, and you're so pretty." Smiling, she wrung her hands together and looked at Snake proudly. "She's pretty," she whispered loudly.

"Gram, stop it," Snake blushed, embarrassed as hell for some reason. "We just friends."

"Thank you," Jaz said to the old lady while suppressing her laughter.

"Well, I need some great babies soon, 'cause I ain't getting no younger. Y'all c'mo' in," she looked at Snake and said pointedly before turning a smile toward Jaz, who giggled and followed the elderly woman into the house and to the kitchen.

Spunky indeed, she thought to herself.

"I'ma run upstairs, Gram. I need to put some stuff up," Snake called out from the foot of the stairs.

His grandmother peeked around the corner of the kitchen doorway to look at him. "Go on, go on," she shooed him away. "Me and ya girlfriend here go' fix ya something to eat."

"She ain't my girlfriend, Gram," he growled.

"Well, she a girl, ain't she? And you said she was ya friend, didn't ya?" she shot back.

Snake sighed and shook his head before mounting the stairs and heading to the spare room across the hall from his own. Ever since he could remember, his grandmother had used the room as a place to store things, but now he saw most of the junk that used to clutter the room had been removed. For the first time in his life, he was seeing the entire room at once. Four walls, a closet, and a doorway. Nothing spectacular.

He looked around for a place to stash the money he had taken the previous night from the Bowen Homes niggas out at the motel. It hadn't been much, only $6,300, and he'd given Jaz $1,500 of that just on the strength of how she had been looking out for him and fucking with his campaign without even asking for anything of monetary value back in return. He also kept a little something for his own pockets, but knowing how shit could get real ugly, real fast, he figured the $4,000 he was about to hide would be enough to help him catch a grip, should he ever need it, although he knew it wasn't much.

Still looking for a place to put the money, he decided to check out the closet. He wasn't really expecting his granny to be snooping around, and he knew even if she did find his small stash, she wouldn't bother or question it, but he didn't want to just leave it lying around some place where she might run across it.

He pulled on a string that dangled down to his waist, and the bare bulb that hung from the ceiling down to his eye level glowed to life in the closet. Looking up, he saw he would have to stand on something to reach the lowest shelf. "Damn," he whispered, looking around while hoping there was an alternative to having to go get something to stand on, but he quickly saw there wasn't if he wanted to use the closet.

He sighed and scratched his head as he turned to go get a chair or something else that would give him a little boost, and after taking only a few steps, he lightly stubbed his toe on something that was sticking up out of the floor, but covered by a worn-out, dusty green rug. He figured maybe it was just a nail or something, but curiosity got the better of him, so he kicked the threadbare rug out of the way and saw what he'd stubbed his toe on was actually a loose plank in the wooden floor. He bent to try to push it back into its right position, and with a little force it slipped back into its place with a little thump.

On a closer inspection of the plank, he saw a very subtle groove had been worn into it at the other end, so he placed his hand in it and pushed. The plank creaked a little and jutted up out of place. He took it up, and with a grunt he got to his knees and peered down into the dark hole. Seeing there was a little opening, he wound up taking up four more loose planks before standing back up and looking down at the opening in the floor. The little hollow space was perfect for what he needed. It was maybe a foot deep and a foot wide, give or take an inch or so.

"What you up to?" Jaz's soft voice asked from behind him.

He jumped and whirled around, spooked a little, and saw her standing in the doorway with a plate. "Don't be creeping up on me like that, for ya own safety, shawdy. What you doing up here anyway?" he asked with squinted eyes.

Jaz shrugged in an unconcerned manner. "She sent me up here with this food for you. I seen them pictures in the living room. That was yo gramma when she was younger?"

"Yeah," Snake said with his mind on something else entirely. "Come in and close the door."

"She was fuckin' beautiful. Like, super model pretty, for real," she said while closing the door. "Who the hell that white man is on them pictures?" she asked before taking a bite out of one of his turkey sandwiches as she made her way to stand next to him.

He glanced at her questioningly, and then at his other sandwhich on the plate she held and thought it would be a good idea to get it before she got to it. Picking it up and taking a large bite out of it, he said around a mouthful of food, "That's my bitch-ass grandaddy."

"But he a white man, though," she said with a slight frown and a tone of voice that suggested maybe Snake didn't know his grandfather was white.

He looked at her like she was crazy for a second. "Duh, I know that piece of shit was white. That don't mean he wasn't my damn grandaddy."

Jaz's frown deepened. "Why you talking about him like that?"

Snake took another bite of his sandwich. "Man, fuck that nigga. Bitch-ass nigga got my muthafuckin' gramma pregnant with my daddy and abandoned her. Good ol' white man like him couldn't be seen sneaking around with no nigga bitch back then, much less getting one pregnant," he said with a sour look on his face. "Don't matter how light-skinned or pretty she was, she still a nigga, and it would've ruined his respectable reputation. My gramma understand that bullshit, I can't. That muthafucka bought my gramma this house and made her raise my daddy by herself. Fuck that nigga," he said disgustedly.

"That's who the other man is on the pictures? Yo' daddy?" she asked softly, feeling a bit uncomfortable after learning about his grandfather.

Snake nodded. "Yeah, that's my pops," he said quietly, and then with a third bite finished off his sandwich.

An uncomfortable silence lasted for about thirty seconds before Jaz spoke again. "What that is?" she nodded at the hole in the floor and took another bite of the sandwich meant for him.

He cleared his throat, grateful for the change of topic. "I don't know. It's about to be my li'l hiding spot, though."

"What you trying to hide?" she asked. He had piqued her curiosity.

When he dropped the four grand in the little hollowed-out space, she was honestly shocked into genuine laughter. "That ain't much to hide right there, sport," she said with a chuckle.

"He-he-he. Hell, nigga, real fuckin' funny," he mocked her laughter with a frown on his face.

Still laughing, she looked back down at the pitiful-looking four grand in the seemingly humongous compartment. "Hold up," she said, setting the plate down and digging in her pocket. She pulled out a $20 bill and dropped it into the hole with the other money. "Now you ready," she said and giggled again as she picked up the plate.

Snake nodded. "Go on and laugh, muthafucka. Make all the li'l jokes you want," he said with a handsome, sneaky little grin. "I got me a li'l plan I know go' fill this li'l spot with cash, just watch."

Jaz laughed again. "Oh really? What is it?" she asked and pecked him on the lips, not actually believing he had a real plan to score big and fast.

He smiled sneakily again, and just when he was about to tell her to mind her own business, a soft knock sounded at the door. "It's a'ight if y'all wanna make me some great babies in there," his grandmother's soft voice called from the other side of the door. "I don't mind. Just pretend I'm not here and have at it."

Snake turned beet red. "Gramma," he yelled as Jaz burst into a fit of laughter.

***

Snake scratched his nuts and sniffed his hand while he lay on the couch in Jaz's living room watching TV. "'Bout time for a ol' shower, buddy," he mumbled absentmindedly to himself. He'd been in chill mode ever since they got back from his granny's house earlier, and being mindful of what he'd done the night before, he knew he needed to just fall back for a while, especially from the area around the motel. So for him, being the pariah he was, that meant he'd be staying inside a lot. When the program he was watching, *The First 48*, went off, he sat up and grabbed a slice of pizza from the box on the coffee table. It was cold, but he had no complaints. It was still good as hell, being that it had been ten years since he'd eaten any Pizza Hut. Just as he was finishing off the slice of pizza, he heard keys jingling. He knew it was Jaz, but he still got up and looked out the peephole before opening the door.

"Hey, boo," she said and rubbed his stomach as she walked into the apartment with her friend, Tasha, right behind her.

"What's hap'ning?" he said, and then with a nod he said to Tasha, "What up, shawdy?"

"Hey, Smoke," Tasha chirped in a friendly tone as he closed the door behind her. She and Jaz both went directly to the kitchen, one raiding the refrigerator while the other raided the cabinets in search of junk food, oblivious to Snake because they were both high as hell and caught up in their girl talk.

He disappeared to the bathroom for his shower, unnoticed by either of them, and by the time he'd finished and gotten dressed, they both were sitting on a couch in the living room, gossiping and watching TV. A blunt of gas was in rotation between them, and he was sure he hadn't left the TV on on the Oxygen channel when he'd left. He plopped down on the couch right next to Jaz and picked up the remote from her her lap. After turning to Sports Center, which neither of the girls seemed to mind too much because they were caught up in their own convo, he interrupted the rotation of the blunt by reaching and grabbing it from Tasha when she was trying to pass it to Jaz.

"Damn, nigga, that ain't yo' weed," Jaz said as he took a long drag on the blunt. "Yo' ass done already came and turnt the damn TV without saying shit."

"Uh-uh, girl, quit being mean." Tasha looked at Snake and said, "It's mine, you can smoke if you want to." She shook her head while rolling her eyes at Jaz and smiling.

Snake held both of his hands up as if to tell Tasha to just chill and let him handle her. "Oh, I can't smoke with y'all," he asked, smoke coming from his nose and mouth when he spoke.

"Nope. Now pass that shit," Jaz said playfully, but still reached for the blunt.

He nodded slowly. "Say no mo'." He passed her the blunt and then dug in his pants pocket. "I guess just me and ol' Tasha go' smoke this then, since she didn't care I smoked her shit," he said, pulling a sandwich bag out of his pocket and opening it up.

The fumes that wafted through the air from his weed was damn near as loud and strong as the weed that was burning. "What the fuck that is, nigga?" Jaz screeched and lunged for the bag he was clutching.

He easily held her at bay while chuckling. "Nah, nigga, yo' ol' stingy, big-head-ass just keep smoking that shit you got right there. Me and shawdy go' smoke this," he shot her a handsome grin and winked. "Roll this up, ma," he said to Tasha and put three large pinches of the weed on the coffee table for her to roll. He deliberately took his time rolling the sandwich bag back up and putting it in his pocket as Jaz evil-eyed him, and in return he puckered his lips and blew her a silent kiss.

"Nigga, what the fuck is this, and where the fuck it come from?" Tasha asked excitedly as she broke the weed down so she could roll it up.

Snake nodded his head. "Yeah, that's that gas pack, straight octane," he bragged.

"Damn sure smell like it. Shit slick, got my fuckin' eyes watering."

Snake nodded even harder and laughed. "Yeah!" he said enthusiastically and reached to get a slice of pizza from the box. He was disappointed when he lifted the lid, though. Only three pieces of nibbled-on crust remained. He bolted up from his seat. "Which one of y'all ate that pizza, shawdy!" he demanded.

"I ate it," Jaz said defiantly with a frown.

"You for real?" he asked, looking at her with eyes as big as saucers.

"Yeah, nigga, I did that," she said with even more defiance.

"Man, I was just about to throw that shit away when I heard y'all at the door. That shit had bugs in it, I meant to throw it out, but I forgot when y'all came in," he said with a frown while shaking his head.

Jaz blanched and Tasha looked up from rolling the weed. She'd eaten one of the slices, too.

"I ain't got no damn bugs. Quit playing with me, nigga," Jaz threatened, but in a questioning, unsure manner.

"Man, I swear to God, bae, that shit had bugs in it," he said with an extremely worried expression on his face.

With a disgusted look on her face, Jaz heaved as she jumped up and ran to the bathroom.

Snake looked at Tasha and smiled evily. "I'ma teach that ass," he said and headed to the bathroom behind her.

Tasha sighed with a little laugh, relieved he was only joking, and started back rolling the weed up.

When he walked into the bathroom, Jaz was bent over the toilet trying to make herself puke. He watched for a few seconds before saying, "I was just playing," while rubbing on her booty.

She stopped heaving and froze solid. "What?" she asked in a low, dangerous tone of voice.

"Wasn't shit wrong with that pizza. I was just fuckin' with

yo' greedy ass 'cause you ate it all up and had a li'l attitude when I asked about it."

She spun around and punched him on the arm. "Nigga!"

He laughed and she pounded on his chest three or four more times before he grabbed and held her. Still laughing, he told her he was sorry and kissed her on the cheek before asking if she was okay.

"Hell naw, nigga, let me go!" she ordered.

He squeezed her a little. "You go' stop beating me up, bae?"

"Yeah," she barked. He let her go and she gave him an icy stare before turning and taking out her toothbrush. "Get the hell on, nigga. I see why yo' name Snake, muthafucka. You ain't shit," she said with a scowl as she looked at him through the mirror.

He laughed again and went back to the living room. Tasha was just sparking the blunt up when Jaz walked back into the room and sat down beside Snake, throwing her legs across his lap. "Damn," she exclaimed when she got a whiff of the weed's pungent aroma.

Tasha took one pull on the blunt and almost choked out. She hit it twice more and seemed to be on the verge of another fit of coughing as she passed it to Snake, shaking her head with tears in her eyes. "That shit smoking!" she burst out and said when she exhaled the potent smoke she couldn't stand to hold in her lungs for a second longer.

He hit the weed a few times, and without hesitating he passed it to Jaz, who choked out just as fast as Tasha had. It took him a little longer to start his coughing, but before the blunt made it's way back around to him again, he did. When everything was said and done, it took the three of them close to an hour just to finish off that one blunt.

***

About an hour after the weed had been smoked, Jaz jumped up from where she'd been snuggled up right next to Snake and turned off all the lights in the apartment. She'd moved so suddenly she actually spooked Snake, and his heart was still pounding when she padded back to the couch and cuddled up next to him again. She offered him her cup of cold Kool-Aid and wound up having to pop him shortly after he accepted it. "Don't drank all of it, boy!" she hissed.

He turned the cup over to her and leaned his head back against the couch, staring at the TV but not really seeing it, too high to focus on anything other than his thoughts. He jumped, startled when Jaz stuck her hand in his shorts and groped his dick. "My pussy wet as hell. I'm horny as fuck," she whispered and ran her tongue around the inside of his ear. "I want some of this dick," she said and squeezed him.

He tried to get up, but she wouldn't let go of his dick. "What you doing? C'mo' to the room," he whispered back urgently. Just that fast he was rock hard and horny as hell himself. He stuck his hand in her pants and felt she was telling the truth. The front of her boy shorts were slick from being soaked through with her juices, and his mouth literally watered.

"Let's do it right here," she whispered with a hint of mischief gleaming in her eyes, her breathing a bit labored because her clit was being teased and toyed with.

"Yo' friend sitting right there," Snake whispered with a confused frown, but it was a front. Jaz had never given him any indication she was into girls, but he had to admit the thought of smashing her and her girl, Tasha, together was currently running through his mind, and it was quite appealing. He wouldn't let on to it, though, not unless she opened the door fully for him to do so.

"That bitch sleep. Watch this. Tasha?" she called softly, but definitely loud enough to be heard by her friend had she been awake. "Told ya," she said when Tasha didn't respond.

The thought of letting him fuck the shit out of her right there while she was asleep became more and more of a turn on with each passing second for some reason.

She ducked her head into his lap and worked his dick free of his shorts. He gave a long sigh of pleasure when her warm, moist mouth closed around him and she let out a few moans herself as she worked on his erection. The more he played with her pussy, the more she got into sucking his dick, and pretty soon he was pulling his and Jaz's bottoms off and maneuvering her light frame on top of him so he could lick her pussy.

With a good 69 in action, the two of them were both moaning and groaning and getting louder by the second, seemingly oblivious to the fact they were't alone. The weed they'd smoked was definitely having an effect. Jaz just so happened to look up as she slobbered up and down on Snake's sloppy-wet dick and saw Tasha staring right at her as if she was in a trance. The look on her face registering surprise, fascination, and interest all at once.

Jaz ignored her. It was too late to stop because they'd already been caught. Plus, if Snake kept licking the spot he was licking at the moment, she was about to come all in his face in just a few seconds, and she didn't want to deprive him of that pleasure. He'd told her a while ago how much he loved for her to come all in his mouth and face. Besides, Tasha was grown, she knew exactly what the fuck was going on. And if she didn't, oh well, Jaz reasoned to herself.

She came hard, and so did Snake shortly after her, but it just wasn't as good as it should've been for either of them because they both were trying to hold back because of Tasha. It took them both a few seconds to recover their strength, and when they did, they got up from the couch and headed to the bedroom as quietly as possible for rounds two, three, four, and however many else the man of steel had in him.

Although she pretended to be asleep when they got up for Snake's benefit, she knew Jaz knew she wasn't. Tasha was wide awake and on the verge of coming on herself, she was so horny. The light from the TV had illuminated the erotic scene between Jaz and Smoke, and she became more and more aroused by it with every second of it she saw. When she heard him pounding into Jaz in the bedroom, she couldn't take it anymore. She got up and tiptoed to the bathroom. Locking the door behind her, she squeezed out of her wet panties and started to play with her pussy, imagining she was watching the scene taking place in the bedroom.

Ambitious

Chapter Eleven

Jaz and Jayla sat at the bar, sipping their drinks. It had become somewhat of a routine of theirs over the past two or three weeks. They would sit and talk shit about this, that, and the other for twenty or thirty minutes or so each night they found themselves getting off around the same time because they both seemed to genuinely enjoy the other's company. That particular night was no different. Nursing their drinks, they were chatting about some new place in Atlantic Station when a small disturbance kicked off in the club.

Jaz took her cue. She drained the last of her drink and grabbed her purse. "Girl, it's time for me to get the hell on. They go' be shooting in a minute and, uh, a bitch ain't got time to be getting gunned down on her overtime day," she chuckled. "Ya feel me? Maybe if I was supposed to be here, but definitely not on my day off."

"Bitch, get yo' crazy-ass on," Jayla laughed and pushed her shoulder playfully. "I gotta wait on Smurf. Bye, girl."

"A'ight, see ya lata, chick," Jaz said with a chuckle and waved with the two free fingers of the hand that she held her keys in before making her way toward the exit. As she got closer to the small crowd that had formed near the door, she saw Tasha and a pissy-drunk Ant were being separated by Vontae, the club's head bouncer. She frowned and rushed over. "What's wrong, Ant?" she asked him because he was closest to her and the more aggressive one.

"Ask yo ol' disrespectful-ass, ungrateful-ass friend," he said while pointing with a limp hand and finger. His speech was slurred and he was spitting uncontrollably with every word that he spoke. "Pun- ass bitch," he said and tried to get at Tasha.

Vontae easily blocked his path, and Ant almost fell when he bounced off the huge bouncer's body. He was wasted.

"What's wrong," Jaz mouthed to Tasha, who looked lost and scared as she shrugged her shoulders in response.

Ant picked his drink up, took a little sip, and then dashed the majority of it in Tasha's face. Vontae got a little bit of it, too, and that explained why he picked Ant's pissy-drunk-ass up like a ragdoll and carried him out of the club. Out of respect for him and his older brother, that was all he did to him. He knew the spoiled rotten young nigga was drunk and just needed to go somewhere to sleep it off.

Tasha, on the other hand, was in tears. All the other dancers were standing around staring at her with smug little smirks on their faces while Jaz rushed over and embraced her friend as Jayla came over with a towel. Jaz took it and blotted Tasha's face dry before draping it around her shoulders. Not in the mood for anything, Tasha just wanted to curl up and die. She was so fucking embarrassed.

Jaz asked Vontae if Ant had left when he came back in the club.

"Yeah, he got in his car, drunk as he was, and smashed out," he answered slowly and with a worried look on his face as he shook his head.

"C'mon, girl, let's go," Jaz said quietly and started to lead Tasha out of the club.

"A'ight, y'all?" Jayla mumbled somberly.

Jaz just nodded in response as they exited the club.

On the way to Jaz's apartment, Tasha opened up and explained how the whole situation back at the club had went down. In a nutshell, Ant had been watching her give some nobody a dance and got jealous. When she'd finished, and after milking the nigga out of $730, Ant had stumbled his drunk-ass over and started complaining about how intimate she'd been with the nigga.

Jaz squinted and wrinkled her nose in confusion. "The fuck he expect? You a damn stripper!" She shook her head, amazed at the stupidity of what she'd just heard.

"I know, right? That's what I was telling his ol' stupid-ass," she said loudly, her embarrassment beginning to give way to anger. "And he got some damn nerve, anyway. All them bitches he be fuckin' up there, but my ol' dumb-ass don't be saying shit," she shook her head, disgusted with herself. "All them hos standing around, laughing at me 'cause my nigga treat them better than he treat me," she said, getting quieter with each word she said as the realization of her statement slammed into her like a ton of bricks. She paused a seconds to even out her breathing and blink away a few tears before she went on to tell about how Ant had snatched her up and how Vontae had come over and stopped him before he could get too far out of hand.

Jaz just shook her head and sighed. When they reached her spot, they walked into a dark, empty apartment. She wondered where Snake was, but didn't think too much of it. He was grown and more than capable of taking care of himself. "But his ass do be needing for somebody to think for his ass sometimes, though," she mumbled to herself with a smile and turned on some lights.

"So it's straight if I crash over here for a few days, girl?"

She looked at Tasha like she had lost her mind. "Bitch, what kinda question is that? Yo' ass ain't never had to ask, and you already know what's mine is yours. As long as you don't care about sleeping on the couch, you can stay as long as you want to."

Tasha grinned slyly. "You know I ain't trying to be intruding on y'all freak, nasty-asses or nothing. Y'all might just decide you wanna fuck on the coffee table while I'm watching TV or something."

"Girl," Jaz stretched the word and laughed as she looked at her friend, scandalized.

"I'ma take this couch," Tasha said and patted the sofa

she'd slept on the night she'd watched Jaz and Snake freaking.

Jaz rolled her eyes and blushed. If only she knew what they'd done on that couch, she'd be willing to bet her bottom dollar she'd rather sleep on the other one. "Girl, remind me to tell you what that nigga did to me the other day in the shower. Had a bitch in tears, singing opera and shit," she laughed and said as she rummaged through her purse for her phone, which had just alerted her. She got it out and responded to a text from Snake.

Tasha sat patiently and watched her friend's facial expression change as she returned the text rapidly. "Girl, yo' ass glowing like a lightbulb. He got you like that?" she asked with a smile, somehow knowing she had just texted Smoke.

She pondered over her response for a few seconds. "Tash, girl, you know I like him. He's good for me. I'm happy as hell. You, of all people, know I be having bad-ass luck with niggas, but this time I think I finally got it right," she said with a ton of emotion and satisfaction.

Tasha smiled sadly, envying her friend's newfound happiness and wondering how she'd wound up getting stuck with Ant's conceited, no-good ass. She had to admit, though, she did love him, no matter how much of a jerk and asshole he was sometimes. "I'm happy for ya, girl," she said quietly and truthfully, and then hugged her bestie. "Now, tell me how yo' ol' alley cat-sounding-ass got around to singing opera, bitch," she said excitedly as she sat back with a big-ass smile on her face.

Jaz covered her face with both of her hands and laughed. "Oh, God!" she exclaimed as she shook her head and peeked between her fingers. "So, we was taking a shower together, right?" She moved her hands away from her face and started talking eagerly. "He love to bathe together, but anyway, that nigga cut off all the hot water without telling me he was about to do it. You talking about a bitch was freezing! He made me stand up under the water while he got down and...."

They kicked it and gossiped for a while before Tasha asked to take a shower. Jaz gave her a brand new pair of her panties and a bra, although they both knew they'd be ridiculously uncomfortable on her, and she went to bathe.

About fifteen minutes later, Snake let himself into the apartment. "What up?" he said, going straight to the kitchen as he tossed his almost-empty keychain on the counter and opened the refrigerator.

"Hey, boo," Jaz replied, flipping through the channels as she unconsciously shook one of her feet.

Snake got himself an apple juice and went to take a seat next to her on the couch. Taking off his Armani bookbag, he dumped it's contents onto the coffee table and sat his new .38 on the floor between his legs.

Jaz saw the money he'd dumped out and was now starting to sort through had bloodstains on a lot of it, and she stared at him unbelievingly.

"Why you looking at me like that, shawdy?" he asked her.

"What the fuck yo' ass done did now, nigga?" she demanded in a hiss with her eyes squinted in suspicion.

"Nothing," he raised his palms and shoulders as he responded like a little child would to its mother when caught in the act of being naughty.

"I ain't crazy, nigga. This blood," she picked up a bill and showed him.

"No, it ain't. That's ink," he said and picked up his juice to take a sip.

Jaz smelled the bill and popped him on the arm. "No, the fuck it ain't! That's blood, nigga!" she said incredulously. She couldn't believe how easily and casually he'd just lied to her.

Snake pouted and shrugged. "So?" he whined, sounding and looking exactly like a little kid.

"Boy," she started to blow on him, but Tasha interrupted

her.

"Gimme some lotion or something, girl. Oh, hey, Smoke. I'm sorry," she said apologetically and hurried back to the bathroom. She knew the panties and bra she wore were inappropriate for him to see her in outside of when she was working at the club, and had she known he was there, there was no way in hell she would've come out of the bathroom dressed that way.

Jaz got up and made a fist at Snake while giving him a look to let him know their little talk would resume later before she went to get some lotion for Tasha.

Later that night, Snake and Jaz were were laying in bed in the dark. Neither of them was sleepy. They both were lost deep in their own thoughts. "Smoke?" Jaz said softly.

"Hm?" he grunted, his deep voice rumbling in his chest.

She climbed on top of his much-larger body and lay her head against his chest as her fingers found his thick, wavy hair and started to rake through it. When she felt his dick stiffen against her, she smiled a little and maneuvered so it slipped inside of her, but then made no other attempt to move again. "You wanna fuck Tasha?" she asked softly, her head still resting on his chest.

"Say what?" He lifted his head to look down at her, but all he saw was the top of her head. He was still sure he had heard her wrong, though. He didn't need to see her face.

"Do you wanna fuck Tasha? Do you wanna fuck my friend?"

He desperately wanted to ask her if she meant the two of them together, but he held his tongue. "Man. Hell naw, man," he mumbled.

"Why not? She got a fat ass and big titties. She thicker than me."

"What's up with you, man? Don't be asking me no shit like that. Just say what's on ya mind. Get to the point," he said and tried to slip his dick out of her, but she stopped him.

"No, I like the way it feel. Leave it in. And I asked you that 'cause I wanna know. I seen the way you was looking at her earlier when she came out the shower," she said, resting her chin on his chest and looking up at him.

Snake frowned, but kept his voice low when he responded. "What you expect, I'm a man. All I know is I seen a half-naked bitch in the spot where I been laying my head. That's enough said right there, shawdy. I ain't gay. I love pussy, so I'ma look."

They both were silent for a few seconds, and then Jaz spoke again. "I like you, Siree. A lot. And I'm starting to get real attached to you." When Snake made no attempt to speak, she went on. "As much as I want you to be my nigga, you ain't, so I can't trip if you fuck a thousand other bitches. But please, please, Siree, don't fuck my friend," she pleaded softly to him. "If you wanna fuck her, I'll let you go on out there now while she feeling fucked up about her own relationship and see if she'll give you some pussy and let that be the end of it, one way or the other. If you don't wanna do that, then I'm begging you not to fuck that bitch behind my back," she said and prayed to God he didn't decide to get up and take her up on her offer.

Snake nodded his head slowly. "Shawdy look good as a muthafucka, right, and I prob'ly could go out there and blast her ass if I tried, but I'm straight. I ain't neva thought about her like that. She yo friend. Even when I seen her in her draws and shit earlier, I ain't think about smashing her," he shrugged. "Don't trip, though, I don't want nobody but you. I see plenty bitches that look good, and a lot of them be trying to holla at a nigga on the low and shit, but that ain't no different than you seeing other niggas that look good to you."

"Yeah, but you the finest nigga in the world to me, though, so I feel like anything other than you is a downgrade."

Snake sucked his teeth. "Man," he drawled and paused for

a second to make sure his words came out the way he wanted them to. "You already know you bad, shawdy. You just a li'l crazy," he joked, and she pinched him. "But nah, though, man, for real, you just was running into sucka's. That's why you was having a hard time finding a real nigga. It's just way too many of these ol' busta-ass, undercover faggot-ass niggas out here polluting the streets now. Giving mufuckas AIDS and other STD's and shit like its fucking legal, shawdy. They making it hard for y'all 'cause they outnumber the real niggas by a billion. But I'm good. I'm where I'm at by choice. I'm right where I wanna be. And nah, I ain't go' lie: I ain't yo' nigga, and you ain't my bitch. But I don't want you fuckin' with nobody else. Yo' li'l ass better not fuck with nobody else."

"Well, I'm just saying, since both of us feel like that, then why don't we just–" she started anxiously, but he cut her off.

He shook his head and sucked his teeth. "Nah, man, we doing straight just how we is now. We go to putting titles and shit on what we got going on, then shit might go' start getting crazy. Let's just keep doing what we been doing. Shit will automatically start to get deeper and deeper if it's s'posed to. We ain't gotta rush nothing."

Jaz sighed and slowly nodded, although she was a bit disappointed. But, looking on the bright side, she knew she did at least have a part of him, and she was determined to make that work for her until she was able to capture his entire heart. She sat up and placed the palms of her small hands on his tattooed and muscled chest so she could brace herself as she began to ride his dick.

Chapter Twelve

Although he had stayed up late, Snake was up bright and early the next morning. He had to go see his P.O., and he wanted to get it out of the way so he would be free to do whatever he wanted for the rest of the day without having to interrupt it. Jaz stumbled into the bathroom after he'd taken a shower, and he was at the sink brushing his teeth when she sat on the toilet to pee. He glanced over at her and grinned. "Yo' ass just look like yo' breath stink right now," he said, joking about her disheveled appearance.

"Shut the fuck up, nigga," she said sleepily and flipped him a lazy bird. "Where you about to go?"

"I told you I had to go see my P.O. today, I'ma go on and knock that shit out early so can be free for the rest of the day."

She nodded as she flushed the toilet and stood up. "What the hell that is on yo' nose, boy?" she asked while giggling and pointing at his face. She'd seen him, but that was the first time she'd really looked at him since she'd come into the bathroom.

Snake snapped his gaze back to his reflection in the mirror and used both of his index fingers to try to bust the big-ass, fire engine red bump on the tip of his nose. "Fuckin' pimple, man. Shit just popped up over night," he said, frowning as much from the pain he was causing himself by trying to bust the pimple as he was distressed at it for even being there in the first place.

Still giggling, Jaz swatted his hands away from his face. "Stop picking at it. You go' make it worse," she said, thwarting his attempt to pop it as she nudged her way over in from of him to wash her hands.

Tasha peeped her head into the bathroom then. "I'm glad y'all up. I'm about to go."

"Damn! Everybody trying to leave me and shit. Where the hell you going early this morning?" she asked with exaggerated sadness.

Tasha rolled her eyes and sighed. "Girl, that nigga was on my line at four-thirty this morning talking about he sorry and shit and I need to come home..."

Jaz hit Tasha with an award-winning deadpan stare. She couldn't believe the stupid bitch was already about to go back, but Ant was her business now, while Snake was her own. She was through voicing her opinions and giving relationship advice Tasha never took, anyway. From now on she'd just be a silent shoulder for her girl to cry on. Sighing, she said, "Alright." She shook her head slowly, and in a defeated tone continued, "Lemme wash up and get myself together. I'll take ya."

Tasha shook her head. "Nah, girl, g'on back to bed. Y'all had a long night," she cracked, and Jaz blushed. "I'll catch the train. I need some fresh air and time to think by myself, anyway," she said as her head and hand disappeared out of the doorway.

Jaz just stood there, shaking her head slowly. She was truly flabbergasted at the stupidity.

Looking at her reflection in the mirror, Snake said, "Stay out them folks' business."

"Shut up, nigga," she said, and then bucked at him before pushing him playfully and scampering out of the bathroom.

Twenty minutes later, Snake and Tasha both were on their way out of the apartment. "Call me if you need me, bitch. And I'll see yo' ass later, Rudolph," Jaz said and squeezed Snake's ass with a giggle on his way out of the door.

He turned and glared at her for a second. "It's yo' damn fault, anyway," he said loudly with a hint of mischief gleaming in his eyes. "If yo' ol' nasty-ass wouldn't poot in my face when I'm eating ya ass, maybe I wouldn't have this shit on my nose in the first place."

Tasha burst out laughing, and Jaz's mouth gaped open in

disbelief. She couldn't fucking believe what he'd just practically announced to the whole world. "Nigga, you dead-ass wrong for that shit! And that only happened once, anyway!" she hissed as she looked around to see who possibly could've heard him. The fact she didn't see anybody else around paying them any attention made her feel a tad bit better.

"Twice," he said, holding up two fingers and smiling.

She scowled at him, but he really was too handsome to stay angry with, plus his sexy-ass smile was making her stomach flutter. "Quit putting my fuckin' business out like that, nigga! What the fuck wrong with you?" she tried to say angrily, but the attempt failed miserably because she couldnt stop herself from cracking a smile. He really was one hell of a dude.

He laughed and blew her a kiss. "Later on, li'l mama."

Jaz sucked her teeth. "Whatever, muthafucka," she said and slammed the door shut. She watched him laugh, turn, and walk away through the peephole in her door before bursting into laughter herself as she walked back to the bedroom.

He and Tasha walked across the street to King Memorial Train Station together, and when they boarded the Westbound to Five Points, they sat together, also. He asked her why she didn't have a car, and she explained she did, sort of. Ant had bought her a new Infinity truck about nine months ago, but the problem was she was absolutely terrified of driving. She'd refused to even get her license. The day he'd surprised her with the truck, she felt kind of pressured into promising him she would at least work on getting it, but she never did. Eventually he got tired of talking to her about it and started driving the SUV himself, which was just fine with her.

"I'm from Hollywood Court. I been riding MARTA my whole life. Ain't nothing wrong with it to me, as bad as traffic be and especially as high as gas is," she said matter-of-factly and shrugged. "I ain't ask that nigga for that truck, anyway," she added as they stepped onto the platform at Five Points.

Snake heard the resentment and hostility in her tone when she spoke of Ant, but the cause of it was none of his business, so he filed it in his mind with the definite intention of revisiting it at a later date, should he need to, and acted as if what she'd said was completely unimportant to him. "A'ight then, I'ma catch up with ya," he said when it came time for them to go their separate ways.

Thirty minutes later, he was at the probation building. He'd called himself smart by trying to be one of the first people at the office, and he was. His P.O., on the other hand, wasn't. It was close to 10:30 a.m. before he'd had enough of waiting around and decided to leave, but on his way out he bumped into none other than his P.O., who turned him right around. The visit was routine, extremely short because Snake had nothing to say, and he was on his way out of the building by 10:45 a.m.

It was still early and warm as hell by the time he made it back to Five Points Station, and with absolutely nothing of importance to handle, he decided to slip upstairs and see what was going on over at Underground Atlanta. He made his mind up on the escalator to check out Sports Profile and U.S.A. Boutique to see if he saw something he might like for Jaz, and when he stepped out of the station onto Peachtree Street, the radiant late morning sun made him squint and use his hand to shield his eyes.

Once they'd adjusted to the bright sunlight, he dropped his hand, glanced around, and was just about to cross Peachtree Street and head over to Underground when he stopped mid-stride to do a double-take. He'd spotted a chick with a big-ass stripper booty that without a doubt would give Nicki Minaj a run for her money. A pair of True Religion booty shorts gripped that big, pretty ass like they'd been painted on, and a pair of brown snakeskin Ferragamo stiletto sandals covered her small feet. Her back was to him, so that was all he could see besides the back of her white tube top, but that was enough. She was looking in the window of Sports Profile, and since he was headed that way anyway, he walked with a little purpose toward her to be sure he got a closer look at that ass.

She surprised the hell out of him once he reached her and she turned around. "Tasha!" he exclaimed while trying not to let his disappointment show. "What the hell yo' ass doing down here?" he asked.

Tasha smiled and pulled off her brown-tinted Gucci aviator frames. 'Rockstar' was emblazoned on her shirt across her plump titties, and for some reason the dog paws tattooed near the tops of her breasts relentlessly beckoned Snake's attention. "Hey, Smoke. What's up," she said with a little wave, pretending not to notice how his eyes kept wandering down to her bosom. "I see that bump ain't shining red no more, Rudolph," she joked and giggled.

Ever self-conscious, he immediately reached for his nose. He had almost forgotten about the damn bump. Almost. "A'ight now," he said in a warning tone as he slowly nodded his head. "You trying to be funny and shit. Jaz teaching me how to work that YouTube and that Instagram shit. Fuck around and some of ya personal business go' be all over the Internet."

Tasha laughed at the threat because she had no idea how serious he was. "You don't know none of my business, nigga. Especially none that would embarrass me," she playfully challenged him.

Snake raised a single eyebrow and smirked. "You right. I don't. Right now," he said in a smug tone.

Understanding him clearly, Tasha laughed again and nodded. "But Jaz do."

"Exactly, nigga," he cut her off and smiled at her with a wink. "All I gotta do is eat that ass and pussy real good before I smash her ass real good, and she go' open up like a book. I bet she even go tell me shit I don't even ask her about yo' ass."

"You ain't shit, nigga," she said good-naturedly and started to look around. "Where my bitch at, anyway?"

"She at home, prob'ly still sleep. What you doing down here?"

She explained to him how she and Ant had argued nonstop as soon as she got home, so she'd showered, changed clothes, and bounced. She said she was just out and about now.

Not knowing what to say about any of that, Snake just nodded, and as he was doing so, a nigga with a small wooden stool and briefcase seemed to pop up out of nowhere. "I see ya spinning and shit, big dog, but ya shit kind of high, though. Ten minutes, not a second longa, and $15, not a penny more, and I'll knock that shit down fa ya. What up?"

Caught off guard by the fast-talking little nigga, Snake impulsively felt his head with his hand. Tasha nodded for him to go ahead, saying she'd wait on him, and he agreed to give the nigga some business.

The little barber flipped his stool and sat it right there on the sidewalk for his newest customer to have a seat. After receiving instructions on how he wanted his hair cut, he draped Snake and, true to his word, he crunk his battery-powered clippers up and was done in actually a little less than ten minutes. "My mirror ain't that big, but check it." He handed Snake a small mirror.

Tapeline was razor sharp, mustache and goatee was precise, bald temp fade was blended to perfection, and his waves looked like a beehive. But even still, there was that got-damn bump on his nose. Distraught inwardly, Snake nodded approvingly at the barber's work and stood up to go in his pocket so he could pay the nigga, but Tasha grabbed his arm, stopping him.

"That shit look good as hell, nigga. Damn!" she said, staring into Snake's eyes. "I'ma pay fa this one. I got it," she reached into her clutch and handed the fast-talking little nigga a $20 bill. "Keep the change," she told him, still staring at Snake.

"I arch eyebrows and shit, too, Miss Lady," the barber said while pocketing the money, and it took just that to make Tasha tear her eyes away from Snake's handsome face.

"What you trying to say," she panicked and instinctively felt her brows.

"Hell nah, shawdy, yours straight," he said as he and Snake both laughed at the way she'd just freaked out. "I'm just saying." He handed them both a card with his name and a number on it. "Just holla at me and I'll come to you or meet ya somewhere or whatever. Y'all be easy," he picked his stool up and headed toward Alabama Street, disappearing just as fast as he'd come.

Snake rubbed his fresh cut with his hand and caught Tasha staring at him. "What up?" he asked, clapping and brushing his hands together to rid them of his hair.

She lowered her gaze and smiled shyly as she shook her head. "Nothing. I'm thirsty. I'ma go over here to Underground and get me something to drink. You coming with me?" she asked softly, finding it a bit hard for some reason to project her voice fully all of a sudden.

Snake shrugged. "Yeah, I'll go. I ain't got shit going on now, anyway," he said.

They crossed Peachtree Street over to Underground and wound up having lunch together instead of just getting something to drink. They sat across from each other at a table in the food court, and the entire time they were eating he kept catching her staring at him. When they finished eating, he got up to throw their trash away, and when he sat back down, he put one elbow on the table, leaned forward to hold his chin in his hand, and stared at her.

Unnerved and unable to stand his meticulous stare for long, Tasha laughed nervously. "What? Why you staring at me like that?" she asked quietly, dropping her gaze to her moist palms, which rested in her lap.

Snake had thought long and hard about this and was certain he, of all people, could and would make the ends justify the means, so he plunged. "You wanna get a room," he asked with a knowing look on his face.

If Tasha was surprised, shocked, or felt any type of way at all about what he'd said, it didn't show in the least way through her facial expression. She cut her eyes up at him, but immediately dropped them back to her lap. "Room? For what?" Her question came out as a half-hearted whisper, although her aim had been for firm and scandalized.

Snake sucked his teeth and scooted his chair closer to the table, then reached and put his hand under her chin so he could lift her head up. "C'mon, shawdy, stop playing. The attraction's apparent. You been looking at a nigga like I was a steak all day. I know you wanna try some of this shit just as much as I wanna see what that fat ass that you got hitting like. What's hap'ning," he questioned with a quiet arrogance that was appealing to her.

"I don't know, Smoke, Jaz," she said hesitantly as she dropped her gaze back to her lap and shook her head slowly.

"Ain't here," he finished the sentence for her. "What you go' do? I ain't go' ask again."

After a few moments of intense thought, Tasha slipped on her aviator frames. "Where we going?" she mumbled, disgusted with herself, but her desire pretty much silencing the disgust as she gave her hand to Snake and allowed him to help her get to her feet.

They decided on the Castleberry Inn on Northside Drive, and all of her hesitant actions and conversation before they reached the room obviously belied her true inner feelings. As soon as the door closed behind them, she pounced. She was especially eager to get his dick in her mouth, and she had gooey saliva bubbling dripping and hanging from her mouth in no time as she used her hands to slurp and suck on his dick. She was breathing hard, moaning, and so into sucking his dick, and he was loving every second of it.

"Hold up," he said, grabbing and holding her head still. He started to move back and forth, real slow at first, sliding his dick in and out of her mouth, but he eventually sped up to the point where he was literally fucking her face, causing her to gag a few times. When he was about to bust, he pulled his dick out of her mouth and started to jack it in her face.

She wiped her mouth with the back of her hand and looked up at him from her knees with an impatient, hungry frown. "What the hell you doing?" she asked.

"I'm about to bust, shawdy," he grunted, still jacking his dick in her face.

"Boy," Tasha scolded in an exasperated tone before she slipped his dick back in her mouth and worked on it at a frantic pace.

He came, and she gladly received him, swallowing as little as possible while spitting most of it back on his dick as she continued to suck him off. When she finally stood up, his entire dick was covered with thick semen and her saliva as she looked at him with pride while squeezing out of her shorts.

"Yeah, take all that shit off. Keep them heels on, though," he ordered as he jacked his dick while watching her undress. Tasha smiled and did as she was told. He sat on the edge of the bed and leaned back on both of his elbows as she stood before him, butt-ass naked with her heels on. His eyes devouring her sexy chocolate body, and he could tell from the self-satisfied look on her face that she knew she was bad as hell, and she was loving the way he was staring at her.

She teased him a bit, dancing slowly and rubbing the head of his dick up and down against her pussy before mounting him. The pussy was hot and wet as fuck, but couldn't ride a dick to save her life, and it took him only a few seconds to reach that conclusion after all she did was scoot around on his dick. All of the dancing and shit she could do looked good, but there was nothing else to it, it was nothing but a front. She was absolutely horrendous on top, so he quickly flipped her and had to resist the urge to hit himself on the forehead with the palm of his hand and say *duh* when he looked down and saw what she was toting. With an ass like her's, he knew damn well the chances of her having much practice riding a dick were highly unlikely. She was built specifically for back shots, and he obliged her.

He bent her ass over the edge of the bed and tried to touch her tonsils with his dick. He didn't play with her at all. He started pounding the pussy and slapping on that big, chocolate ass, and she bucked like a rodeo horse. When she screamed out and squirted all over him and the bed sheets, all it did was geek him up even more. He'd never actually seen a bitch squirt like that outside of a porn movie, but he liked it.

Tasha took the dick and threw all that ass back like a pro, and he had to admit she was damn good, but not great. They fucked eight times in half as many hours, and after wearing each other out, they both fell asleep, exhausted.

It was half past seven when she woke up in panic mode. She went and showered, and that seemed to calm her down a little. "Listen, Smoke," she started as she sat on the bed, putting her clothes on. Snake knew the guilt lecture was coming, so he sat quietly and pretended to be interested in what she was saying. "You can't tell Jaz about this shit," she said fearfully with a scared look on her face. "I can't fuckin' believe I just did this shit," she shook her head and sighed. "That's my girl, man. We been best friends since the sixth grade at C.E.P. She go' fuckin' kill me if she find out we done fucked," she pleaded quietly as tears came to her eyes.

Snake smirked. "Look, Jaz my girl. For real. That's where

I wanna be. I just wanted to see what that fat ass you got was hitting like," he shook his head slowly to reassure her. "Don't trip, I ain't go' say shit to fuck up what me and shawdy got going on. Both of us grown, we saw something we liked, we fucked," he shrugged in an unconcerned manner. She had no idea that, to him, the whole ordeal truly was no big deal and nothing more than a minor accomplishment in his major scheme to come up. "That's it, no strings or feelings attached. Ain't no reason why we both can't leave here today and this shit never come up again. You go yo' way, and I go mine. A'ight?" He spoke with so much calm and poise it assured Tasha a little that everything would be okay.

"Deal," she said with a smile, knowing their little secret would be safe with Smoke.

They shook on it and left together after he took a quick shower. They sat separately when they got on the bus and completely lost sight of each other when they made it back to Five Points Station.

Ambitious

Chapter Thirteen

Summer slowly gave way to Fall, and things got back on track for Snake. He'd eased his way back into the motel out on Fulton Industrial Boulevard, to Rambo's delight. Ant was still fucking with him the long way on the work, looking out for him with a little something extra almost every time he shopped with him, and they had even started to hang out together occasionally. He and Jaz were doing better than ever, and he'd even managed to put a sizeable dent in the little hiding spot at his grandmother's place. He was still on his low-key, incognito shit, but that was just plain old Snake.

One evening when he let himself into Jaz's apartment, Tasha was sitting on the couch watching TV. "What up, fool?" he said in his lazy drawl as he tossed his keys on the counter.

"Hey, crazy," she chirped back without even bothering to look away from the television.

"Hey, bae," Jaz said with a smile as she walked into the living room.

"What a vision," he said, picking her up and kissing her once she was close enough for him to grab. He'd really missed her. The trap had been rolling hard as hell for the past three straight days, not giving him a chance to get away from it and back to her.

Jaz laugh and demanded he put her down when he started to twirl her around. Still giggling and feeling jubilant from his presence, she sauntered into the kitchen and started back on dinner as he went to their bedroom. After taking a nice, hot shower, he put on a comfortable pair of baggy Polo sweats and a wife beater. Jaz was chopping onions and bell peppers and gossiping with Tasha when he walked back into the living room.

Tasha's eyes burned holes in him from the second he emerged into the short hallway from the bedroom until he walked into the kitchen, wearing the Armani cologne she loved and bought for him to wear for her, not Jaz.

Jaz caught the tail end of Tasha's stare down and wondered what it was about, but she didn't say anything.

"Smell good in this muthafucka, bae! What we eating?" Snake asked, walking up behind Jaz and nuzzling her neck while pushing his wood up against her ass.

"Cubed steak and rice. Get off me," she said curtly and shrugged him away. Honestly, her intentions hadn't been to be mean or harsh, but that was exactly how she came off because she was still pondering on the look Tasha had given him. Something about it just didn't feel right in the pit of her stomach.

He backed up and looked at her with a slight frown on his face for a few seconds, and then shrugged it off. "Must be that time of the month. Guess that mean no poo-nani for me, then, huh," he joked and picked up a big bag of Four Cheese Doritos before walking into the living room.

"Fuckin' asshole," she mumbled and mean-mugged his retreating back before turning her gaze to Tasha who, for a split second, had a little smirk on her face. It was so quick, though, gone before she could even blink, that she questioned if she'd actually seen it or not, but she was sure she had.

When Snake sat down and tried to take the remote from Tasha, she had enough. Something wasn't right. Maybe it was the look in Tasha's eyes. Or the way she giggled and struggled with him for the remote. Maybe it was the way she'd said, "Uh-uh, Smoke," that made her gut clench. She honestly didn't know, but whatever it was, she was damn sure about to check it. When she stormed into the living room, Snake and Tasha were so surprised they both still held on to the TV remote as they looked up at her with shocked faces.

"What's up with y'all two? What the fuck y'all got going on?" she demanded, her eyes shooting back and forth between them.

"What?" Snake frowned.

Jaz raised a single eyebrow and cut an icy look at Tasha. "How long you been fuckin' my nigga, stinking bitch?"

Tasha recoiled as if she'd been slapped. "Jaz," she said slowly, "I ain't." She shook her head with a baffled look on her face.

Jaz snapped her angry gaze to Snake. "Bitch told you she got herpes yet, dumb-ass nigga!"

"What the fuck you talking about, man," Snake snapped.

"Jazmine, what the fuck wrong with you? I ain't got no fuckin' herpes!"

"Shut up, nasty bitch! Get the fuck out my house!" When nobody moved or said anything, she yelled, "Now, bitch!"

Tasha shook her head no as she stared into her friend's face. "I ain't going nowhere 'til you–"

Jaz laughed. "Wanna bet?" she said sadistically and turned toward the kitchen.

Snake jumped up and took two steps after her. "Go on and leave," he said over his shoulder to Tasha, who sucked her teeth and stood up.

"I ain't going nowhere, nigga!" she exclaimed.

By that time Jaz had picked up the big-ass knife she'd been cutting vegetables with earlier and was trying to get around Snake. "Bitch, get the hell out! I ain't about to keep holding her back!" he exploded.

"Naw, bitch, don't leave now," Jaz goaded in a deadly calm voice as she nodded her head. "Please, just stay yo' dumb-ass right there so I can shish-kebab yo' stupid ass, ho. Move, boy!" she said and took a swipe – halfheartedly, but none the less a swipe – at Snake with the knife just as Tasha squeezed by him and scampered out of the apartment.

"Bitch, if you cut me," he said and paused, looking at Jaz with fire in his eyes. "Don't swing that fuckin' knife at me no more, shawdy," he warned her calmly and took a menacing-looking step toward her.

She stared into his eyes before she let the knife slip from her grasp and clatter on the floor as she broke down. "How you go' do me like this, nigga? Good as I been to yo' ass, what more you want from me? What else you need me to do?" she said between sobs.

Snake sighed. "Jazmine, what the hell wrong with you? What you tripping on?" he asked quietly, pulling her to him and hugging her, his threatening demeanor seeming to have dissipated completely.

"I know y'all fuckin', nigga. That shit was all over both of y'all faces," she sobbed, pushing away from his embrace.

He swallowed hard. "I don't know what you think you saw, but I swear to God, bae, I ain't never fucked that bitch. You is tripping, bae." His voice pleaded for her to believe him.

She leaned back on the counter and shook her head slowly. "I know you lying. I know you fuckin' lying, nigga," she said aloud, but moreso to convince herself than to him as she looked into his eyes.

He returned her stare without blinking. "No, the fuck I ain't! Stop saying that shit! Don't you know I love yo' li'l ass, girl? Ain't no way in the hell I would fuck yo' best friend, shawdy. You fuckin' tripping!" It was his turn to be angry.

"You ain't never told me you loved me in all this time we been fuckin' around. Why the hell you wanna say some shit like that now?" she asked, suspicious of his convenient timing and his motive because she knew he thought he had been blessed with a little more sense than everybody else in the world.

"'Cause you ain't never accused me of fuckin' yo' best friend before. 'Cause it's true. Or maybe 'cause this shit was what it took to make me realize that losing you is a definite possibility and what we got could end right here, right now," he shrugged and looked down at his feet. "I don't know, but I meant that shit when I said it," he said quietly and cut his eyes up at her, looking exactly like a handsome, scared little boy.

"Look me in my face and tell me you ain't never fucked that bitch, Siree," she demanded in an attempted firm tone.

"Bitch ain't never seen this dick, ma, I swear to God. That's Ant girl!" he said with no hesitation as he raised his gaze and stared straight into her eyes. He could basically hear her resolve cracking and knew it wouldn't be long before she succumbed to his relentless lies and fierce denials.

Jaz dropped her head and stared at the floor for a long moment, contemplating. She didn't believe him. She knew he possessed the ability to lie easily and convincingly at the drop of a hat, but as much as she hated it, she owed him the benefit of the doubt because before now, he'd never, not even once, given her reason to doubt or so much as question his loyalty to her, or even if he'd fucked other bitches, let alone Tasha. Ever since they'd met, he had always made her feel like everything had been solely about her. She sucked her teeth and frowned as she shook her head. "I love yo' ass, boy," she said, pouting as she walked over to him.

"I love yo' li'l ass, too, but I'ma tell you some real shit, shawdy," he opened his arms and welcomed her. "Don't blow up on me like that again, man. I don't want to, but I swear, I will pack up my li'l shit and get the fuck on. If you really do love me, then you should trust me and believe me when I tell you something, bae, especially about some serious-ass shit like this."

Jaz nodded and buried her face in his chest. "Okay," she mumbled while her intuition screamed in protest for her not to believe him, but he was planting soft little kisses on the top of her head, swaying her judgement in his favor.

***

"Nigga, hell nah! You know good and damn well I ain't got no fuckin' herpes! As much as you done had yo' dick and tongue in this pussy, yo' ass of all people would know if I had some shit," Tasha said with mock attitude as she lay naked on top of the covers in a room at the Castleberry Inn, her and Snake's little creep spot since the first time they'd fucked the past summer. It had been close to a month since the big blow-up at Jaz's apartment, and this was their first little rendezvous since then. "Ain't no bumps, discharge, or funny li'l odors coming out this coota," she said with a laugh and accidentally brushed her thumb against her clit, causing her to shiver a little.

"I don't know, man. Shit done had a li'l tang to it the last few times I done blasted. I just ain't wanna say nothing," Snake joked as he came out of the bathroom.

"Yeah fuckin' right, nigga! Don't play with me! This pussy stay clean and ready to bust open anytime. Yo' ass better act like ya know," she laughed and threw a pillow at him.

He knocked it away effortlessly and lay on the bed next to her. "What time you going to work?"

"In a few minutes," she answered, preoccupied with picking at one of her fingernails.

"You and shawdy still ain't talking?"

She sucked her teeth. "Hell nah, her and that ol' retarded-ass bitch, Jayla, always be together and shit now. You know, they don't really talk to nobody else," she said with an attitude, jealous of how quickly Jayla seemed to take her place as Jaz's friend.

Snake nodded. "What's up with ol' boy?"

"Fuck that pussy-ass nigga!" Tasha scowled and said. "Done moved some li'l bitch in the house with us and go' tell me if I wanna fuck with him, I gotta fuck her and let her fuck me, too! That nigga ain't sniffed this pussy in three weeks, and that li'l bitch ain't go' never have the pleasure," she said matter-of-factly.

"He go' put yo' ass out if you don't get with the program. You need to be trying to get you somewhere to stay at lined up if you ain't go' do it," he said uninterestedly as he flipped through the channels on the television.

"I'ma come stay with y'all," she joked and snickered.

"No, fuck you ain't! I don't need you fuckin' up my happy home with yo' ol' homewrecking-ass."

"Nigga, no the fuck you didn't just call me!" she punched him on the arm and laughed.

"Aye, man!" he exclaimed and rubbed his arm, pretending to be in pain. "I'm just saying, yo' ass better eat some pussy before you be homeless. That's all I'm saying," he threw both his hands up and joked with a grin.

"See," she shook her head, "now, you wrong fa that, nigga. I ain't about to eat shit. I'll suck some dick and lick some balls. I'll even eat some ass, but I just ain't with the tits and clits being shoved in my mouth, boo-boo. And that nigga ain't go' do shit. He love him some chocolate thunder," she said sexily and rubbed her hips and thighs.

Snake smirked at her. "So, what the hell yo' ass doing here with me all the time, then?"

"'Cause, he ain't got that golden stroke or platinum tongue like you do, boo." She winked and flashed a quick smile at him before she frowned and asked, "What the hell you be doing here with me if yo' ass love Jaz so much, the way you say you do, nigga?"

He smiled devilishly at her. "That's fa me to know and you not to even worry about. But I will say this, though: part of it is 'cause yo' ass and titties a li'l bigger. That got a li'l something to do with it. Both of y'all ass pretty as fuck, but she a li'l prettier than you," he said in a joking manner.

Tasha rolled her eyes. "Whatever. I'm about to go. My cab should be here in a minute." She got up and dressed quickly, feeling some type of way because she'd seen right through his little joke, and for some reason it had bothered her, although they were supposedly just fucking.

"Yeah, I'ma go on and dip, too," he said and sat up with a groan. "I need to head back over to the room, anyway."

Chapter Fourteen

As soon as Jaz walked into the club, Jayla rushed up to her with the news. "Girl, that nigga beat that bitch like she fuckin' stole something," she said excitedly.

"Who?" Jaz asked eagerly as she made her way to the bar with Jayla matching her step-for-step.

"Girl, Ant! That nigga just pulverized Tasha ol' trifling-ass about a hour ago!"

Jaz frowned. "For real? Why? Where at?"

"Hell yeah. He beat that bitch like she was a nigga, right out there in the parking lot. They was arguing about something in here, then the next thing I know he was snatching her ass out the club."

For the past three or four weeks, Jaz had thought she'd be happy to hear about or see some shit like that happen, but now that it had actually happened, she didn't like it. Not one bit. Her deep hatred for Ant started to bubble in her blood. "Why the fuck ain't nobody stop the shit?" she asked, anger evident through her tone and expression.

"Ant pulled a gun on Vontae when he tried to stop it, so he backed off," Jayla said as a confused frown creased her pretty face. "I'm saying, though, it seem like you mad about it or something."

"Shit, I am!" Jaz fumed.

Jayla's frown deepened. She was beyond confused. "Why?" she asked.

"'Cause Tasha was my friend."

"Yeah, until she fucked yo' nigga, remember?" She looked at Jaz incredulously. "If that bitch was yo' friend, then I would hate to see one of yo' enemies," she said while shaking her head.

Jaz sucked her teeth and walked away. No, she didn't fuck with Tasha anymore, but she realized then she really didn't want to see her hurt, either. They had been such good friends for so long that it was hard to just stop caring about her in the blink of an eye, no matter what she did. Besides, she really didn't have any proof she'd even had sex with Snake. It was just a feeling she had.

Beyond annoyed at everything and with everybody, she completed her shift and went home.

***

Snake had cooked a late dinner and placed fresh red roses along with scented candles all over the apartment by the time Jaz walked in late that night. "What's all this, bae?" she asked, surprised and all smiles as she looked around excitedly.

"Nothing major, right," he said in his super-cool, super-sexy drawl. "Just thought I would do a li'l something 'cause I love and appreciate ya so much."

Jaz beamed as he took her purse and helped her out of her coat, her mood improving tremendously the instant she saw her apartment and her man. After dinner, he popped a bottle of champagne and they toasted to themselves before clinking glasses.

Later that night, while they lay in bed, Jaz told Snake what had happened to Tasha, and judging by his reaction, she couldn't tell if he cared or not. He didn't say a word about it, just continued to lay there, holding on to her.

"Promise you won't ever do no shit like that to me, Siree," she said quietly.

"As long as yo' ass don't attack me with knives or nothing no more, I won't," he joked and kissed the back of her neck. "Now, what about us getting married or something and having some kids and shit?"

Jaz was speechless for a moment. "You wanna get married, baby?" she asked quietly even though she was overwhelmed with happiness.

Snake thought about it for a second before he answered. "Not right now, but eventually, hell yeah. And to you, I think. I mean, I'm getting old, shawdy. I had to pluck a gray hair out my head the other day, and I ain't even got no kids yet."

Jaz giggled. "You ain't getting old, baby. You like a bottle of wine. You just get better with time," she said and ground her plump little ass against him.

"You right, I do, don't I?" he said arrogantly, but was joking. "And hold up with all that shit there," he scooted away from her. "You know damn well you on ya period. Don't start nothing you can't finish."

"Ha," she laughed and rolled her eyes. "I forgot you know my cycle like clockwork. And anyway, nigga, just 'cause I'm on my period, that don't mean I don't get horny." She scooted back against him and ground on him harder to prove her point. "Ain't nothing wrong with my mouth," she said seductively. Snake's dick bulging against her ass and back was driving her wild. When she couldn't take it anymore, she rolled him over and gave him the best head she had to give.

After his last nut, they went to shower again so she could get herself off and he made sure she brought her vibrator along. It was about to be a pretty interesting shower.

***

True enough, what Ant had done to that beautiful-ass girl was way past fucked up, but honestly, Snake didn't give two fucks about it. It was virtually impossible for him to care any less about Tasha's wellbeing or her dysfunctional-ass relationship. Period! But, it was in his best interest at the moment to pretend otherwise, because his moment of golden opportunity had presented itself. Finally! After months and months of patiently lying in wait, it had finally decided to show it's beautiful face. He silently thanked God for the opportunity, but kept in mind he still had to plot and plan with precision and execute to the tee, or else shit could go terribly wrong.

"Listen, Tasha, this the last time I'ma ask ya: is you sure? I mean, absolutely positive you wanna help me do this shit? I done already told you how I play. Ain't no going back. Once it's done, it's done, shawdy. You sure you wanna be a part of this shit?" he stared at her and said seriously in an attempt to make her aware of the grave dangers and possibilities they faced if something should go wrong.

She removed her shades slowly, the same pair of Gucci aviator shots she'd worn the first time she let him blast. "Look at my fuckin' face," she said with quiet anger. "I'm beyond sure. Fuck that nigga. He knocked out three of my teeth and broke my fuckin' finger. I want his ass to burn in hell."

When she took her shades off, he desperately wanted to tell her to put them back on. Ant had fucked her face up pretty damn bad. The scene from the classic movie *Friday* where Red took his shades off to show Smokey and Craig what Debo had done to his eye instantly came to his mind. Snake imagined himself recoiling and saying, *Damn! Put ya glasses back on,* and had to fight tooth and nail to keep himself from busting out in laughter.

He nodded and said, "Say no more. You already know what I need you to do, so just make sure you make it happen. Now," he said while laying her back on the bed, "I ain't had none of this cat in about two weeks. You know I been missing hitting this fat ass, bae," he pouted and said sadly.

"You know it's yours, daddy," Tasha purred and flashed her fixed smile as he helped her out of her clothes.

***

Snake crept quickly through the big back yard of the house

on Collier Road. It was cold as hell out, but his body had become more and more immune to the weather as he became more and more anxious to pull off his latest caper. Adrenaline was already coursing through his veins as he approached the back door of the house. He could thank Tasha for the key, which he was now easing into the deadbolt and turning slowly. He could also thank her for the security code to the alarm system of the house, which he was currently repeating quietly to himself so he wouldn't forget it.

He'd laid in wait for as long as possible. It was now 4:03 a.m., and he'd been camped out in a thicket of bushes near the edge of the backyard since 11:30 p.m. He had wanted to be sure Ant was counting sheep before going in, so he'd waited patiently, so long, in fact, he now had to worry he might be up and getting ready to start his day. He doubted it, but shit would be ugly if that was the case.

The lock turned and he left the key sticking in the door. He took a deep breath and exhaled slowly as he turned the knob. "Here we go," he whispered to himself.

Once he cracked the door, the seal of the alarm broke, and it started to beep loudly. He had ten seconds to shut it off before it started wailing, but that was no problem. He followed Tasha's directions to the keypad and quickly punched in the code. The beeping died immediately, but left a seemingly louder silence in its wake. Now all he hoped was Ant had been asleep and the beeping hadn't woken him up, Tasha had told him there was a keypad for the alarm system in his bedroom, also.

Easing his .38 from his waistband, Snake crouched down and stayed extremely still. He held his breath so the sound of his own breathing wouldn't interfere with what he was straining his ears to hear: any signs of life, any kind of movement, anything. He heard nothing. After a minute or two of intense listening, he was satisfied his entrance had not been detected, nor had he disturbed anything or anyone. He eased back over to the door as carefully and quietly as he possibly could and closed it back before duck-walking ever so slowly and quietly to where Tasha had told him the stairs would be, and voila! There they were.

He smiled broadly and made a mental note to commend her for her efforts in this caper, and then shook his head quickly, silently cursing himself for allowing his mind to wander. He knew better than to be silly while he was on the battlefield. That was a sure-fire way to not make it off of it with his life. He needed to be focused. He shook his head quickly again and returned his mind to the business at hand.

He started to creep up the steps and was sure to skip over the fourth and fifth ones because Tasha, once again, had warned him they creak loud as hell, and Ant had come to use them as an extra warning against intruders. *The fourth, fifth, and eleventh, wasn't it?* he questioned himself silently with a deepening frown. *Or was it the twelfth?* he thought. "Shit!" he mouthed quietly, cursing his own stupidity. He stood right there on the sixth stair, debating with himself and refusing to take another step until he convinced himself it was the twelfth stair all along he'd been warned to avoid, but just to be on the safe side, he'd step from the tenth to the thirteenth to avoid everything in question. Fuck it.

When he reached the tenth step, just as he'd done every other, he put his tiptoe down first, slowly, and then applied the rest of his weight.

Creak!

A light came on and his heart skipped several beats.

***

Not knowing what exactly had woke him up, Ant sat up in bed. Sleep-disoriented, he rubbed his bleary eyes and glanced at the clock on his nightstand. 4:06 a.m., it read. He looked at the bitch sleeping on her stomach beside him, and for some reason a strong feeling of disgust washed over him. He missed Tasha. He wished now he hadn't went so hard on her, and maybe she wouldn't have moved back in with her mom a few days ago. He knew she'd come back, though. She always did. He just didn't know when.

That was the first time she'd took it so far as to move out. He had a few things working in his favor, though. She and her mom didn't get along too well, plus she still lived in the projects, so with him having spoiled her so much for so long, for her to have to go back to the projects and be content for good was a long shot, he knew. He just hoped it wouldn't be too long before she came back.

Throwing back the Louis Vuitton sheet and comforter, he swung his legs over the side of his gigantic bed, slipped his feet into his warm, fur-lined Louis Vuitton slippers, and headed to the bathroom. He had to use the one out in the hall because the toilet in his master bathroom was broken thanks to the slut currently asleep in his bed dropping her fucking tree logs. He knew it was natural, but just the thought of her doing it, and then fucking up the toilet on top of it, grossed him out so much and made his skin crawl to the point where he vowed right then and there, unaware he was scowling, to put the bitch out later and slide over to Hollywood Court to bring Tasha back home where she belonged. She had never broken his toilet. Hell, it would take an act of God for her to even take a shit if he was in the house. But the new bitch? He tossed an angry glance in her direction and shook his head.

On his way out of the bedroom, something caught his eye. The colors on the keypad to his alarm system weren't what they should've been. "I know I set this muthafucka last night," he said quietly, a pensive look coming over his face as he thought hard about it, but couldn't quite remember if he actually had or not.

After a few seconds, he shrugged it off and continued to the bathroom in darkness. When he reached his destination, like he'd gotten used to doing for Tasha's benefit, and to her delight, he dropped his Louis Vuitton pajama bottoms and sat on the toilet to piss. That way he wouldn't misfire in the dark, and it also prevented him from splattering the seat or leaving it up. After milking his dick and blotting the tip of it dry with tissue, he stood and tied his pants back up, but completely forgot to flush or wash his hands before heading back to the bedroom.

He'd taken only one step out in the hall when he heard the loud squeak of the stairs, and instantly, without a doubt in his mind, he knew an intruder was in his home. He immediately hit the light switch, sending light to every corner of the hallway and staircase, and saw the nigga dressed in all black, wielding a gun, and halfway up the steps.

Comprehension first, and then panic quickly registered in Ant's eyes. "Fuck!" he exploded and took off for his room.

"Uh-uh, bitch!" Snake grunted and leapt the rest of the stairs by twos and threes with little grunts.

The chase was on. Ant ran right out of his slippers, kicking one back that just so happened to hit Snake square in the face.

"Umph." He grunted and grabbed his face with his free hand, the unexpected blow slowing him and even causing him to stumble a little, but he kept going.

Ant reached his room and used both of his hands and all the strength he could to slam the door closed behind him in stride. Snake unintentionally and unexpectedly ran right into the path of the swinging door, and the force with which it slammed into him knocked him backward and sent his .38 flying out of his grasp. Ant hit the light switch and rushed to his nightstand.

Dazed, Snake shook his head to clear it and bounded into

the bedroom after him. Acutely aware his life was in serious danger at the moment, he knew he needed to get to Ant before he was able to get to a weapon.

Too late. He rushed into the room just in time to see Ant turning while cocking a big-ass .45. A pretty bitch in the bed looked on in horror as she glanced back and forth between Snake and Ant with her small titties exposed, looking like she wanted to scream, but thank God she didn't.

With rage bordering on insanity flashing in his eyes, the hand Ant was holding the gun in began to tremble – not out of fear or hesitation, though, but with anger. "All this time, after all the shit I done did for you, yo' ass ain't been shit but a fuckin' snake in the fuckin' grass, bitch-ass nigga!" He spat the words at him and took a step forward.

Snake didn't hesitate. He picked up the closest thing to him he could use as a weapon, a glass plate, and rushed toward Ant, fearless as he thought about the reason he and Jaz couldn't get along.

Ant closed his eyes and squeezed the trigger three quick times, but nothing happened. When he next opened his eyes, he saw the same glass plate that Snake had charged him with for a split second before it smashed into his forehead and broke. He felt warm blood on his face, and then nothing, blackness surrounding him.

Snake kicked the unloaded .45 away from where Ant had crumpled to the floor and looked over at the chick in the bed. "Don't move. Don't make a sound, bitch. If yo' ass even breathe too loud, I'ma kill ya, ho. You got me?" he warned her.

With tears leaking from her eyes, she quickly nodded her understanding.

Snake disappeared into the hallway for a few seconds, and then came back with his .38 in hand. He calmly walked right over to the trembling chick, picked up a pillow, and put a bullet through her head. The slug went into the pillow and out the other side of her head, splattering blood everywhere before it lodged into the wall. Picking up another pillow, he was about to shoot Ant, too, but he paused, thinking better of it. He could possibly need him later, so he tore some strips of the Louis Vuitton sheets and tied his hands and feet together.

Once he was sure the binds were inescapable, he went over to the safe that had been installed into the wall. Reaching into his pocket, he pulled out a slip of paper as he shrugged off the backpack he was wearing, and then blew on his gloved fingers before spinning the safe's tumbler. Looking at the little slip of paper, he was just about to begin entering the combination when Ant groaned, signaling he was beginning to come to. Annoyed at himself for not gagging him, he walked over to him and kicked his ass in the back of the head with all the strength he possessed, causing Ant to go back out like a light, and that time he snored.

Snake went back to the safe and put in the first piece of the combination: 12-23-84, Ant's birthday. He entered the next piece: 06-13-86, Tasha's birthday. The next piece, 03-04-09, was their anniversary, and the last piece was 09-01-10, the birthdate of their stillborn daughter. He turned the latch and pulled the heavy door of the safe open.

He dropped to his knees along with a few tears when his eyes gazed upon the contents of the safe, and he thanked Tasha repeatedly for making shit so much easier for him. He'd been plotting to take Ant off ever since the very first day he'd offered to give him a ride from the bus station, but all of his plans and schemes had always seemed half-baked and missing the crucial element that would allow him to reap the maximum benefits for his efforts. Every single one of them had lacked something.

All of them except one.

Deciding to fuck Tasha and manipulate her into crossing Ant out had been his greatest brainchild thus far. Sure, Ant hadn't helped himself out with all of the bullshit he put her through, but all he really did was just speed up the process because his ass was going to get got, and Tasha was going to be the one to turn his ass in, no matter how good he might've been to her. His fate had been sealed the second she allowed him to stick his dick in her. He simply had that kind of effect and could be just that manipulative when he needed to be, and now, because of that, he was staring at what he knew had to be well over a million dollars in cash. Finally!

Looking at the neatly-stacked rows of money in awe, he picked up his book bag, but sat it right back down. "First things first," he said with a sniffle while pulling out his .38 and drying his face and eyes with the back of his other hand. He got up and grabbed the pillow he'd had earlier, put it to Ant's head with the barrel of his gun jammed into it, and without so much as a blink, fuck a conscience, he put two bullets in his head. "Nice knowing ya, buddy," he mumbled with a little laugh and smirk.

He quickly packed up the money and left the house just the way he'd come, unseen and under the cover of darkness. It was 4:47 a.m.

Ambitious

Chapter Fifteen

Snake stayed away from Ant's funeral. Too many people plus the police equaled not his type of shindig. He laid low and waited on Jaz to get home so she could tell him all about it. Turns out she had plenty of hot gossip to report, and she let it rip as soon as she came into the apartment.

"Hey, baby," she said, happy to see him when he opened the door for her. She tiptoed to kiss his lips, and then walked inside. "God knows I hated Ant, but his funeral was sad as hell," she said in a down tone as she stepped out of her Christian Louboutin heels and walked into the kitchen. Picking up a big red apple out of her fruit bowl, she washed it off and crunched into it as she went and sat next to Snake on the couch. "Wee Baby and them did it real big for that boy. He used to love Louis Vuitton, so they did everythang in Louie for him. His casket was even Louie."

"You talking about Wee Baby from the South?" Snake asked as he pulled her legs up into his lap and started to massage her feet.

"Ooh, thank ya, bae," she said appreciatively and smiled at him. "Yeah, you know him and Ant was brothers? I think they got different daddies or some shit. Anyway," she shrugged, "it was sad as hell, but it was nice, though. A big-ass fashion show," she said with a little excitement and smiled. "Wee Baby had the whole Jonesboro Road and Cleveland Avenue up there with him. All them niggas and they girls was Louie down. Killa and Choppa had a few of them Boulevard niggas with them. I think that nigga Ro came with them, too. All of them was in the Gucci. Nico and Major brought the whole Summer Hill and Lakewood with them, and Vito and a handful of his folks from the East Side was there, too. All of them was playing that Louie shit, too." She bit her apple again and laughed as she thought about something while her free hand found Snake's head. "Vito and Killa, with they ol' retarded asses, was about to get to fighting and shit." She shook her head slowly with a small smile playing at the corners of her her lips. "A muthafucka would never know them niggas was cousins if they ain't look so much alike, especially how they be at each other's throats. Them niggas hate each other," she said with a laugh.

"Other than that, though, and a few other things, it was real nice. After it was over, Wee Baby had got a li'l drunk and started tripping," she frowned and continued. "He was talking about the nigga that did it was there at the funeral, and how he got a hundred thousand on whoever the nigga s'posed to be head, and all type of other crazy shit. Kind of made me wish I knew who did it so I could get that li'l hundred grand up out his ass. I know that nigga good for it," she laughed sadly as she absentmindedly rubbed Snake's head, loving the way his hair felt when it got long and thick, like it was at the moment. "You need a haircut, bae."

"I know," he said, unconsciously rubbing his head himself before asking, "Tasha was there?"

"Hell yeah," Jaz winced and shook her head. "Right there on the front row with the rest of his family, boo-hooing like a damn baby. I felt bad as hell for her. She loved Ant ol' no-good ass. I wanted to say something to her, but I don't know," she shrugged unsurely. "I don't think I'm ready for that just yet."

Snake nodded knowingly. "They close to finding out who did it yet?" he asked.

"Hell naw, not that I heard. Wee Baby stuck on that 'somebody that fuck with Ant did it' shit. He really think Smurf slick had something to do with it. He wasn't even go' let him and Jayla into the funeral if his mama hadn't made him."

Snake grabbed Jaz's hand and stared earnestly into her eyes. Without letting go, he stood up from the couch. "Come here for a second," he said softly, gently pulling her up and leading her toward their bedroom.

She didn't know what she was expecting, but her heart beat fast with anticipation, and she fought hard to calm the butterflies flitting around in her stomach. He let her hand go when they reached the bedroom, and he walked over to the bed. Picking up a medium-sized Atlanta Hawks gym bag, he emptied out its contents, causing Jaz to frown as complete and total anti-climax set in.

"Aw, nigga, why the fuck I thought you was about to ask me to marry you or some shit? What you showing me money for? Where the fuck yo' ass get all that shit from, anyway?" she asked disinterestedly.

Instead of answering vocally, he picked up another bag and, being sure to keep the two piles separated, he dumped it on the bed, too.

Okay, now he had her attention. He'd just dumped a lot of fucking cash on their bed. And wait. It looked like. Was he? Yes! He was about to dump another bag of it on the floor beside the bed. "Where the hell yo' ass get all that money from, Siree?" she shrieked, looking between the three piles of cash.

Snake looked pointedly into her eyes while she slowly put it together.

She gasped and covered her mouth. "No, you didn't! I know you didn't. Are you fuckin' crazy, boy?" she hissed, and then another reality hit home. "Oh my God, Ant. And that other girl. Oh my God," she said quietly with an appalled expression on her face that quickly turned to one of incredulous disbelief. "I thought you and Ant was friends, baby. Y'all was just at Central Station together the other weekend. Why you do," she whispered until another reality came crashing down on her. "That bitch!" she exclaimed, but tried to keep it down as she squinted her eyes and frowned at him.

Snake nodded and shifted all the blame to Tasha. "She set the whole play up. Told me where they lived, gave me the key, the codes, took all the bullets out the nigga's gun, everything," he said quickly, trying his damnedest to make her believe he'd been just a pawn in Tasha's masterplan.

Jaz shook her head. "That ol' scheming, dirty, fake-ass bitch!" She punched her palm with her fist and scowled. "Sat her treacherous ass up there with that man family and cried a fuckin' river all damn day!"

"I been wanted to tell ya, but I had wanted to wait 'til after you went to the funeral and shit. I ain't want you to be acting funny or nothing while you was there."

Dazed, Jaz just stood there, shaking her head. She was really starting to grasp the fact Snake was just that: a fucking snake. And while he was always the nicest, sweetest man in the world to her, he was completely evil to everybody else and never to be trusted, under any circumstances. Nobody appeared to be safe from his evil except for maybe her and his grandmother, but everybody else seemed to be fair game. He was a real slimeball, and for some reason, in a weird, twisted kind of way, knowing he felt she was special to him made her feel good about herself. It made her feel loved and wanted, and quite frankly, it turned her on a bit. She felt her nipples stiffen and her panties moisten a little, but it wasn't the time for freaking. She closed her eyes and shook her head rapidly so she could clear her mind and focus on what he was saying to her.

"...me count it?"

She caught the last part of what he'd been saying. "Huh?" she asked.

"I said, is you go' help me count it?"

She looked at the large piles of money warily. "I guess so. I really ain't got no damn choice, do I," she said unenthusiastically as she shook her head slowly.

"That's my girl! I love ya, bae!" he clapped his hands once and said excitedly with a Mad Hatter grin on his face.

Jaz rolled her eyes, and the two of them picked a pile.

***

Many, many hours and painkillers for hand cramps later, Snake and Jaz both were too tired to even fuck. After a shower, they lay naked together in the dark, sharing a big cup of apple juice with $2.8 million in cold, hard cash sitting casually at the side of their bed.

"Baby, why you do that shit?" she asked quietly as she walked her fingers across his chest and stomach.

"Do what?" he asked sleepily.

"You did that shit to Ant 'cause of what he did to Tasha, didn't you?"

"Man, hell nah," he said, wide awake now. He couldn't have her misconstruing the facts of the matter now that the cat was out of the bag.

Even though she couldn't see his face too good in the darkness, she lifted her head from his massive shoulder and fixed him with an unbelieving stare. "So you telling me this bitch just came to you, of all people, and set all that shit up on GP?" She shook her head no. "Uh-uh, nigga, you got to be thinking I'm slow or something, 'cause that shit don't even sound right. I know y'all fuckin', nigga. Yo' ass better not let me find out for sure, though, muthafucka. You hear me, nigga?" she said with an attitude and pinched him.

"Ouch, man! Yeah, ma, stop! Damn!" he whined and knocked her pinching fingers away. "I hear ya, bae."

"Let me fuckin' find out, nigga. I'ma kill you and that ol' stankin'-ass bitch," she said so calmly Snake just kissed her and dismissed the comment for exactly what it wasn't: an idle threat.

***

Just as Jaz had seen how Ant's older brother, Wee Baby,

had treated Smurf at the funeral, so had plenty of other people, and it took no time at all for word in the streets to be Smurf had a hundred grand on his top. Whether it was true or not, muthafuckas didn't know or even care enough to try to find out. It was just what *shawdy and them* had said, and they were just passing it along, unknowingly helping the rumor burn through the city like a wildfire.

The first few times Smurf heard the off-the-wall-ass rumor, he brushed it off because he knew he'd had nothing to do with the shit. Ant was his pahtna. They'd chopped money together on more than a few occasions, and the whole city knew it. There was no way in fuck he'd slime his homie like that, especially not about a few chips. He had his own money! But the more he heard it from different people, some of them credible, at that, and the longer he went without hearing a single word from Wee Baby to straighten it up, the more he began to believe maybe there was some truth to it.

It came to a point after a few weeks of the rumor burning through Atlanta that Smurf wouldn't leave his Cobb County condo unless it was absolutely necessary. And when he did, he had a special set of wheels just for it. He'd purchased a '98 Honda Accord with blacked-out windows and three missing hubcaps. He knew anybody who had ever even heard of him wouldn't be expecting him to be behind the wheel of a piece of shit like that.

One afternoon after a quick run to pick up some money, he built up enough nerve to call Wee Baby and at least try to see what was up, if he couldn't straighten the whole mess out. Jayla had gone out with her new friend, Jaz, so he had the perfect opportunity to make the call and maybe even kiss a little ass if he needed to.

Scrolling through his contacts, he stopped on the desired name and thought about it for a second before taking a deep, steeling breath and tapping the green call indicator. The phone rang twice before a man answered. "Aye, Wee. This Smurf, man. What's up?" he said, trying not to sound so timid.

"What you mean, *what's up*, nigga?" came Wee Baby's aggressive reply.

All of a sudden thinking of a million reasons why making the call was a terrible idea, Smurf swallowed, which took a lot more effort than it should've, and tried to explain. "Nah, man, it ain't even like that, man. I ain't calling you on no gangsta shit, big dog. You already know I don't want no problems with you or nobody, man. I'm just trying to see what's up?" he said, clearly afraid.

"With what, nigga?" Wee Baby turned the aggression up. He didn't want to talk to the nigga.

"Everybody saying you got some paper on me, bruh." Smurf's voice was barely louder than a whisper before Wee Baby's thunderous baritone cut him off.

"Nah, Jones, I ain't ya bruh! My li'l brother dead, nigga, thanks to yo' ass. Fuck this nigga talking?" Smurf heard him say before the line went dead while he was still talking. Too scared to do anything, he just sat there, staring at his phone, paralyzed by fear until all of a sudden he clutched at his stomach. He had to take a shit, bad as hell.

***

"Nah, I'm good, keep going," Wee Baby said to his wife in a calmer tone as he grabbed her head. She'd been sucking his dick before Smurf had called and while he was talking to him. When he snapped on him and hung up the phone, she asked him if he wanted her to stop, but now she was back at it as he made a call. "What up, fool? Where ya at?" he spoke into the phone, all business. He paused for a few seconds to listen, and then spoke again. "Man, shoot over there to Thomasville and get Trigga. I want y'all niggas to slide through Herndon

Homes and turn that nigga Smurf lights out, shawdy. I got the check," he said and paused again to listen. He nodded once he heard what he wanted to hear. "A'ight homie," he said and hung up. With a sigh, he put his phone down and looked down at his wife, only then realizing she'd stopped again.

She stared at him with an impatient frown. "What you doing, William?" she asked with a little shrug and shake of her head.

Wee Baby frowned at her. "Stay out my business, Ronique. Shit don't concern you, man," he said in an exasperated tone as he pulled her head back to his dick.

***

Snake was in the shower, so he didn't hear when Jaz and Jayla came into the apartment. She told Jayla to have a seat on the couch and turned the TV on for her. "If you want something to eat or drink, just go on and get it from the kitchen," she said, handing Jayla the remote and heading to the back. "Hey, boo, what's up?" she stuck her head in the bathroom and said.

"Hey, love," Snake called back over the running shower water.

"Listen, I got some company, so make sure you're decent before you come out, bae," she said and ducked out of the bathroom, heading to their bedroom.

Snake's phone was going crazy when she walked in the room, but she went on about her business, trying to the best of her ability to ignore it. In the end she caved in and told herself she was trying to be helpful when she decided to answer it and tell whoever it was Snake was in the shower. When she reached to grab it, it stopped buzzing, but she picked it up anyway and saw four missed calls and a text message, all from a nigga named Kevin.

She opened the text for the sole purpose of sending a reply, and her eyes seemed to take on a mind of their own as they quickly scanned the message.

What you doing, Smoke, pick up the phone!

Jaz frowned and started to just put the phone down, but something, she didn't know what, told her not to.

That same something told her to text back instead, and that was exactly what she did as she slowly lowered herself to the bed. *Yeah?* she keyed in and sent the message, her heartbeat two times its normal rate as she nervously awaited a response.

She didn't have to wait long. A return message came through just seconds later.

Answer the phone.

Can't talk now. What's up? Jaz texted back.

I'm prego again, and I need more $, another message came through saying.

Feeling as if she'd been slapped, Jaz's eyes darted back to the name of the person who had sent the message. Obviously it wasn't from some nigga named Kevin. A tear dropped from her eye and splattered when it hit the screen of the phone as she read the message again. She couldn't fucking believe it. She had to read the text message six more times before she could make her brain respond to it. *By who?* she typed in and sent, her fingers moving at the speed of light.

You, fool! Who else! came an almost instantaneous reply.

You positive? Jaz shook her head slowly while keying in the letters, not wanting to believe what was going on.

Nigga, hit my line, ASAP!

Jaz was in all-out tears when Snake came into the room rapping some song. He immediately hit the brakes, stopping mid-stride. "What the fuck? What's up, bae?" he asked with a frown.

Jaz looked up at him slowly through wet, puffy eyes. "It's kind of hard for a nigga named Kevin to get pregnant once, much less twice by you, nigga," she said in a low tone.

"What?" Snake's frown deepened, and then it dawned on him as he scanned the room for his phone.

"Me and Tasha the only people that call you Smoke, Siree." Jaz shook her head and handed him his phone with tears streaming from her eyes. "Put ya clothes on and leave. I don't even wanna look at you right now," she said quietly.

Looking at her with a pleading expression on his face, he looked as if he was about to attempt some kind of explanation, but Jaz was in no mood for any of his bullshit antics and lies. It was nothing he could say to right this wrong or make it go away. "Don't say shit. Just leave. Please," she pleaded with him in a devestated tone of voice and with an identical expression on her face.

Knowing he was caught and seeing the pain in her eyes fucked with the inkling of a conscience he had, so much so he didn't even try to argue or deny it. He simply put his clothes on, and with one last longing look back at her, he left without saying a single word.

Shortly after he left, Jaz came out of the bedroom. She looked a mess, her eyes were red and swollen, and Jayla just knew she'd been crying. "What's going on, girl? Tonio just left, and it looked like that nigga might've been crying or something," she said, concerned as Jaz sat down beside her.

"Girl," Jaz said quietly with a sigh as she shook her head, refusing to fully believe it herself, "that nigga done got that bitch pregnant, and this ain't even the first time." Her tears started anew.

"Who?" Jayla asked, shocked.

"Tonio," she said, still shaking her head, but being careful not to expose Snake's true identity. Even though she hated his guts at the moment, hated his mother and father for getting together and having him, she didn't want even the slightest bit of harm to come to a single strand of hair on his beautiful head.

"Who pregnant? Not Tasha?" Jayla asked incredulously.

With a shamed, embarrassed expression on her face, Jaz nodded her head and answered, "Girl, yeah." The words came out in an unintentional whisper.

Jayla dropped her head and Jaz broke down. She confided all sorts of things in her without getting too loose-lipped, being mindful some things were never to be spoken of.

She found that although Jayla was a good listener, by the time she finished venting and pouring her heart out, she felt an emptiness inside, an unhealthy void, and try as she might, she couldn't shake the feeling. She longed to be held and loved.

Jayla was patting her hand, trying to console her when they made eye contact, and after a second or two, Jaz leaned over and kissed her square on the lips.

Taken by surprise, Jayla found herself kissing her back before breaking the connection. She jumped up quickly. "I, uh, need to use the bathroom," she said nervously, avoiding looking directly at Jaz before rushing off to the bathroom and closing the door behind her.

Bitch! If you don't get yo' country-ass back out there! What the fuck is you doin!

"Uh-uh, Tab! That crazy bitch just kissed me!" Jayla hissed urgently.

So what? If she wanna kiss again, then kiss her ass again, stupid!

"No! That's nasty! She a girl! I love Smurf!"

Listen, dumbass, can't you see the bitch is weak and vulnerable as fuck right now? Tab scolded. *If she wanna kiss, kiss the bitch! If she wanna bump pussies, then there need to be some pussy bumping in this bitch. Whatever! Ain't no telling how much info she can give us about this nigga that's go' help us get his ass.*

Jayla shook her head, unconvinced. "I don't know, Tab," she started firmly.

Bitch, get! End of discussion! Tab said with finality and caused Jayla to unintentionally jerk toward the door.

Nervous as hell and not knowing exactly what to expect, she went back out to the living room.

"Look, I'm sorry," Jaz said apologetically when Jayla came walking back into the living room. "I don't know what the hell all that was about."

Jayla cut her off by bending and kissing her on the mouth, and in the next couple of minutes they both were naked and exploring each other's bodies right there on Jaz's living room couch.

Chapter Sixteen

The Department of Corrections' Blue Bird bus pulled into the shipping yard at Jackson State Prison and unloaded its passengers.

"Terrell Dyer!"

Boon heard the transfer sergeant fuck up the pronunciation of his name. "Right here. And it's D-A, not Dyer," he corrected him as he stepped forward.

The racist, redneck-looking sergeant took his mirror-tinted shades off and looked Boon in the face. He spit a long stream of brown tobacco juice out of his mouth. A few little beads of the spittle dribbled down his chin, and he wiped them away with the back of his hand as he walked over to him. "Boy, do I look like I give a pregnant coon's ass about saying your got-damn name right? You better take your li'l narrow ass over to that line before you have a real reason to be going to Augusta State Medical Prison," he snapped, towering over Boon threateningly as he pointed out the line he wanted him to get in.

Not wanting any problems with the scumbag, lower-than-dirt correctional officers, Boon followed the instructions he was given without saying a word. He knew all it would take was a dirty look from little ol' five-foot-six, 120-pound him and the lowlife, scum-of-the-earth C.O.s would pounce on him like a pack of wild dogs just to boost their self-esteem. He wasn't trying to go through all of that.

Carrying all of his property and with leg irons biting into his ankles with every step he took, he was slowly making his way over to the line for Augusta State when he heard somebody calling his name. He turned and saw his pahtna, Slug, from Dixie Hill and smiled. "What up, fool?" he drawled excitedly in his raspy voice.

"Shit, cooling, right? What the fuck you doing in prison, young nigga? I ain't know yo' li'l ass was even old enough to come to chain-gang," Slug joked while smiling as he got closer, glad to see his li'l pahtna again, but wishing it was under different circumstances.

"Man, they got me fucked up, big homie. Twenty years, shawdy," he rasped slowly.

"Damn," Slug winced and shook his head. It hurt him to hear that, but he tried to keep shit positive because they only had a few minutes to talk before some lowlife C.O. came over and made them go on about their business. "That ain't shit, my nigga. You can give that shit right back to they ass, li'l bruh. Just don't lay down on that shit. You gotta stay in the law library. What you going to Augusta for?"

Boon smirked. "Some of ya Blood homies tried to kill me when I was in Rice Street 'cause I ain't wanna get down with they shit, bruh. Fuck-nigga Trap, from Lakewood, poisoned me, shawdy. Put some shit in my food. I'ma kill that nigga if I eva catch his bitch-ass. But yeah, though, them folks got me down there to Grady in time, but that shit fucked up my liver and my kidneys. I was just down there at Smith State Prison with my cousin, Red Bull, but since I gotta go to Augusta twice a month for treatment, they just decided to transfer me down there."

Slug shook his head. "Some of the homies on some bullshit. How old you is now, young nigga?" he asked.

"Shit, I'ma be eighteen in about three more months."

"Damn, my nigga." Slug winced and shook his head again. "Look, I gotta dip, right? I'm about to go down here to Ware State and turn up on them folks. You know I be getting it in whereva I go, right? But yeah, though, gimme ya info, bruh, and I'ma bust at some of the IF homies down there and tell them to fuck with ya. We got a couple Muslim homeboys tha's down there, too. I'ma holla at everybody about ya."

Boon nodded and they quickly exchanged info before Slug moved as fast as his leg irons would allow him over to the

Ware State Prison line and bus. Boon loaded up and waited for his bus to carry him to Augusta State Medical Prison.

***

At one point, Smurf used to wonder if Wee Baby had wanted him dead. Lately, though, there was no longer need to wonder. He knew. He'd seen the car full of Wee Baby's flunkies or what not lurking in and around the projects he'd grown up in while behind the wheel of his inconspicuous Honda. And from what his pahtnas that still lived in Herndon Homes told him, a car full of Wee Baby's shooters religiously made a pass through the projects at least three time a day. Ever since that day, almost a month ago now, when he'd called him to try to put the situation right, they'd been putting in appearances and it wasn't a doubt in Smurf's mind they were laying on him.

And now, because of some pussy he just couldn't seem to get enough of, here he was, caught. Well, stuck, rather. He was halfway to the Honda he'd left parked on John Street as a car full of Wee Baby's thugs slowly approached. Turning around and going back into Tiara's apartment was out of the question. It would be too obvious, plus she had her 18-month-old son in there with her. Yet his only other option was to try to make it to the Honda, which was risky as hell, also. He was willing to bet he hadn't been spotted yet, but the car creeped ever closer. What should he do? One thing was for certain, though: if he kept doing what he was currently doing, which was standing still and looking crazy, he might as well jump up and down and scream, "Hey! Here I go! Gun me down!"

In the end, although he hated to do so, he concluded the final result was inevitable. "If I'm about to go, I'ma go out blazing," Smurf grunted to himself as he drew his twin forty-fours. An unfamiliar feeling of courage and bravery surging through his body. The extended clips to his pistols gave him a grand total of forty rounds, and he let loose.

Boc, boc, boc, boc, boc boc!

He stood his ground and squeezed both triggers repeatedly, trying to put all fourty of his shots into the old LTD.

The driver and the nigga sitting right behind him never had a chance, but that was all the damage he was able to inflict before the other two passengers of the car cut him down with choppas. Of the forty rounds his forty-fours had, he plugged the car 16 times. He, along with the the two niggas he'd shot, were pronounced dead on the scene when the ambulance arrived.

They shot Smurf 37 times, but true to his word, he most definitely went out blazing.

***

"So, when the last time you fucked ya other bitch?" Jaz asked in a deceptively calm, conversational tone of voice.

Snake frowned. "Don't start that shit, bae. We been doing good," he muttered while shaking and dropping his head. He was leaning back against the front door of Jaz's apartment, holding onto her by her waist.

"Oh, I know," she said matter-of-factly, "but I still want to know. When the last time you seen the bitch?"

He sighed loudly and told the truth. "I gave her some money about a week ago. It's about time for me to give her some more, though, she prob'ly done ran through that li'l shit I gave her last time."

Jaz rolled her eyes and shook her head. "You always kicking all this shit about you wanna come home and get back with me, but you still fuckin' with that ho," she said and shrugged as if to say *what the fuck?* "You need to cut the check with that bitch and tell her ass to kick rocks."

"With my baby?"

She looked at him pointedly. "Who fault that is? That's the purpose of you cutting that bum-ass ho a check!"

A skeptical look came over Snake's face. "That shit ain't go' work, bae. She don't really care too much about that money. Prob'ly 'cause I ain't neva tell her how much it really was. She think it was only a few hundred grand," he was saying until he noticed the impatience on Jaz's face. He cleared his throat and said, "But that don't even matter, though. That's what you want me to do? That's go' make shit back right with us?"

"I ain't go' say all that, but it would damn sure be a good start. That ol' stinkin'-pussy bitch need to be completely out the picture before I even think about starting over with you."

Snake squinted his eyes suspiciously at her. "How you know that pussy stink? You been snooping around down there, too?" he joked, referring to what she'd told him had happened between herself and Jayla.

It had only happened once, and it had been nearly a month ago. It hadn't been a bad experience, but she really wasn't interested in trying it again. Maybe, and only maybe, if Snake wanted to try it, but never again with just herself and another woman alone. The whole girl-on-girl frenzy was completely overrated to her. She needed a nigga with a hard dick to truly satisfy her, and Snake was more than capable, plus his head game was outstanding.

She pinched his stomach and popped him on the arm at the same time. "Get out," she said in a no-bullshit tone.

"Ouch, man," he said with a laugh and grabbed her. "A'ight, bae, a'ight. For real, though," he said seriously. "You know I love you, right?"

Jaz nodded. *I love yo' ol' no-good ass, too, nigga,* her heart screamed, but she sighed, electing to remain quiet.

"I would do anything for ya, bae. You my heartbeat, man.

I'ma try to cut shawdy a check and tell her to fall back. I'ma swing by there when I leave here. In the meantime, though, you know that money there if you need anything." He was talking about the cash they'd counted together.

"Yeah, I know it's there. I'm straight, though. You know it ain't ya money I want," she cut him off.

"A'ight, but just in case. I love you, Jazmine Sinkfield. Don't ever doubt that shit," he said quietly and bent to kiss her lips before turning and leaving.

With a loud sigh, she closed the door behind him and made her way to the couch. She was tired as hell. She and Snake had been fucking like jackrabbits all morning. The last thing she remembered was lying down on the sofa before dozing off to sleep.

***

The sound of her phone ringing roused her from a deep sleep. "Hello?" she answered sleepily without looking at the display.

"Bitch, where you get off telling my baby daddy to quit fuckin' with me! Tonio mine now, bitch. Face it, I took that—"

Jaz snatched the phone away from her ear and, while frowning, looked at the name *Stupid Bitch* on the display. "Bitch, you so fuckin' stupid. You don't even know him," she said with a mirthless laugh as she put the phone back to her ear. "You ain't shit but a fat ass that got pregnant by mistake, ho! You don't mean shit to him! Tha's my nigga, bitch, believe that! Now, don't call my phone with this lame-ass bullshit no more or you ain't go' have to worry about having that ol' ugly-ass baby, bitch." She hung up and turned off all of her alerts.

Fully awake now, mad as hell, and adrenaline pumping through her body, Jaz jumped up and paced back and forth in front of her couch. She had a good mind to throw some clothes on and pull up on Tasha. "What's up now, bitch?" she hissed as she imagined herself standing over Tasha's slightly-showing body and kicking her repeatedly and as hard as she could in the stomach. "With my steel-toe Timms on, too," she said and kicked the air how she wanted to kick Tasha. She abruptly stopped pacing and ran to her bedroom. When she came back to the living room, she had her Timms on, and for some strange reason it seemed to comfort her a little, just knowing they would be the boots she wore to stomp a bitch's head in if Tasha called her again.

After pacing her living room floor a little more, she went and brushed her teeth and then ate an apple. Still fuming and seeing her anger wasn't abating, she dropped to her knees and leaned her elbows on the couch with her hands clasped together in prayer.

"God, it's me, Jazmine," she began earnestly. "I don't be asking for much 'cause I know you be busy helping other people a lot, and I don't be wanting to bug ya with my li'l problems. But I gotta ask ya, please, don't let that bitch have that baby, I swear to you I hate her ass, and I don't think it would be fair. If Siree really love me and don't really care about her ol' stinkin'-ass like he say he don't, then please, don't let her have that baby. Amen. Oh! And let my daddy know I miss him. Okay, bye," she finished quickly, then stood up and went to the bedroom.

When she walked back into the living room, a big blunt of the gas Snake had left her was between her lips, and she fixed herself a big cup of juice before having a seat on the sofa. After firing up the gas, she flipped through the channels on the TV in search of something funny to lighten her mood. She really needed a laugh because she was still seriously considering pulling up on Tasha and beating her ass until she was at the very least sure her ol' bald-headed-ass, gremlin-looking-ass baby was dead as fuck, hence cutting off all ties between her and Snake.

It took somebody bamming on her door to make her realize she'd drifted off into a daze and snap her back to reality. She took a quick pull on the blunt before setting it on the ashtray and hurrying to the door. Her soul literally begging for it to be Tasha, come to get herself and her stinkin'-breath-ass baby killed.

She tiptoed to look out the peephole and saw Jayla. "What's up, girl?" she said, swinging the door open. The instant she got a good look at her distraught friend, she knew something was wrong. "What is it?" she asked with a concerned frown.

Jayla threw her arms around Jaz and erupted in tears. "They killed Smurf!" she sobbed.

"Oh my God, girl, no," Jaz said softly as she hugged her friend.

"They shot him up a few hours ago in Herndon Homes. They say he killed two of the people that was trying to kill him. The niggas they was with left them there to die," she sobbed through her tears.

"Who did it?" Jaz asked while shaking her head slowly.

With a sniffle, Jayla said, "Everybody on Facebook and Instagram saying Wee Baby paid some niggas to do it. You know he think Smurf had something to do with Ant getting killed, anyway," her face turned to an angry frown.

Automatically protecting Snake at any and all costs popped into Jaz's mind. "No, girl, he ain't have nothing to do with that shit!"

Jayla shook her head and went to sit on the couch and Jaz continued.

"Girl, Tasha the reason behind all that shit," she said, closing the door and having a seat next to Jayla.

"What?" Confused anger registering on her face.

"Yeah," Jaz said matter-of-factly with a nod. "She the one

that got Ant robbed and killed in the first place."

"How the hell you know that?" Jayla squinted her eyes and asked.

"She told Tonio how she set it up with the keys, alarm codes, everything," she said, still nodding and in a tone that was encouraging hate for Tasha.

"That ol' dirty-ass bitch!"

"I know, right? That's the same fuckin' shit I said when Tonio told me!"

"I'ma kill that bitch! Her ass the reason Smurf," Jayla started saying, and then paused. Looking at Jaz square in the face, she asked skeptically, "Tonio told you all that shit, Jaz?"

"Yeah, girl," she said solemnly with a nod.

"And you believe him?" she asked seriously.

Jaz thought about the close to $3 million she'd helped count sitting in her bedroom closet. "I swear to God, girl, I would bet my life on that shit, that it's true."

"I'ma kill her and Wee Baby bitch ass!" Jayla exploded.

On board to assist Jayla in committing at least one of those murders, Jaz jumped up and hurried to her bedroom. When she came back, she had on a pair of black jeans in place of her faded, pink flannel pajama bottoms, the same pair of Timberland boots, a black hoodie, and an all-black Atlanta Braves fitted hat. "Let's go get that bitch," she said in a sinister tone, clutching an aluminum baseball bat in her right hand.

Jayla shook her head. "Nah, I got something better."

"Better than swinging for the fence with that bitch head and stomach?" she said and looked at Jayla with a look that said *bitch, please*. "I doubt it," she scoffed, and took a practice swing with all of her might, almost letting the bat slip from her grip while doing so.

Jayla frowned and moved her hand back and forth in a negative gesture. "Hell nah, girl. Trust me, I got something for that bitch and that nigga. This what we go' do."

***

"Who am I about to murder, bae? What the fuck going on?" Snake said the second he walked into Jaz's apartment that night.

"Nobody, baby. Relax. I just wanted to be with you right now so we could talk, face-to-face."

"Why the fuck you text me all that shit about some nigga bothering you, shawdy?" he asked angrily while frowning at her.

"'Cause, I knew you was go' come as soon as you got it. I'm sorry," she said quietly with an apologetic look on her face. "We need to talk, though."

Still frowning, he took his coat off and went to the bathroom. When he came back into the living room drying his hands on his shirt, Jaz motioned for him to come sit next to her, and she climbed into his lap, straddling him.

"You know that bitch called me after you talked to her earlier, right?" she said softly.

The slight frown that had been creasing Snake's face vanished and was instantly replaced with a look of the deepest regret. He sighed deeply and rubbed his head. "What she say?" he asked.

"Talking shit, but she made me do some thinking, though. I don't think it's right to make you stop fuckin' with the bitch completely. That baby she go' have is yours, too. So, I guess what I'm saying is it's okay," she said with a sour face, "if you keep some kind of relationship with her stinkin'-ass, 'cause it would be fucked up to make her take care of a baby by herself that didn't ask to be born."

Snake sighed again, but that time it was out of relief. "Good, 'cause she was talking some crazy bullshit earlier when I told her I wanted to just cut her a check and go on about my business," he said, not bothering to volunteer the information she had stated: that because of what the two of them had done, they were obligated to each other for life. She had said that with a very subtle insinuation of *or else*.

Clearly understanding her meaning, Snake had immediately cowered down and became compliant with the nonsense she was talking, but at the same time he began to seriously think about the best way he could kill her ass and get away with it. After she had the baby, though, of course. The thought of him becoming a dad had grown on him and was exciting. He didn't want to miss out on the blessing she was carrying just because he was going to kill her ass, not if he didn't have to. He'd decided to just try to play it cool until she spit the baby out, and then he'd smoke her ass. It was as simple as that.

Jaz moved closer and rubbed her nose against his. "Don't hurt me, Siree. Never again. If you start back fuckin' with that bitch, I swear to holy God," she said, grabbing his shirt and pulling him even closer, "that bitch or any other bitch while me and you together, I'ma shoot yo' ass. Right here," she whispered seriously while touching him between his eyes. "And then I'ma kill myself. I don't think you know how fuckin' much I love yo' ass, nigga, and I'm a damn good girl. Don't hurt me again, I'm begging you. Please."

Snake wiped her tears away and kissed her lips. "I love you, bae. I know I fucked up, and even though you know why I did that shit, I'm sorry. I swear it ain't go' happen again," he said and pulled her to him, and they simply hugged and rocked each other.

***

"Well, that went smooth, li'l one," Tasha sighed contentedly and said aloud to her baby as she rubbed her barely-protruding stomach. She was full from the late dinner Wee Baby had treated her to. "I thought it was go' be kind of weird or something," she said with a little smile, still clutching the envelope of money he'd given her right before he dropped her off.

She stood watching his Porsche truck ease up the block, but when it stopped and his reverse lights glowed white, she pulled her knee-length leather jacket close around her to fight off the chill of the night air and started to walk toward the SUV, thinking either he or she had forgotten something.

She didn't hear the two niggas creeping up on her, but the sound of the assault rifles they carried being cocked behind her made her whirl around in fear to see what the fuck was going on. She dropped the money-filled envelope to the ground and threw her hands up as if she was really about to shield herself from the onslaught.

"Nah, it's too late for all that shit, bitch! This for li'l Ant!" one of the niggas barked.

Tasha's scream was cut extremely short. The spark from the barrels and the sounds the choppas made as they spit round after round lit up the night. Each of the black-clad gunmen reloaded once they ran out of bullets, and then stood directly over her already-mutilated body and gave her fifty more rounds each before they ran off in different directions, choppas steaming in the cold night air.

Then, and only then, did Wee Baby shift his truck back into drive and pull off.

Chapter Seventeen

"You ready for ya dance now, mister?"

"I don't remember asking for one, shawdy, to tell ya the truth."

"But I give the best dances in the house. You don't wanna pass on this opportunity, trust me," she said sexily.

Irritated and intrigued all at once by the super-sexy stripper rolling her body in tune with the music, he reluctantly accepted the dance offer and handed her a crisp hundred dollar bill before checking his Breitling. "Try not to get too much of ya body oil and glitter and shit all over me. I ain't no regular, I'm just here on a li'l business," he said with a ton of arrogance.

She nodded and began to dance. Using her well-equipped body to do so, she slowly and sensually seduced him. Bending over, she softly clapped her ass less than an inch away from his face, and every time it clapped, the sweet scent of strawberries coupled with fresh, clean pussy brushed his nostrils. She knew she had him reeling when he gave her two more crisp hundred dollar bills. "Is this to keep me dancing, or a tip?" she asked, looking over her shoulder as she tucked the bills under the band around her thigh.

"Both," he replied with no less arrogance than the last time he spoke.

Still dancing, she laughed a little and turned around.

"Why the fuck you the only one in here with a mask on?" he asked, obviously annoyed by it.

"It's part of my outfit. You don't like?" She'd stopped dancing to ask, but was flashing a pretty smile.

"Hell nah. Take it off. I wanna see ya face," he ordered.

"Damn, you bossy," she laughed.

"I'm a boss," he said seriously. "I wanna see ya face."

She laughed again. "You can see my face, just not the area

around my eyes. My stage name is Mystique. This mask is part of it."

"I don't like it. Lose it," he demanded.

Unfazed by his rudeness, she smiled sweetly. "The only way this mask comes off is if my panties and bra go with it."

Although she stood before him now with her titties and ass bared, he clearly understood her meaning, and for the first time since she'd been dancing for him, he showed a sign that suggested maybe he wasn't an asshole one hundred percent of the time by chuckling. "Tempting, I swear, but I'm married," he said, holding up his ring finger for her to see and twisting his wedding band with his thumb. "Working on twelve years now."

"Aw, that's sweet. Stay faithful, boo, lord knows us women sure do appreciate it when we find a man who knows how to," she said and started dancing without making any other attempts at conversation for a while. When he started to check his watch every other minute or so, she frowned. "Is something wrong? You want me to stop dancing?"

Sensing a slight attitude from her, he quickly let her know what was up. "Nah, you good. I was s'posed to be meeting somebody up here, but it don't look like they coming, though." He checked his watch again.

"Too bad."

"Yeah, for them," he said smugly as he pulled the Prada knapsack beside him closer and threw a quick glance over the club.

Catching his eyes, she stared into them for a second. "I'm thirsty. You want another drink? It's on me," she said sweetly and smiled.

He thought about it and didn't see a reason not to have another, so he agreed. "Uh, yeah. Gimme a Goose and cranberry with a li'l ice."

She said okay and headed to the bar while his dick grew

harder and harder as he watched her ass bounce and jiggle with every step she took. He imagined himself smashing her from the back. *Her li'l short, red ass sexy as hell and thick as fuck!* he thought to himself, and when she came back with his drink, he let her know exactly what was on his mind.

"How much to let a nigga smash?" He asked the question in a tone and manner that suggested somehow he was doing her some sort of favor by inquiring.

She laughed. "What happened to keeping it faithful?"

Not one to play games, he just stared at her pointedly in response.

She got the message loud and clear. "For a big shot like you, three for this pussy, two for some head," she said, all business.

Taken aback, he started to laugh and tell her to go fuck herself, but there was just something about her. Maybe it was that fucking mask. Whatever it was, he wanted her ass bad. And truth be told, he probably would've given the bitch a fucking Benz had she asked. She was just that bad, and he was just that infatuated and intrigued by her and her damn mask.

"I tell ya what," he paused and took a swallow of his drink while her eyes burned holes in him. "You can keep the pussy for now, 'cause I'm going home tonight. But I'ma give ya the li'l two hunnid for the head. My wife won't trip about that. Go get ya shit. Nah, hold up!" He took another swallow of his drink. "You gotta lose that fuckin' mask first, though. Or just slide that muthafucka up so I can see ya at least one time or something."

She licked her thick, full lips seductively and slowly shook her head no. "When I'm done with that dick, you can keep it if you want," she said with a sexy little laugh and walked to the back.

When she came back and said she was ready, he downed the last of his drink and led the way out of the club. He hit a button on his keyring, and the alarm to his Audi TT chirped before he opened the passenger door and helped her into the car. When he got in the little coupe, he crunk it up, and the big engine roared ferociously to life before idling down to a deep purr. He blasted the heat to combat the chilly night and pulled out his throbbing dick while clearing his throat.

She wasted no time getting on it. Leaning over, she took him into her mouth and sucked him to a quick nut. The head was pretty good, but he knew it would've been better if they weren't cramped up in the car. Plus she was excessively sloppy with it. His clothes were fucked up when she finished, and he couldn't really enjoy it because he had to keep clearing his throat to relieve himself of a persistent itch at the back of it.

"How ya liked it?" she asked as she watched him dry his dick off with some napkins from fast food joints before stuffing his dick back in his pants.

"It was decent. Give me ya number," he said arrogantly while blinking rapidly.

"You got my money?" she asked, and when he reached for his pocket, she stopped him by grabbing his hand. "I'm talking about my hundred grand, nigga," she said in a not-too-friendly tone.

His eyes grew wide with surprise, and he was still blinking fast as hell as he began to cough. "That was you?" he struggled to get out between coughs. She nodded and smiled. "The only reason I'ma," he started as he reached between his feet for the knapsack but a violent fit of coughing stopped him.

She looked him in the eyes as he hacked, and her smile brightened. "And that would be the shit I put in ya drink starting to work on ya."

His eyes bulged and flashed terror, but it was too late.

"It fuck with ya nervous system first. That's why the corner of ya mouth keep twitching like that and why you blinking like a muthafucka," she said conversationally and picked an imaginary piece of lint from his collar. "It's more than likely eating away at the tissue in and around ya lungs now. That would explain that runaway cough that's pestering you. Next, it's going to pretty much paralyze ya, and you gonna feel a badass burn, like your blood is boiling in ya veins."

His head lolled to the side, and he found himself staring at her, but not really seeing her. The pain was too intense to be concerned with seeing anything. He let out a horrible-sounding groan, and she laughed.

"Ah! That's prob'ly happening now," she said and laughed again as his face involuntarily twitched in pain.

"Why?" he managed to gurgle just loud and clear enough for her to interpret what he meant.

She slid her little costume mask off, and recognition registered in his bulging eyes before he began to foam at the mouth. "'Cause Smurf didn't do shit to deserve what you made happen to him, you piece of fuckin' shit!" Jayla yelled hysterically and resisted the urge to hit him with her hand. Instead, she put her hand to his neck to feel for a pulse and felt it fade completely away under her fingertips. "And that, Mr. Wee Baby, means yo' ass is done," she said when she heard and smelled his bowels release.

Bravo. Bravo! I must admit, Jay, I. Am. Impressed. That was a fine body of work you put together there, if I must say so myself. I didn't think you had it in ya, boo.

"I don't know why. After all, we are one and the same, Tab," Jayla said arrogantly as she looked in the visor mirror and doctored her makeup a little.

Amen. For Smurf.

"For my baby," Jayla said and took a deep breath to get her mind right for the next task. After grabbing the knapsack with the hundred grand in it, she forced a few fake tears from her eyes and jumped out of the Audi, screaming at the top of her lungs.

***

Snake woke early the next morning to the sound of his phone ringing, but when he didn't recognize the number on the display, he ignored it and sat it back down. Jaz was still asleep, and after fucking her brains out the previous night, she'd allowed him to spend the night for the first time in weeks. She was beginning to come around and accept the fact he'd fucked up and gotten Tasha pregnant. And now, after allowing some time to pass and him vowing relentlessly to not screw up again, things were finally starting to look up.

He got out of bed and headed to the bathroom. While brushing his teeth, he decided he'd cook her a real nice breakfast and feed it to her in bed. After that he'd eat her pussy until she begged for him to fuck the shit out of her, and then he'd take her shopping. For a ring. Maybe even a house and whatever else her little heart might desire. He knew Jaz was all right for him and completely for him. He'd fucked up a few licks in his lifetime, but right now he was willing to bet the house he wouldn't blow this one. While doing his ten years in the can, he'd met more than a few niggas who would've killed, literally, to have a broad like her on their team, including himself. She was a real trooper, and now he was about to try to show her how much he appreciated and valued everything about her being.

She was awake when he walked back into the room. She'd covered her head with her pillow. "Will you please answer that damn phone before I break that muthafucka! A bitch trying to damn sleep!" she grumbled sleepily when she heard him come back into the room.

"My bad, love," he said with a little smile, hurrying over to his ringing phone. "Who the hell this is, man?" he answered the phone, seeing the same number from earlier on the display. After a brief pause, he spoke again. "Oh, what up, fool? Everything a'ight? You sound a lil wheezy, bruh. Where Tasha at?"

Jaz took her head from under the pillow and peeked at him when she heard him ask that.

"Nah, I ain't sitting down. Why?" Snake asked apprehensively with a frown. "I don't wanna sit down, nigga. What up? Where Tasha at?" he asked with a touch of anger in his voice before he stood quietly for a few seconds, obviously listening. And then he exploded. "*What!*"

Jaz jumped at the sound of his thunderous voice, a frightened look on her face.

"When?" he managed to ask, his voice barely louder than a whisper as he dropped his head and sat on the bed. After a few more seconds of listening, he shook his head slowly. "Tell ya mama I'ma be over there in a few, bruh," he mumbled and tossed the phone on the bed after disconnecting the call.

"What's wrong, baby?" Jaz asked softly as she walked across the bed on her knees and placed her arms around Snake's neck.

He grabbed her arms and pulled her closer still. "Somebody killed Tasha last night, man," he croaked and swallowed the lump in his throat before going on, "her and my baby. They killed my baby, shawdy," he said, growing tired of fighting it as sobs began to rack his body.

Jaz wound up dropping a few tears of her own while she comforted him. She didn't care what had happened to Tasha, or her little Crypt-Keeper-looking baby, for that matter. In fact, she silently thanked God for answering her prayers, but what she couldn't stand was the sight of Snake in so much anguish. It stabbed at her heart and caused her unbelievable, almost unbearable pain. For a second she kind of wished she and Jayla hadn't conspired to get the stinkin' bitch killed, but who the fuck was she kidding? That feeling only lasted for maybe a millisecond.

Once Snake got control of his emotions, he sighed a deep, weary sigh and stood up. "I'ma slide through there and check shawdy folks, man. See if I can find out what the fuck happened and shit."

"You want me to come with you?" she got up and asked.

He thought about it for a second while he pulled on a thick pair of Gucci sweats. "Nah, you good. Stay here. I can't pull up over there with you, bae. Kind of disrespectful," he said somberly. "All her folks know y'all was beefing and shit."

Jaz nodded okay and trailed him to lock the door behind him.

***

In the first few weeks after Tasha's funeral, Snake walked around moping and sulking all day, everyday. He wasn't sleeping much and he didn't want to eat, fuck, or pretty much do anything that involved him having to interact with other people. He seemed to be perfectly content with just sitting around, smoking gas, playing with some big-ass machine gun he'd popped up with out of nowhere, and brooding. Jaz, although she was trying to be patient with him, quickly grew tired of all the gloomy, sad shit. The not-wanting-to-fuck part a little more so than the others.

One particular bright, sunny Saturday afternoon she'd taken all she could from him. She stalked into her bedroom and rested her hands on her hips with an impatient scowl on her face. "Get yo' ass up! Go take a fuckin' shower and get dressed, Siree! Yo' gramma said she about to cook dinner, and she want us to come over there. I'm about sick of yo' ass, nigga," she said, snatching the covers off of him and opening the blinds in her bedroom, allowing the bright March sunlight to shine through the window. "It's damn near seventy degrees out there, nigga! We about to go over yo' gramma house and eat, then we go' get in traffic and enjoy this fuckin' day!"

After fixing her with a blank stare, Snake blinked slowly and got up to take a shower like he was told.

On the way over to his grandmother's house, Jaz tried desperately to get through to him, but when he shut her down with silence time after time, she swerved over to the side of the road and threw the car in park. "I wish you would stop brooding over that bitch! You got any idea how the fuck that shit make me feel? You s'posed to be my nigga!" she yelled at him, her expression a mixture of anger and pain.

He hit her with another blank stare and blinked slowly before he chuckled as his face transformed into an angry mask. "Man, fuck Tasha!" he exploded. "If you think I'm fucked up about that bitch, yo' ass wrong! I was go' kill the bitch myself. Yo' ass did me a favor! The baby? So-so," he screwed his face up and turned his outstretched hand back and forth as if to say a little. "I'm even over that shit now, though. But them people shot her ass over a hundred times. Bitch had bullet holes all in her fuckin' feet, shawdy. Why you think they went so far with the overkill, Jazmine?"

Suddenly not as riled up and and aggressive as she'd been a couple of seconds ago, Jaz shrugged slowly and shook her head.

Snake gave a little laugh, but it sounded threatening, menacing. "I know why," he said. "I know what the fuck you did, Jazmine," he said knowingly. "And believed it or not, I can even understand why you did it. But what I can't seem to put my finger on is why you would want to get back at me like that, and if that was yo' true intentions in the first place.

Jaz was stuck. "I-I-I," she stammered.

"Yeah, I know. Money make muthafuckas do the worst," he said matter-of-factly. "Why you think I ain't been sleeping?

Grieving about Tasha ol' nothing-ass?" He gave another sinister-sounding laugh as he put his .38 in his lap. "Nah, Jones. I been laying on whoever you got to knock Tasha off to kick the door in trying to get at me and my money. Three million in cash is enough to get anybody's check canceled, muthafuck love. You think I'm about to go out bad? I thought about putting a bullet in ya head and just taking off at first, right?" he admitted. "But after the first few nights of watching, waiting, and nothing happened, something told me not to kill ya, to just hold off a li'l longer, 'cause something wasn't right," he nodded his head slowly.

"So, this what we go' do." Snake deliberately made a show of pulling the hammer back on his .38, and Jaz inhaled sharply as tears streamed from her eyes. He looked directly into her glossy orbs so she'd know he meant nothing but business in its purest, most unadulterated form. "You about to tell me everything, shawdy. From the beginning to the end. You ain't go' leave out the slightest, smallest piece of detail." He held his thumb and index finger up with a fraction of an inch between them for her to see. "And lying ain't even go' begin to become a option in yo' mind, or I swear to high God, girl, I'ma shoot yo' ass in the face and leave ya ass right here on the side of the road. You got me?"

With her face balled up in terror, Jaz swallowed around the lump in her throat and nodded. "It all started that day I text you and told you a nigga was fuckin' wit' me," she began.

***

Jaz popped the shit out of Snake as he loaded another bullet back in his revolver. "I don't give a fuck 'cause it wasn't loaded, nigga! You scared the shit out of me! I almost peed in my fuckin' clothes, nigga!" she yelled at him as she parked in front of his grandmother's house. "After we eat, yo' ass can just stay right on over here with her, muthafucka!"

Snake frowned. "Nah, nigga," he said as they got out of the car and walked to the front door. "One thing I ain't about to let you do is play that reverse psychology shit and turn this shit around on me to make it seem like I'm the bad guy. Yo' ass the one that did that bullshit! You the one that threw a fuckin' tantrum like a little-ass fuckin' kid and killed my fuckin' baby. All 'cause that stupid-ass bitch made you mad. All you had to do was be patient and I was go' whack the bitch myself, but naw, yo' ass just had to go and do the shit yo' way. You need yo fuckin' ass beat for that shit, that's what the fuck you need, bitch!"

"You and me both, nigga, 'cause you should've never fucked the bitch and got her ass pregnant in the first place! I don't give a fuck about you wanting to take Ant off! You should've found another fuckin' way to do it! So that shit make us even, bastard! And now ain't the time to talk about this shit. We go' finish this shit later!" she hissed as she smoothed a loose strand of hair into place and rang the doorbell.

"Nah, fuck that," he muttered. "Who the hell you think you is to be dictating when we – hey, Gram!" he said and instantly adjusted his attitude when his grandmother answered the door. He and Jaz both exchanged their masks of anger for happy-go-lucky smiles immediately.

"Hi!" Jaz squealed excitedly and waved.

"Hey, babies. Y'all c'mo' in here," she said with a smile and turned to head back to the kitchen, waving them in behind her.

Jaz looked over at Snake and flashed him a murderous scowl. "Forget that bitch and that ol' shit-bomb-ass baby! They ass is in the past. I'm the only bitch that's about to be having yo' damn kids, nigga, so you need to accept that shit and move the fuck on!" she whispered furiously and headed into the house.

"Crazy-ass bitch!" he hissed back and pushed her a little too hard while she was stepping over the threshold, causing her to trip, lose her balance, and fall face-first. "Oh, I'm sorry, bae!" he said loudly while stepping over her, his apology dripping with sarcasm.

She bounced up quickly without any offered help from him and straightened her clothes while Snake's grandmother looked to see what all the fuss was about. "Oh, it's okay," she said with a forced smile on her face. "You can be so clumsy sometimes." She laughed a loud, extremely artificial-sounding laugh. "My big doofus!" she exclaimed as she drew back and slapped the shit out of him on the back under the pretense of showing loving affection.

Snake winced and laughed, but the smile went no further than his mouth. His eyes flashed fire as he looked at a smiling Jaz.

His grandmother raised a single eyebrow at their weird behavior. "You two crazies quit fooling around and come get something to eat," she reprimanded as a mother would and went back to the kitchen.

Once the young couple was seated, Snake's grandmother fixed both of them plates, and she made sure to pile Jaz's with a ton of food. Snake glanced between his own plate and Jaz's and frowned as he looked at his grandmother. "You think she go' eat all that, Gram? I know she greedy, but damn."

"Shut the fuck up, nigga," Jaz mouthed silently as she shot him a bird and rolled her eyes.

"Aw, hush up, boy. She eating for two. We tend to eat a bit more when we get with child, ya know," she said while waving him off.

He looked back and forth between his grandmother and Jaz, perplexed.

After being shocked the old lady knew her secret Jaz smiled sheepishly. "Surprise! I'm pregnant," she said lamely while looking at Snake.

"When the hell you was go' tell me? You done told my damn gramma," he frowned and snapped at her, angry as hell because he had really came within moments of killing her a few weeks ago.

Not knowing what to expect from him, but definitely not expecting him to react like that, Jaz looked at him incredulously before she responded. "No, I didn't, fool! I ain't told no-damn-body. She just guessed somehow!"

"Look at her, boy! She practically glowing! I don't know how you missed it, but I knew she was with child the instant I laid eyes on her when she was standing out there on my stoop!" the old woman said with a wise smile that reached her eyes.

The news of the baby eventually improved Snake and Jaz's moods, and it excited all three of them. All of the fuss and talk of babies was the reason the two of them didn't get around to leaving until after dark, and although both of them told her it wasn't necessary, his grandmother insisted on walking out to the car with them.

"Hey, Mama Ellis, you doing a'ight tonight?" one of the local young hustlas called out as he walked by the house.

"Hey, Jock. Yeah, I'm doing just fine," she said with a wave of her hand.

The young nigga made no attempt to speak to either Jaz or Snake, and Snake frowned when he turned to his grandmother. "Mama Ellis? Who that li'l nigga ism Grammy?" Snake asked, a little jealous.

"Oh, that's just Jock," she said dismissively with a wave. "He go grocery shopping and do other li'l stuff for me when you ain't around. Sell more dope than a li'l bit, but he's a good kid. Got a good head on his shoulders. He go' make it away from here one day."

Snake nodded apprehensively and was just about to ask another question about the young nigga when he heard someone call out, "Jaz! Tonio!" He and Jaz looked and saw Jayla behind the wheel of her Pontiac G6 in the middle of the street.

"What's up, girl?" Jaz called out as she hurried over to Jayla's car while Snake just threw up his hand and waved.

"Who is that? And who the hell is Tonio?" Snake's grandmother asked with a puzzled look on her face.

"I don't know, Grammy. She crazy. That's one of Jazmine friends. You should go back inside. It's kinda cool out here. I love you." He kissed his grandmother's cheek and ushered her toward the house.

"Hey, Ms. Ellis!" Jayla called from her car.

"Hey, baby!" Snake's grandmother turned and said with a wave before going inside for the night.

"You should've seen her face when shawdy called me Tonio," Snake said with a laugh when Jaz finished talking to Jayla and got in the car.

She laughed because she could only imagine what the spunky old woman's reaction had been like. When her laughter died away, she looked into Snake's happy, smiling face and knew she didn't want to fight with him anymore. "I love you, baby, And I'm sorry for what I did, but only 'cause it hurt you, though."

He thought about what she said for a few seconds before responding. "I love yo' li'l evil ass, too."

Relieved, Jaz caressed his cheek and looked into his eyes. "Truce?" she asked.

He leaned over and kissed her. "Truce, bae," he agreed before Jaz put the car in gear and pulled away from the curb.

***

Later that night, Jayla turned the covers back on her bed and climbed in. After swallowing two sleeping pills, she fluffed her pillows and lay back down with a little smile on her face. It was finally time to take action and have her revenge. She closed her eyes and burrowed down into her mattress, knowing she would need as much rest as possible because tomorrow promised to be a long, but fruitful day for her. She clocked out and snored very lightly as she slept peacefully through the whole night.

Ambitious

Chapter Eighteen

Jayla and Jaz both laughed at the little joke she'd made about Snake as she rang his grandmother's doorbell.

"Hey, baby! What a surprise this is!" the old woman answered her door and said with a smile.

"Hey, Ms. Ellis," Jaz said with a smile and wave as she stepped inside. "This is my friend, Jayla. She's the one who spoke to you last night from her car."

"Hi," Jayla waved and stepped inside behind Jaz.

"Hello, sweetie," the old woman smiled warmly at Jayla and wrung her hands together. "Tell me y'all came to watch C.S.I. with me?" she asked with a hopeful smile as she looked back and forth between her two visitors.

Jaz and Jayla quickly glanced at each other briefly with humor in their eyes before Jaz spoke up. "Uh, no ma'am. I was just stopping by to see how you were doing and to see if you had any more of that peach cobbler you made. I was telling her about it, and she wants to taste some."

"Sure I do! It's almost gone, though. I knew Siree loved it, but I found out last night how much you do, too," she said with a smile. "Y'all sure y'all don't want to stay?" She shook her head. "I think somebody's finally about to kill Horacio's corny ass." she turned and headed into the living room where the TV was on.

Jayla gripped her pistol, a small Glock tucked in the pocket of her jacket, and snatched her blackjack from the other pocket. When she hit Snake's grandmother with a violent blow across the back of the head, Jaz jumped back in shock, not fully understanding or believing the images her eyes were relaying to her brain. "What the fuck?" she started before Jayla thrust the barrel of her pistol into her face.

"Shut the fuck up, bitch, and turn yo' ass the fuck around," Jayla sneered.

Still not quite understanding what the hell was going on, Jaz turned around and felt the blackjack slam against the back of her head just before everything went black. She fell to the floor, unconscious, only a few feet away from where Snake's grandmother lay sprawled out.

When she regained consciousness, she found herself bound and gagged. Her head hurt like a bitch, and she had to pee bad as hell. Obviously she'd been carried – or more than likely drug to – and put on the couch in the living room, because when she opened her eyes she saw C.S.I. on the TV set. Blinking away the fogginess from her mind, she sat up slowly, wincing from the pain it caused her tender head.

"It's about damn time! I was starting to think I might've clocked yo' ass a li'l too damn hard," Jaz heard Jayla say, but she couldn't see her as she surveyed her surroundings. She spotted Snake's grandmother, though, also bound and gagged, sitting in an old recliner across the room from her. Her wide eyes revealed not a trace of fear. Instead, they showed only a calmness that clearly belied the situation at hand.

"Okay, Jaz," Jayla said as she came into view with a phone in her hand. "Call Snake and get his ass over here A.S.A.P. And don't try to be slick and let him know what the fuck going on."

Wondering exactly who the fuck Jayla was, Jaz balled her face up in defiance and yelled all types of profanities into her gag while shaking her head, no. She'd never, not even accidentally, referred to Siree as Snake in front of anyone, so it was eating her up to know exactly how the fuck Jayla knew his name.

"A'ight," Jayla said with a frown. "Either you go' make the call or I'ma shoot this old bitch." She drew her pistol and put it to Snake's grandmother's head. "And then I'ma shoot yo' ass. You make the choice."

Tears sprang to Jaz's eyes. She'd just been asked to make

one hell of a decision. *How the fuck you get yaself into this one, Jazzy?* she thought to herself as she slowly dropped her head and shook it. *I should've never trusted this bitch! And how the fuck my dumb ass let her talk me into coming over here? She don't even fuckin' know Snake or his damn grandma! I should've fuckin' known better!*

"I ain't go' wait all day," Jayla said impatiently.

Jaz looked at Snake's grandmother and still saw no sign of panic or fear. She shook her head no just slightly, enough for Jaz to catch it, but she was too weak. She couldn't bear to have the old woman's blood on her conscience. Jaz nodded her head yes, and that was when the old woman's tears came. With a sigh, she closed her eyes and began to cry quietly.

Before Jayla removed the gag, she assured Jaz any attempts to warn Snake or tip him off in any kind of way would mean instant death for the old lady and herself. "That mean the baby, too, hon," she added as a reminder and held Jaz's phone up for her to talk into it.

"What's up, bae?" Snake answered after the second ring.

"Hey," Jaz said. Her voice was a little choppy from crying, so she cleared her throat. Jayla slapped the shit out of her on the back of the head and threatened her with her eyes. Blinding pain shot through her body and brought fresh tears to her eyes, she'd hit her in the exact same spot she'd hit her with the blackjack earlier. Fighting tooth and nail not to protest aloud in pain, she squeezed her eyes shut and took a deep breath. "Hey, what you doing?" she asked.

"Shit. Watching the Hawks' garbage-ass get they ass smashed. What up?" he asked, figuring she wanted something.

"How fast can you make it over here to yo' grandma house?"

"Why, what up?" he asked, alert.

"I stopped by to check on her earlier and she wasn't feeling too good," she said with a grimace, hating being forced to lie to and trick him like she was.

"What's wrong with her?" he cut her off and asked in a panic. She could hear a lot of rustling around coming from his end of the connection.

"She complained about a headache. She took something for it, though, and lay down, but she had asked me to see if you would come over."

"I'm on the way now. Tell her I'ma be there in about twenty," he said and hung up without saying another word.

***

He parked his '08 Lacrosse right behind Jaz's Impala and jumped out, worried sick about his granny. As he made his way around the car, he saw the kid she'd spoken to the night before walking up the street. "Aye, say, Jack! Sock!" He couldn't quite remember his name. "Aye, say, bruh?" Once the young nigga looked at him, he spoke again. "You seen my gramma today? What's wrong with her?" he asked, worry evident in his tone.

"Nah, I ain't seen her, bruh. I ain't even slid through there to check on her today, big dog," Jock said.

Snake nodded okay and quickly walked to the front door of his grandmother's house. He ignored the questioning look the young nigga was giving him and used his key to let himself in so the doorbell wouldn't disturb her, just in case she was asleep.

***

Jaz winced when she heard the unmistakable sound of Jayla's blackjack cracking against Snake's skull. She saw his upper body crumple to the floor from where she sat tied up, but a wall blocked her from seeing him from the waist down.

Jayla made quick work of restraining him, although she tied him up a little differently than herself and his grandmother. She rolled him onto his stomach and put his hands behind his back, then bent his legs at the knees and tied his right wrist to his right ankle and his left wrist to his left ankle. Once she'd finished tying his restraints, she slowly dragged his heavy body into the living room and plopped down on the couch beside Jaz. "Whew," she said and wiped away a few beads of sweat from her forehead. "That nigga heavy as hell, girl!"

After regaining control of her breathing, she went to the kitchen and came back with a pitcher full of ice water. "It's showtime," she exclaimed and dashed Snake full in the face with the freezing cold water.

He woke up gasping for air and sputtering as he flailed around to the best of his restrained ability. "What the fuck?" he shouted before he noticed Jaz and his grandmother tied up and looking at him.

The first complete thought that came to his foggy mind was all along it had been Tasha who had run her mouth and gotten herself killed, and it was her who was responsible for what was happening to him now. But then he remembered Jaz had admitted to what she and her friend had done, so that left him with a blank. What the fuck was this shit about? Then he saw Jayla walk into his limited line of sight.

"Hi, Snake," she said with a pretty-ass smile. He frowned and started to say something, but she spoke first. "What's wrong? You don't look too excited to see me, baby."

"I barely even know you, bitch, and it seem like you the one that got us tied the fuck up, so why the fuck would I be happy to see yo' ass?" he growled.

"That ain't true, baby. We know each other pretty damn well. Here," she moved closer to him. "Get a good look at me," she squatted down in front of him.

Snake racked his brain just as he did the very first time

he'd seen her in the club almost a year ago. Nothing. He drew a big blank. She looked vaguely familiar, but he just couldn't place her pretty face. With a sigh and a shrug of his shoulders, he gave up. "Man, I don't fuckin' know you, you crazy-ass bitch. You got me confused with another nigga."

Jayla stood up and smiled. "Maybe this might help you some." She took her time and undressed slowly, then stood before him butt-ass naked. "What about now? Is it starting to come back to you now?" she asked as she cupped and squeezed her right breast seductively.

At that point Jaz's fear of what was to come had decided to take a backseat and let her more aggressive curiosity dominate her brain. She stared between Snake and Jayla, scared to even blink because she thought she might miss something, damn the fact she was possibly about to die. Knowing exactly what the fuck Snake and Jayla had going on was way more important to her at the moment.

Snake laughed. "Look, lady, I. Don't. Know. You! I'm telling ya, man, you got me confused with somebody else. And you need a li'l help, but it's cool. They, got a place for folks like you. Just let us go and we go' make sure you get some help, shawdy," he said with a handsome little smirk, one hundred percent sure that even though the bitch was as crazy as a bat bug, all of what was happening was some kind of mistake. He knew all he needed to do was somehow talk some sense into her crazy-ass and get her to untie them.

Anger flashed in Jayla's eyes, but she smiled and started to dress. "Oh, you think this shit funny? It's some kind of game or something, right?" Her smile turned to a deadly serious look. "I assure you, it's neither. And just to let you know how serious yo' predicament is, I want you to think back, what, close to eleven years ago now? Jason Phillips was my daddy, and you?" She laughed softly once. "You was my very first."

Lightbulb! The recognition and realization was

instantaneous on Snake's facial features. A bit of shock and even fear could be seen.

"Ah! I thought that li'l piece of information might help you out a bit," Jayla exclaimed as Snake closed his eyes, dropped his head, and sighed. "What's wrong? Hold ya head up, baby. Be proud! Surely yo' ol' nasty-ass ain't ashamed of what you did to a fourteen-year-old virgin girl, are you?" she goaded him. "Fuckin' pedophile," she sneered and spit in his face.

Snake flinched when the spit hit him, and not being able to wipe it away, of all things, is what infuriated him the most. Reigning in his anger, he sighed and said in a forced calm tone, "Look, man, this shit don't concern nobody but me an–"

Jayla shook her head and cut him off. "Nah, this shit way bigga than just me and you, nigga," she said in a warning tone. "But they don't know what you did," she said, pointing at Jaz and his grandmother. "They don't even know why they tied up and shit."

Snake sighed again and shook his head, defeated.

"I think I'ma let they ass know what happened. I mean, it's only fair they know what's going on, too," she said and sat on the couch next to Jaz before she began to speak slowly. "One night, about eleven years ago, this piece of shit," she said and nodded her head toward Snake, "decided to kick in me and my daddy's door. Apparently he had gave my daddy some dope to sell, and it was time to collect. Well, when good ol' Snake came for his money, my daddy didn't have it because my fuckin' crackhead-ass auntie had broke in our house and found my daddy's hiding spot. That bitch stole everythang we had. But him," she pointed at Snake, "cold-hearted piece of shit that he is, he didn't give a damn about any of that. He just wanted his money. My daddy begged yo' ass, nigga, to just give him a few days. A few fuckin' days was all he asked you for! He would've had ya li'l money, but no. Good ol' Snake had some other shit on his mind.

"He beat the shit out of my daddy with a gun 'til he was damn-near incoherent while I begged him not to kill him. And then he took me, a fourteen-year-old child, and fuckin' raped me. Piece of shit forced my daddy to watch as he destroyed my body, but he didn't stop there. No, not him. That would've been too civilized for this nigga." She closed her eyes and shook her head matter-of-factly. "When I woke up, after he had knocked me out, this muthafucka walked right over to my weeping, broken daddy and shot him in the face. All of that shit, all of that fuckin' pain and torture he caused, all of it for less than ten thousand petty-ass dollars," she finished quietly with tears running from her eyes as she relived that horrible night through her memories.

A deafening silence fell over the room as all eyes fell and rested on Snake, who closed his own.

"And now," she took a deep breath and stood up, wiping her tears away, "after all these long years, I'ma have my revenge. Tit-for-tat, and then some," she laughed lightly and walked over to Snake.

"Hold up, man. What the fu–" he said as Jayla gagged him.

"Shut the fuck up, nigga," she whispered in his ear and then kissed his cheek. "Be right back, baby. Don't go nowhere. I got a surprise for ya," she smiled and winked at him before leaving the room, only to return a few seconds later carrying a huge, onyx-black dildo.

Snake's eyes bulged, and he thrashed about wildly, undoubtedly cursing like a sailor into his gag, but in the end all he accomplished was tiring himself out.

Jayla laughed quietly, but constantly as she wrestled with his resisting body to position him just right at the center of the room so Jaz and his grandmother could easily see the show. Because of the way she'd tied him up she had to struggle a little bit, but eventually she managed to wiggle his pants down just far enough for her to be comfortable while she worked. "Girl, this nigga got the cutest butt I ever seen on a man," Jayla looked at Jaz and said as she caressed and squeezed Snake's bare ass. She slapped one of his cheeks hard enough to make it sting and turn his light skin an angry-looking red. "What a shame it is, though," she said in a sarcastic, wistful manner and tone as she picked up the obscenely large dildo and stroked it lovingly with her hand while an evil grin played at her lips. "I thought about using a li'l K-Y, but it might lessen the pain I so desperately need for you to feel, so I decided against it. I hope you don't mind too much. I do have a little lube, though."

She stuck the tip of the dildo in her mouth and very slowly, as if she was giving a real blow job, took as much of it as possible into her mouth. She got really into it, moaning and groaning as if she was somehow taking some kind of weird form of pleasure from sliding the fake dick in and out of her mouth, and then she abruptly stopped. When she pulled it out of her mouth for the last time, her saliva glistened on the first few inches of it, but the other foot plus of it was bone dry.

"You ready baby?" she asked sexily as she positioned the dildo just right.

Snake wiggled and thrashed desperately but there was nothing at all he could do.

Jayla laughed mirthlessly. "I know it, boo. Neither was I," she said calmly, and then went into a rage. "But that shit still didn't stop yo' ol' sick-ass! You nasty bastard," she exploded and slammed the dildo into Snake's ass as hard and as fast as she could.

Tears of excruciating pain immediately sprung to his eyes, and he squeezed them closed to keep them from falling. Jayla didn't lighten up, though. In and out, harder and harder, faster and faster. She fell into a rhythm, and every time she shoved the dildo into him, he screamed an inhuman, animalistic noise into his gag. Drawing an unbelievable amount of pleasure from the sounds he was making, she would snatch the dildo out, do a quick two-count, and then ram it right back into his ass again.

In agony and embarrassed beyond measures he thought were even possible, Snake braved a glance at Jaz. Their eyes locked for a brief second before Jayla rammed his ass with the dildo again. His eyeballs threatened to explode from his head, and the big vein in the middle of his forehead looked like it was about to burst. Jaz cringed in pain every time Jayla went in with the dildo, and she was crying relentlessly. His grandmother had fainted long ago.

And then, finally, she stopped. "You liked that, daddy?" Jayla asked seductively.

In too much pain to even think straight, Snake just sat there, crying.

She snatched the bloody, shit-smeared dildo out of his ass roughly and sat it to the side. She drug his heavy, bleeding body right in front of the couch Jaz was sitting on and positioned him so he could see what was about to go down next. He couldn't see Jaz, but she maneuvered her legs so they were touching him so he'd know they were in the situation together.

"And now, the tit-for-tat gets a little deeper," Jayla said as she walked over to his grandmother and slapped her lightly until she woke up. "Yo' turn," she said and pulled her old, frail body from the chair she was sitting in. "Quit resisting, you ol' old-ass hag!" she yelled, annoyed at the old lady's stubbornness.

She was much easier to prep for the degrading. Only her ankles and wrists were bound together, plus she had on a long, billowing gown that almost dragged on the floor. Jayla leaned the old woman over the arm of a chair, hiked her dress all the way up, and went directly to work.

Fury burned through Snake as he watched his grandmother

tortured by the psychotic bitch he and Jaz both had thought was harmless. His beloved Gram looked at him with so much pain and agony in her eyes while tears dripped from them, and he'd had enough. He writhed and wriggled, causing himself excruciating pain while trying to get free, but it truly was no use. She had tied him up good.

Not wanting to see the gruesome scene any longer, Snake closed his eyes, but opened them right back at the sound of Jayla's voice.

"What's wrong, baby? You tired of looking like my daddy was?" She laughed and shoved the dildo in as hard and as deep as she could until she was positive it was the old woman's pelvis it was touching, and then she got up, leaving it exactly where it was, buried deep inside the old lady. "Did I mention that the night you took this pussy, you destroyed my body to the point where I would never be able to give birth to my own kids?" she asked in a conversational tone as she walked over to Snake.

He shook his head and whimpered.

"Well, you did, so I figure why the hell should you be able to have any without me?" she said with a shrug. Jayla drew her pistol, pointed it at Jaz, and squeezed the trigger without so much as a blink.

Snake couldn't see Jaz because she was above and behind him, but he felt her legs get tense, and then go slack. He knew Jayla had shot her. "No!" he screamed into his gag, fresh tears coming to his eyes while Jaz's body lay sprawled on the couch limp, bleeding. Dying.

He was stunned, completely out of it. He didn't know or even care anymore whether he was coming or going. He watched Jayla go back to work on his grandmother, but she quickly grew tired of degrading the old lady and slammed the dildo down. When she put the pistol to her head and squeezed the trigger, he didn't even blink. He was looking through the scene, forward to death, which he was ready for. He heard police sirens in the distance, but they were too late. All he hoped for now was they took a little longer to arrive so she would have enough time to finish him off.

"And now, the coup de gras," she walked over to Snake and pointed the pistol so close to his face the barrel of it touched the tip of his nose, causing it to sizzle a little as it burned him. Then a stroke of genius hit her. She lowered the gun until it was just a few inches away from his dick. "Say goodbye," she said sweetly and laughed before squeezing the trigger.

His entire body ignited in fire and pain, and with her mission accomplished, Jayla quickly surveyed her surroundings and then fled from the house.

Chapter Nineteen

Jock had been in the motion of raising his hand to ring Ms. Ellis' doorbell when he heard the gunshot. Curious and afraid because he knew Ms. Ellis was damn near eighty years old, he jumped off the porch instead of ringing the doorbell, ran around to the side of the house, and called the police to report the gunshot he'd heard. From his little spot on the side of the house he heard two more gunshots, and then saw somebody run out of the front door carrying something in their hand.

Only when he saw the police surround whoever it was who had run out of the house did he come out and flag down one of the late-arriving officers. His main concern was Ms. Ellis, and he knew she couldn't run that fast, so he didn't give a damn about whoever it was the police had boxed in down the street. He was in the process of explaining to the officer he was the one who had called for them and they should check the house when a volley of gunfire erupted behind them. He and the officer both ducked and whirled around just in time to see the figure who had run out of the house drop to the ground after being spun all kinds of ways by the officers' bullets.

The officer with Jock called for an ambulance and drew his service-issued Glock before he began to approach the house. "Stay here," he ordered.

***

A'ight, Jayla, listen. They got us surrounded, but don't panic. Whatever you do, don't fuckin' panic. Just put the gun down and raise ya hands, Tab said slowly, trying to calm Jayla down. She needed to take control of the situation because she could feel Jayla was close to losing it.

Tears rolled down Jayla's face. "We going to jail forever, Tab. We go' be some girl's bitch forever, Tab," she murmured.

No the fuck we ain't, bitch! Don't fuckin' say that shit!
Tab snapped before softening her tone. *Just relax, Jay.*
Everything go' be a'ight. All that money and shit Smurf left us,
we go' get the best lawyers money can buy, and we go' get off
on some insanity shit, trust me. All kind of doctors and shit will
vouch for us. We straight. Just put the gun down, Jayla. Why
you clutching it like that? Just drop it!

"Uh-uh, Tab." Jayla shook her head with tears in her eyes.
"I ain't listening to you this time. I can't go to jail. I'm sorry."

No! You stupid-ass bitch, what the fuck you doing? Don't
raise that pistol!

***

When officer Branson walked into the house, everything
seemed normal until he walked a little further and looked to his
right. He got on his radio for an ambulance immediately upon
seeing the gruesome scene in the living room. Holstering his
weapon, he rushed over to the woman on the couch and felt for
a pulse. There was just barely a hint of one, but he knew that
more than likely she was going to die, apparently from a
gunshot wound to her shoulder or upper chest, it looked like.
He couldn't be sure because of all the blood. She'd probably
fade away due to loss of blood.

He moved to the man who lay bound and gagged on the
floor and felt for a pulse. His was stronger than the woman's on
the couch, but still weak and fading fast. He had a chance, but
only if the God-damned ambulance would hurry! He rolled the
man over and visibly cringed when he saw he'd been shot in
the groin. Literally feeling his pain, Officer Branson radioed
for an ambulance again and started talking to the man. "Sir, can
you hear me? Sir? Help is on the way, sir. Any second now and
they'll be here!" He removed the gag and used his personal
pocketknife to cut the restraints off of him. Other officers had

begun to swarm the house by that time, and the paramedics weren't that far behind them.

When Officer Branson stood up to let the medics do what they did, he looked over to his left and saw a third victim, an obvious fatality. He shook his head and sent up a silent prayer for the man on the floor and the woman on the couch, who the paramedics were bustling around and trying to get loaded onto gurneys. Apparently they thought both of them had a chance. He knew if either one of them survived, they could only thank God and that fourteen-year-old kid who'd called for the police.

He eased his way out of the house, careful to stay out of everybody's way. What a hell of a first day on the job.

***

When Snake opened his eyes, there was a nurse standing over him. "Hey, handsome," she said quietly with a smile. She was young and pretty. "I didn't mean to disturb you. I thought you were out like a light, like you've been since you got here. I'll get your doctor," she said and left.

A few minutes later, a short black man knocked softly and came into the room. His long, white jacket had *David Emblasheer, M.D.* stitched over the left breast pocket, which had way too many pens clipped to it. "How are you feeling, Mr. Ellis?" he asked.

Snake groaned in response.

"That's what I figured. Okay, let me get straight to the point. Emergency reconstructive surgery was performed by myself, along with a resident Dr. Roy Swanson when you were brought in the other night. You suffered extensive nerve damge to you upper and lower," he paused and thought for a second. With a sigh, he continued speaking, but in layman terms. "Mr. Ellis, we were able to salvage and reconstruct the majority of you genitalia, but quite naturally when one takes a bullet to that region, there is only so much that man can do. You'll be maimed and scarred for the rest of your life. I'm sorry," he said in a hard, all-business tone he'd perfected after years and years of learning that, for his own good, he couldn't get attached to any of his patients, no matter the circumstances. His job was to save them and fix them, not care about them.

Snake squeezed his eyes shut and tears spilled forth from them when he opened them back.

"As far as sexual intercourse goes," Dr. Emblasheer, the bearer of bad news, went on to say, "due to the amount of nerve damage sustained, if you did by some miracle manage to become erect, I'd advise you to take full advantage of it. You wouldn't be able to feel a thing, but at the same time it could possibly be years before you were able to accomplish," he paused, considering his words, "getting a rise out of it again. As for passing waste, I'd advise the use of a catheter and a leg collection bag."

Snake nodded absentmindedly at everything as the doctor droned on and on after that point, he didn't want or need to hear anything more. He found himself shaking his head no, and then, to his relief, the doctor turned and left. He just wanted to be left alone. He needed some time to think by himself.

He reached to feel his nuts, but a steel handcuff bit into his wrist. "Why the fuck am I cuffed?" he groaned to himself as he snatched his wrist against the steel while using his other hand to try to feel his nuts. He was bandaged too heavily to feel a thing, though.

A soft knock sounded at the door again, and two white men in cheap suits came into the room. They introduced themselves as A.P.D. Homicide Detectives Lite and Morrow, then got straight to the point. "We found this gun," they showed him a picture of a black, forty-caliber Glock, "with your prints all over it, along with $180,000 stashed away together in a nice and cozy little spot inside your grandmother's house. Ballistics came back positive. This was the same weapon used in a robbery and multiple homicide last summer. You want to talk to us about it, buddy?"

Snake groaned loudly, closed his eyes, and shook his head. *Damn!*

Ambitious

Epilogue

Almost Four Years Later

He felt extremely blessed. True enough, his dick basically didn't work at all and he'd just arrived at his home for the next three and a half years of his life, but that was it. He'd only been sentenced to seven years! An up-and-coming defense attorney by the name of Marcus Thomas had literally bedazzled and hoodwinked a jury of Snake's peers into believing such a handsome man like his client, who'd been through so much tragedy recently, couldn't possibly be responsible for those horrendous murders at that motel over on Fulton Industrial Boulevard. Yes, he'd wound up with the murder weapon, but he'd purchased it off the street from some guy after those crimes had been committed. Marcus Thomas not only convinced the jury, he even convinced Snake, himself, that had his client known what had happened with the weapon, he would've carried it to the nearest police headquarters straight away so justice could begin to be sought.

Yes, quite frankly, Marcus Thomas had put on one hell of a show, and the jury had eaten it up, all to District Attorney Saul Poward's dismay. He had been so outraged when the not guilty verdict on the malicious murder counts came down that he literally had to be physically restrained and threatened with pepper spray in the courtroom. In the end, Snake was only convicted of tax evasion and possession of a firearm by a convicted felon and sentenced to serve seven years in prison, which was one of the few things he had to smile about lately.

He hobbled to his new housing unit. The bullet he'd taken to the dick had not only disfigured him, but it had also left him with a permanent, awkward-looking and -feeling gait. He would also have to undergo treatment and therapy more than likely for the rest of his life.

After another convict helped him to his cell, he plopped down on his bunk. He needed to take a load off. He'd been up and moving since before three that morning. He checked his G-Shock and saw it was now a little after five, so he lay back with the intention of unpacking and using the phone after a short nap. He needed to let his family know he'd been transferred.

***

The pipsqueak of a kid had grown into a strapping young lad, a man, and also a leader of sorts. He and three of his pahtnas had been sitting, as they always did on Tuesdays and Thursdays, watching to see if they knew any of the new arrivals. When he tied his knife to his wrist so it wouldn't slip away and stood up, his pahtnas followed suit.

"Nah, shawdy, y'all niggas fall back. I'm good. Just make sure y'all get my phone when Kebo pull them out. And get that money from the white boy, Steve, bruh. He s'posed to have two hundred in dots for me today. Just send all that shit to me in the hole. Y'all keep fifty of it," he rasped quietly, but firmly, and then left them.

Taking the stairs two at a time, he was on the ground floor and sliding into the room of the nigga who'd just come in in no time. "Guns up, nigga! You know what it is," he rasped just loud enough to wake the nigga on the bed right before he stabbed him in his right eye.

Recognition dawned on Snake's face a few seconds before the final darkness of death from being stabbed repeatedly enveloped him.

The young nigga stabbing him was the same young nigga he'd knocked out and robbed at Five Points Station years ago. His name was Boon.

***

"C'mere, baby!" she called out sweetly.

"No," came his immediate response.

"Boy! If you don't get yo' li'l bad-ass in here right the fuck now, Siree Jabril Ellis Jr., I'ma whup that butt-butt," Jaz yelled as she stood up.

Her three-year-old son came speeding into her bedroom with both of his fat little hands covering his butt. "No butt-butt, Mama! No butt-butt," he whined, already near tears just from the thought of yet another whipping so soon after he'd earned his last one.

"It's time to call Daddy. You wanna talk to Daddy?" she asked enthusiastically, her threatening demeanor disappearing instantly.

"Daddy! Daddy! Daddy!" he jumped around and chanted excitedly.

Jaz looked at her handsome baby boy and couldn't help but smile. He was a carbon copy of his father. She dug around in her Gucci purse and got out her phone, along with the greendot she had purchased for her and her son's snake in the grass.

The End

Stay Connected with Us!

Text **LOCKDOWN** to 22828 to stay up-to-date with new releases, sneak peaks, contests and more…

Thank you!

<u>Coming Soon from Lock Down Publications/Ca$h Presents</u>

BOW DOWN TO MY GANGSTA

By **Ca$h & Jamaica**

TORN BETWEEN TWO

By **Coffee**

BLOOD OF A BOSS **IV**

By **Askari**

BRIDE OF A HUSTLA **III**

THE FETTI GIRLS **III**

By **Destiny Skai**

WHEN A GOOD GIRL GOES BAD **II**

By **Adrienne**

LOVE & CHASIN' PAPER **II**

By **Qay Crockett**

THE HEART OF A GANGSTA **II**

By **Jerry Jackson**

TO DIE IN VAIN **II**

By **ASAD**

LOYAL TO THE GAME **IV**

By **T.J. & Jelissa**

A DOPEBOY'S PRAYER **II**

By **Eddie "Wolf" Lee**

A HUSTLER'S DECEIT **III**

THE BOSS MAN'S DAUGHTERS **III**

BAE BELONGS TO ME **II**

By **Aryanna**

TRUE SAVAGE **III**

By **Chris Green**

RAISED AS A GOON **III**

By **Ghost**

IF LOVING YOU IS WRONG…

By **Jelissa**

BLOODY COMMAS **II**

By **T.J. Edwards**

Available Now

(CLICK TO PURCHASE)

RESTRAINING ORDER **I & II**

By **CA$H & Coffee**

LOVE KNOWS NO BOUNDARIES **I II & III**

By **Coffee**

RAISED AS A GOON I & II

By **Ghost**

LAY IT DOWN **I & II**

LAST OF A DYING BREED

By **Jamaica**

LOYAL TO THE GAME

LOYAL TO THE GAME II

LOYAL TO THE GAME III

By **TJ & Jelissa**

PUSH IT TO THE LIMIT

By **Bre' Hayes**

BLOOD OF A BOSS **I II & III**

By **Askari**

THE STREETS BLEED MURDER **I, II & III**

THE HEART OF A GANGSTA

By **Jerry Jackson**

CUM FOR ME

CUM FOR ME 2

CUM FOR ME 3

An **LDP Erotica Collaboration**

BRIDE OF A HUSTLA **I & II**

THE FETTI GIRLS **I & II**

By **Destiny Skai**

WHEN A GOOD GIRL GOES BAD

By **Adrienne**

A GANGSTER'S REVENGE **I II III & IV**

THE BOSS MAN'S DAUGHTERS

THE BOSS MAN'S DAUGHTERS II

A SAVAGE LOVE **I & II**

BAE BELONGS TO ME

A HUSTLER'S DECEIT I, II

By **Aryanna**

A KINGPIN'S AMBITON

A KINGPIN'S AMBITION **II**

By **Ambitious**

TRUE SAVAGE

TRUE SAVAGE II

By **Chris Green**

A DOPEBOY'S PRAYER

By **Eddie "Wolf" Lee**

WHAT ABOUT US **I & II**

NEVER LOVE AGAIN

THUG ADDICTION

By **Kim Kaye**

THE KING CARTEL **I, II & III**

By **Frank Gresham**

THESE NIGGAS AIN'T LOYAL **I, II & III**

By **Nikki Tee**

GANGSTA SHYT **I II &III**

By **CATO**

THE ULTIMATE BETRAYAL

By **Phoenix**

BOSS'N UP **I & II**

By **Royal Nicole**

I LOVE YOU TO DEATH

By Destiny J

I RIDE FOR MY HITTA

I STILL RIDE FOR MY HITTA

By **Misty Holt**

LOVE & CHASIN' PAPER

By **Qay Crockett**

TO DIE IN VAIN

By **ASAD**

BOOKS BY LDP'S CEO, CA$H

(CLICK TO PURCHASE)

TRUST IN NO MAN

TRUST IN NO MAN 2

TRUST IN NO MAN 3

BONDED BY BLOOD

SHORTY GOT A THUG

THUGS CRY

THUGS CRY 2

THUGS CRY 3

TRUST NO BITCH

TRUST NO BITCH 2

TRUST NO BITCH 3

TIL MY CASKET DROPS

RESTRAINING ORDER

RESTRAINING ORDER 2

IN LOVE WITH A CONVICT

Coming Soon

BONDED BY BLOOD 2

BOW DOWN TO MY GANGSTA

Ambitious